Praise for THREADS

Great fun. It goes at a cracking pace and girls will love it.

... the next Princess Diaries – *only hotter.*
AMANDA CRAIG, THE TIMES

A magical tale ...
BLISS MAGAZINE

... a must read ...
INDEPENDENT ON SUNDAY

Miss it, miss out.
MIZZ MAGAZINE

Bang on trend, with some hilarious fashion faux pas ...
TBK MAGAZINE

The fashion story everyone's talking about ...
SUGAR MAGAZINE

A treat ... elegant and funny and has real narrative verve.
DAVID ALMOND, AUTHOR

*The perfect stocking-filler for the girl who knows
her Marni from her Matalan ...*
EVENING STANDARD

... upbeat and thoroughly entertaining.
BOOKS FOR KEEPS

A MESSAGE FROM CHICKEN HOUSE

Sophia, no! This can't be the end of the trilogy. We'll miss the girls too much!
   I never thought it would end like *that* – but I *loved* it all and your readers will love it too.

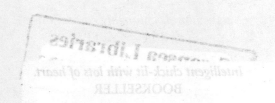

BARRY CUNNINGHAM
Publisher
Chicken House

Stars

SOPHIA BENNETT

Chicken House

2 Palmer Street, Frome, Somerset BA11 1DS
www.doublecluck.com

Text © Sophia Bennett 2011
First published in Great Britain in 2011
This edition published 2015
Chicken House
2 Palmer Street
Frome, Somerset BA11 1DS
United Kingdom
www.doublecluck.com

Cover design and interior design by Helen Crawford-White
Typeset by Dorchester Typesetting Group Ltd
Printed and bound in Great Britain by CPI Group (UK) Ltd, Croydon CR0 4YY

The paper used in this Chicken House book is made from wood grown
in sustainable forests.

1 3 5 7 9 10 8 6 4 2

British Library Cataloguing in Publication data available.

ISBN 978-1-910002-96-4
eISBN 978-1-910655-38-2

To my mother, Marie, who
tells the best stories

Also by Sophia Bennett

Threads
Beads
The Look
You Don't Know Me
The Castle

Chapter 1

I'm sitting in the back row of a mega-tent in Paris, surrounded by fashion students, buyers, editors and movie stars, and watching THE MOST BEAUTIFUL CATWALK SHOW I WILL EVER SEE IN MY LIFE.

It doesn't matter that it's hot in here. It doesn't matter that everyone around me looks so unbelievably chic I might as well have shown up in my pyjamas (actually, the kimono I'm wearing does have a hint of pyjamas about it). It doesn't matter that beside me a fifteen-year-old in a serious afro is jiggling with excitement and making her chair wobble.

It's just good to be here. Dior Haute Couture. John Galliano at his most incredible best. Skirts and jackets that are so huge and theatrical they're almost impossible to wear, but so exquisite you want to spend the next year examining every inch of them. Fabrics that burst with colour and drape like magic. Shoes that are perfect pieces of sculpture in their own right and belong in a museum.

Hair that . . . Well, you get the picture. Galliano didn't exactly skimp on this one. And we've only seen ten outfits so far. We're not even halfway through.

My friend Crow – the girl in the afro beside me – is a designer. She's constantly thinking up new ideas for beautiful clothes, and drawing them, and making them. She's been doing it for years and has a queue of people who want to wear her outfits. But she is a teenager. She does most of it from a workroom in the basement of my house in Kensington, in between GCSE classes and remedial maths. She doesn't have a building full of seam-stresses on tap, like they do at Dior. Or access to the best makeup artist, hairdresser, DJ and set designer in the world, like John Galliano does. Actually, she does have access to the best DJ, or one of them. He happens to be my brother. But that's beside the point.

What I mean is that my friend makes clothes in a spare room and here we are, witnessing the absolute height of fashion. This is as bold and creative and luxurious and EXPENSIVE as it can possibly get. It's the toughest ticket to get hold of in the fashion world, and when my brother said he could wangle two of them for us, we practically fell over. Now, sitting in the middle of it all, surrounded by models, lights, photographers, music and fashionistas, I'm still recovering from shock.

The outfits keep on coming. Galliano seems to have hired pretty much every supermodel in the world to wear them. And the skirts are getting bigger and longer. As we sensation, but even after this happened to Galliano, he still struggled. His most famous collection was made in two weeks, out of bits of black silk because that's all he could afford, and he drove it to Paris himself in a friend's Mini and got the best girls to model for him as a favour. This is why I love Galliano so much. Not because of where he is now, but because he came so far and never gave up, and just when you thought it was all going to go horribly pear-shaped, he made something amazing happen.

Do I sound like I could give classes on The History of Galliano? I probably could. Such a pity it's not an A-level subject. Anyway, I'm busy daydreaming about him driving that Mini to Paris all those years ago when I suddenly realise there's a shushing sound in the air and something strange is happening.

Galliano has handed the roses to Isabelle and whispered something to her, before turning to leave the catwalk. However, you can't whisper in front of that many telephoto lenses without somebody working out what you just said. Another whisper is making its way around the tent as everyone struggles to get in on the secret.

'What?' everyone's asking. 'What did he say?'

It takes ages to reach the back row. By the time it gets to us it sounds as though he's just congratulated Isabelle on getting engaged in real life. But that can't be right. Because if Isabelle's engaged, there can be only one person she can possibly be engaged to, and that person is my big brother. Which would make me the future sister-in-law of the most beautiful girl in the world.

Crow looks at me, confused. She's probably wondering if the future sister-in-law had the faintest idea this was about to happen.

I didn't. I'm in shock. I'm staring at the spot where Isabelle was just standing: a stunning vision in a Dior gold dress, cradling a bouquet of roses and holding hands with a fashion icon. Who, by the way, was dressed in doublet and hose, thigh boots, two silk sashes and a cloak.

I simply have to be dreaming.

Chapter 2

Crow rubs my arm. It's her way of asking how I am. I rub hers back, very lightly, which is my way of saying, 'Fine, but don't talk to me about it.' I need to find Harry quite badly. Can it be true? I have to know. But it's going to take him ages to sort his decks out and fiddle with kit before he's ready to go. I don't know why this is. I've just watched him often enough to know it's a long process and that he doesn't like to be disturbed while he's doing it. Especially to be asked if he is really GETTING MARRIED and accidentally forgot to tell his FAMILY before it got leaked out to THE WHOLE WORLD.

Crow and I join the queue to leave the tent. We get several looks from the other people in the crowd. I assume they're mostly aimed at Crow, who has recently grown tall for her age, and is fragile-looking, black and beautiful. She may look fragile, but she's about as brittle as a steel girder. A very brightly dressed girder. Today her outfit consists of a red, tightly pleated silk poncho that makes her look like a poppy, with homemade gold rubber boots (she's experimenting with footwear) and an origami paper headdress that Galliano happened to have lying around yesterday, when we came to watch rehearsals, and gave her. As you do.

As we head into the gardens of the Musée Rodin, a few people come over to air-kiss us and ask Crow what she's up to. She's sort of 'on the radar' for fashion people. Not totally famous yet, but people who know fashion know to look out for her. And, of course, she's hard to miss, especially in her origami headgear. By the time we get clear of the tent, she has a little cluster of fans around her and it takes a while for a lanky young man wearing a bright yellow fleece and a satchel to make it through to us.

'Henry!' Crow shouts, as if he's the only person there. She is good at many things, but schmoozing fashionistas isn't one of them. Not if there's family around to be hugged.

'Crow-bird! Was it good?' he asks.

Henry Lamogi is Crow's older brother (currently single, as far as I know, and not rumoured to be engaged to any supermodels whatsoever) and, if possible, where she goes, he goes. Their parents are still in Uganda with their little sister, Victoria, so she and Henry stick as close as they can.

'It was incredible,' she breathes. Her hands, as usual,

start dancing as she attempts to describe the show. She's about to go through it, outfit by outfit, when Henry stops her.

'There are some people who want to meet you. I said I'd find you for them. They're waiting over there.'

He guides us across the gravel to a spot where three men in suits and matching camel overcoats are waiting. They are clearly not fashion people. Men in fashion don't do suits and matching overcoats, unless it's for a shoot. They do wacky velvet jackets, or wacky oversize scarves, or wacky cashmere layering, or something clever with a hat, but the whole suit/overcoat thing is just too easy, unless the overcoat is in some way wacky, which these are not.

Crow does her shy smile and Henry introduces us. The men hold out their hands and say they're from some company I've never heard of. One is English, one is American and one, I think, is German, although his accent is so slight it's hard to tell. The American does most of the talking. He goes on about how impressive it is that Crow already has a dress in the Victoria and Albert Museum, and how quickly her first high street collection sold out at Miss Teen last winter.

It's true. Crow may do her designs in a basement, but one was worn by a starlet to the Oscars (sounds great, nearly killed me) and her Miss Teen party outfits became prized bestsellers on eBay. Unlike my designs, by the way, which were made in the same basement and have only managed to get me GCSE Textiles. I did get an A, though. Yay!

However, Crow's eyes quickly glaze over. Talking about what she's already done doesn't interest her very much. She's too busy thinking about what she's going to do next. That's one of the reasons why she needs me as her business manager. I am the schmoozer of the operation, and also the schmoozee, if required.

Annoyingly, the men persist in not catching my eye. Is there something wrong with me? Do I have cappuccino foam on my lip again? Even though I'm the one nodding and saying 'absolutely' and 'how interesting', they insist on talking only to Henry (who hates fashion and is wearing a YELLOW FLEECE, for goodness' sake) and Crow, who isn't listening.

Eventually, I give up. I have other things on my mind right now. Like how cold it is in the Paris winter in nothing but a kimono, how stupid I was to leave my embroidered pashmina (a present from my granny) at Dad's apartment, and how MY BROTHER MIGHT BE MARRYING A SUPERMODEL.

I notice that the American keeps glancing behind me, distractedly. I look round and spot a mini-stampede going on near a side entrance to the tent. Every photographer in the vicinity – and there are lots – is rushing over to get into position. Somebody mega-famous is about to emerge. And then I spot the halo of blonde ringlets and see Isabelle Carruthers, caught for a second like a deer in the headlights as the flashbulbs pop and the pack of paparazzi shout out their questions.

A tall, good-looking young man with floppy hair comes to stand beside her. My brother. The flashbulbs go into a frenzy. Harry puts a protective arm around Isabelle. I strain to hear what they're saying in answer to the questions, but we're too far away. However, what they are not doing is shaking their heads and denying all knowledge of whatever's being shouted out to them. In fact, Harry is kissing Isabelle for the cameras and grinning, which is a bit of a clue.

So maybe Galliano was right. I can't see an engagement ring, but Isabelle is stroking the empty space on her finger as if there might be one there any minute.

Meanwhile, German guy has taken over from American guy. I hear the words 'investment vehicle' and 'archive potential' and 'major breakthrough opportunity'. Compared with 'your brother is about to get married', they don't really register on the Richter scale.

Crow's eyes are still glazed. I tune out again and try to watch Harry and Isabelle's body language. Isabelle is smiling and posing and doing clever things with her hair. She is a supermodel after all. Harry still seems a bit wary, but the way he's snuggled up to Isabelle suggests that here is a man who found himself in Paris last night with the most beautiful girl in the world and decided to round off the evening by proposing.

He might have mentioned it, that's all. So I could

congratulate them before every paparazzo in Paris and practically every magazine editor in the world.

I look back and the overcoat men are shaking hands. The English one is giving me a funny look, as if he's noticed that I haven't really been paying attention. I'd explain why, but it would sound too totally weird for words. Instead, I just say goodbye politely and flick my eyes back to the press posse hovering around Harry and Isabelle. I mean, it seems normal when you see it happening to George Clooney or Angelina Jolie, but when it's happening to somebody you know, it's just bizarre.

'What's going on?' Henry Lamogi asks, now that we're alone.

I explain as best I can. Henry takes in my shocked expression and puts a kindly arm around me. This is one of his specialities. He has world-class kindly arms and I instantly feel a bit better.

'We'd better go over and rescue them,' he says.

This seems an excellent idea.

We get to Harry and Isabelle just as they're about to make their getaway. But for a split second we're caught beside them, in the midst of the flashbulbs, and I realise I'd have thought a bit harder about the whole kimono thing if I'd known there was a chance of it appearing in *Hello!* magazine in a couple of days' time.

I catch sight of the overcoat men across the gravel, staring back at us thoughtfully.

'Who were they?' I ask Crow.

She shrugs. We have better things to think about right now. I assume.

Chapter 3

'Oh my God! Harry! Isabelle! Oh my GOD!'

Twenty-four hours later, Mum is meeting us off the Eurostar at St Pancras station in London. Or at least, I think it's Mum. It's how Mum would be if you seriously speeded up the video and turned the sound up to max. I've never seen her like this before.

'I'm so THRILLED! You dark horses! I had no IDEA! You're so amazing! Come here! Let me hug you.'

Henry, Crow and I huddle around the luggage trolley, waiting for the enormous hugs and crying to die down so we can say hello.

It's been a bit like this since yesterday evening, except mostly on the phone. We were whisked by limo back to Isabelle's hotel room (massive, and overlooking the Eiffel Tower, naturally) and over the next few hours I opened the door to increasingly large bouquets of flowers and intriguing designer shopping bags with big bows, while Isabelle and Harry answered non-stop calls from people all around the world, checking the story was true and shouting their congratulations. Crow and her brother headed back to my dad's apartment after a while. They just couldn't take the excitement any more.

'Hi, darling,' Mum manages eventually, with a peck on the cheek for me and a quick hug for Crow. 'Isn't it thrilling? Granny's on her way up, of course. Oh, and Harry, Vicente will be here at the weekend. Isn't that wonderful? We must organise something for him. Big celebrations!'

Vicente (pronounced Veh-SEN-te – it's a Portuguese thing) is Harry's dad. Mum used to go out with him before she met my dad. He lives in Brazil, where he's a gazillionaire with loads of land and hundreds of eco-projects on the go. We like him, but we hardly ever see him. Isabelle's never met him. So the news that he's coming is the cause of more hugs and squealing.

At this point, Henry Lamogi makes his excuses and goes home on his own by Tube. I don't blame him. Crow accepts a lift with us in Mum's car and spends the journey staring at me, wide-eyed. As Crow makes her dresses in our house, she sees Mum all the time, so she knows what she's like normally – and this is SO not normal. You'd honestly think Mum had never had a wedding to look forward to before.

And then it hits me.

She hasn't.

And she's obviously really potty about them. And it's all my fault.

Crow sees me suddenly crumple and holds out her hand to me. I take it, and I'm grateful that it's she who's here and not one of my other friends. They'd be asking me what the matter was, and of course I couldn't possibly tell them. Crow doesn't ask. She's just there, and that's all I need right now.

The next hour is a blur. We get home and the downstairs is full to the brim with yet more flowers and packages. There is a man in a black pac-a-mac lurking outside and it's quite possible he's our first very own paparazzo. Isabelle and Harry quickly disappear to Harry's room and turn the music up loud. Everyone pretends they've gone to unpack. Mum makes a hot chocolate for Crow and cappuccino for me (new obsession – still haven't got the knack of maintaining foam-free lips) and goes on and on about how perfect Isabelle is for Harry, and how she'd been hoping he'd find the right girl, but how amazing it is that he's managed to do it so soon – he's only twenty-three – and when are they going to set a date?

As soon as I can, I drag Crow up to my room and we slump into a couple of chairs and just stare at each other.

'Things are going to be different,' she says.

I nod. My eyes brim. I don't want things to be different. I like them just the way they are.

I look around my room at the curling posters from the

V&A, my wall of *Vogue* shoots stuck up with Blu-Tack, the butterfly duvet cover I haven't replaced since I was ten, the view of treetops from my window and the old, familiar mess. I meant to tidy up before we went to Paris for the Dior show, but it didn't quite happen and actually the place is worse than usual. The wardrobe doors are open and several pairs of leggings are trying to make their getaway from the bottom shelf. My scarf collection is hanging precariously from the top of one of the doors and judging by the tee-shirts, tops and underwear on the floor, I'm pretty sure my chest of drawers must be nearly empty.

Mum asked me to 'edit' my magazine collection before I went (by which she meant throw most of it away) but I only got as far as piling everything in the middle of the room, where it looks like a piece of modern sculpture. The nearest pile makes a very useful footstool. I rest my feet on it and pick up an old *Grazia* from another pile to take my mind off things, while Crow goes through my book collection, looking for something inspirational. By which I don't, of course, mean Thomas Hardy or Jane Austen, but a guide to platform shoes through the ages.

She still doesn't talk. I know exactly what she means.

She means, 'I love Harry too, and I'm sorry we'll be seeing less of him.' She means, 'Your mother's gone totally loopy, hasn't she? What is it with all that conversation? She's usually too busy to say hello.' She means, 'I can tell you're not OK about something. I'm not sure exactly what, but if you wanted to talk about it, you could. I'm here if you need me.'

'Crow?' I say eventually.

She looks up from a Salvatore Ferragamo gold padded platform illustration. 'Yes?'

'Thanks.'

She smiles and nods. She doesn't ask what for. I've known her since I was fourteen and she was twelve. She's practically lived in my house for most of that time. She just knows.

Chapter 4

Next morning is triple Business Studies at school. The perfect antidote to Dior. I sit at the back of the class on my own, mentally designing the outfit I should have worn to the show if I'd wanted to look cool. It's not till break that I finally get the chance to talk to Edie, one of my best friends, who is – I assume – dying to hear all about our trip.

Edie is a pretty, blonde super-genius who I always thought had a bit of a thing for Harry until she started going out with her new boyfriend, Hot Phil. He lives in California, and by 'going out with' I mean messaging, emailing and moping over. I wonder what her reaction will be.

I tell her the news.

'That's great!' she says, without missing a beat.

'Mmm. It is, isn't it?'

'Isabelle's lovely. And I s'pose that means you get to be bridesmaid.'

'Yaaay.'

'Oh God, I'm sorry,' she adds, finally sensing the lack of enthusiasm in my 'yaaay'. 'You must be exhausted. How was Paris?'

And so I tell her about Paris, but after five minutes of 'mm hmms' I remember that Edie isn't really interested in fashion and never will be, so I stop.

'And how are Crow and Henry?' she prompts, politely.

This reminds me to mention the men in matching overcoats, but very quickly I start getting 'mm hmms' again. Edie's mind is clearly somewhere else.

'Is something the matter?' I ask. 'Have I missed anything?'

She pauses for a while to consider.

'Have you noticed something odd about Jenny recently?'

Jenny is our other best friend. Redhead, actress, with slightly diva-ish tendencies and an allergy to men since a rather unfortunate incident with a Hollywood Teenage Sex God while filming a movie. Nothing about Jenny is completely normal, but I must admit, I haven't noticed anything unusually unusual.

I shake my head.

'You know she's missing school for a week next month?' Edie clearly finds this astonishing.

I nod, trying to keep a straight face. Edie simply cannot imagine how anyone could POSSIBLY miss school for a week in their second term of A levels. Even if they have four more terms to catch up. Even if it's to go to New York and perform in a workshop for a new musical.

'And?'

'Well, she's been asking me to help her out with a couple of English assignments, so she can get them out of the way. I said I'd go round to her flat and she practically shouted at me not to. She looked almost tearful. And since then I've been watching her. She's got these grey shadows under her eyes. She looks exhausted. Of course I've asked and asked what the problem is' – Edie would – 'but she won't say.'

'Perhaps she's been busy practising.'

This workshop in New York is to try out a musical written by a playwright friend of Jenny's called Bill. She performed in a play of his last summer, which is how he knows how good she is. The musical is called *Elizabeth and Margaret*. Not the world's snappiest title. And it's about the Queen and her sister when they were growing up. Not the world's most gripping news item. But you never know with musicals. 'Guy gets disfigured at the opera', 'Abba songs', 'miner's son does ballet', 'chess'. None of them sound too amazing to start with. So we're giving Bill the benefit of the doubt.

Jenny's got four weeks to prepare for this workshop, learning every note of a dozen new numbers. She's a brilliant singer, but even so, it's a lot to ask. I'm not at all surprised about the shadows under her eyes. I am surprised about the shouting and tearfulness, though. To be honest, if anyone was going to be shouty and tearful right now, I'd expect it to be Edie.

It's Edie's year for being mega-stressed. Her plan is to join the United Nations as soon as possible, and become some sort of ambassador – like Angelina Jolie, but without the acting career and multiple children (or Brad Pitt) and with an uber-degree from Harvard instead. So with that in mind, she's doing six AS levels this summer, grade seven clarinet, American SATs (don't ask), her Harvard essays in the autumn and Oxford interviews 'as backup'. And meanwhile, she's still running her save-the-world website, where she talks all about the projects she's interested in and raises money to save children who need basic stuff like water and computers. AND if Hot Phil doesn't message her at least eight times a day she assumes he's gone off her and gets spotty with distress.

'Look, if you want me to talk to Jenny, I will,' I say. Edie really doesn't need any more stress right now. 'She's got today off to go over some songs with the casting director—'

Edie cuts me off with a shocked look that says it all. *Another* day off? How will Jenny ever recover?

I ignore her. '—but I'll go round to her place tonight. Promise. OK? And by the way, which assignments?'

It's worrying me slightly that I now remember something about essay preparation that should have happened before the Dior show, but hasn't quite.

'*King Lear*,' Edie says with a patient sigh. 'And *The Canterbury Tales*. But that's not due until half-term.'

I mentally dismiss *The Canterbury Tales*. Any assignment due in more than a week is a bridge I don't have to cross yet. But Lear is due in by Friday, I've just realised. Hopefully Edie will be able to give me a few tips, and my English teacher won't mind if I give them to her in bullet points and say I'm practising my presentation technique. It worked last time. Sort of. Anyway, I have shouty, tearful friends to worry about, apparently. Bullet points will have to do.

Chapter 5

I get home after school and call Jenny's mobile. No answer. So I try her landline and a strange thing happens. After about eight rings, the answerphone kicks in, then someone picks up and I can hear breathing on the line. It sounds slow and heavy, like the person at the other end had trouble getting to the phone.

'Jenny?' I ask, worried. The breathing continues, but there's no answer. 'Gloria?'

Gloria is Jenny's mum. It can't be Jenny's dad because he's living with his fourth wife in the Cotswolds.

'It's Nonie,' I say. Nothing. I'm starting to get slightly freaked out. I wonder if it's a heavy breather, except I definitely made the call. You can't randomly call a heavy breather, can you? Anyway, I heard two seconds of the answerphone, and it was Jenny's voice on the message. I've heard it a million times.

I hang up and grab my bag and a warm scarf.

Downstairs, the kitchen is full of family and yet more wedding talk.

'Granny's on her way,' Mum yells after me. 'Be back soon. And have you done that Shakespeare thing yet?'

'Just working on it with Jenny,' I shout virtuously. 'See you later.'

Outside, I feel the cool evening air on my face and suddenly I'm a bit calmer. The lurking paparazzo checks that I'm not a golden-ringletted supermodel and goes back to skulking in a dark corner. Fifteen minutes later, I'm at the door of Jenny's flat in a big apartment block near the Albert Hall, determined to knock and ring the bell until someone lets me in and explains what's going on.

Eventually, Jenny opens the door and stands behind it for a moment, staring at me and not saying anything. I notice how white her face is under the red hair, and those grey shadows under her eyes, which seem almost purple in this light.

'Oh, hi, Nonie. You're back,' she says dully, holding the door half closed.

Edie's right. This is odd. I pretend it isn't.

'How did it go with the casting director?' I ask brightly.

'Fine,' Jenny says. The door doesn't move.

I smile politely, hoping my worried frown lines aren't showing. 'Can I come in?'

She looks behind her. 'Er, maybe tomorrow?'

'Don't be silly. I'm here now. I have vital info on *King Lear*. And we need to chat.'

Jenny can see that I'm not moving, so she steps back and lets me in.

'Sorry about the mess,' she says.

I'm about to say for goodness' sake, I'm used to it, when I look around and realise that actually, I'm not. The narrow hallway is truly cluttered, littered with dirty laundry, bulging plastic bags and piles of plates that belong in the sink. Even on my bad days I'm not this bad, and if I was, Mum would totally freak out and probably ground me for a week.

'Er, everything OK?' I ask, as we pick our way through the piles and head for Jenny's room.

'Fine,' she says. Her voice hardly makes it past her lips. Edie is right. She is SO not fine.

When we get to her room, she curls up on her bed, where her cat, Stella, is waiting for her, and gently strokes Stella's fur. I move a couple of piles of books from the chair beside her desk and sit down near her. I sense Jenny's been here for a while, curled up like that, and whatever she's been thinking, it hasn't been good.

'Tell me about it,' I say.

Instead, she tries to change the subject and asks me about Paris, but suddenly I have no interest in talking about Paris, or brothers, or engagements, or any of that stuff, so I ask her again what the matter is and make it clear I'm not moving until she tells me.

'Well . . . I can't go to New York,' she says eventually, and a tear hits Stella's nose, which the cat crossly pats away.

'Why not?' I ask, appalled. 'Won't school let you? Has Bill changed his mind? Or this casting guy?'

'It's not school. Or Bill. I've got nowhere to stay, OK?'

Jenny's eyes flash defiantly at me.

'But I thought you had a hotel all sorted out. I mean . . . New York's full of hotel rooms, isn't it?'

She ignores me for a while and focuses on stroking Stella. Then she sighs.

'They won't let me stay on my own. Or even if they would, Mum won't let me stay in a hotel by myself. And she can't go with me.'

'Why?'

Jenny looks flustered. Then furious. 'Look, she can't, OK? She can't get the insurance, and she doesn't want to go, and that's it. It was only a workshop, anyway – not a real show or anything. Look, I'm fine. Just leave it. Shouldn't you be doing an assignment?'

I have three choices. I can sit here silently. I can go home and work on *King Lear*, with Mum and Granny popping in every five seconds to ask what colour bouquet I think Isabelle should have. Or I can argue with Jenny. I go for option three.

'It's not "only" a workshop! How can you even say that?'

True, the musical people only need Jenny for a week, to help perform the songs for some producers so they can raise the money to put on a proper show. But it's her chance to sing and do a bit of acting with the top professionals in the business. She's been so excited about it she hasn't been able to think or talk about anything else since Christmas.

'I don't even know if I'm a good enough singer,' she says listlessly.

'Yes you do. You *do*, Jen. You did all those tests for them. You were incredible in *Annie* when we did it at school. And you sing all the time. Even when it's really annoying. You are TOTALLY a good enough singer, Jenny Merritt.'

Actually, I'm quite enjoying the arguing option. It's getting a lot of things out of my system. I wait for the next thing I can disagree with.

'Well, where am I supposed to stay?' she asks.

'Can't you just explain about Gloria not going and ask Bill or someone to put you up?'

'No.' Jenny's lips tremble and she shakes her head. I realise she didn't really want to tell *me* what was going on, so she's not going to do it to anyone else – even an old friend of the family like Bill. Even if that means staying in London and missing out on her big chance.

28

Then I have my genius idea.

'Isabelle's flat! You know Isabelle. She's got this flat in SoHo.'

'Soho? Near Oxford Street?'

'No, dummy. SoHo New York. It's her second home. I don't know how big it is, but I'm sure she could give you floor space. It isn't for very long. And she could get her friends to look out for you. Models are quite used to girls being on their own in big cities.'

We both shudder at this. Mum has told us some hairy stories about young, pretty girls left to their own devices in big cities by modelling agencies. Why the agencies let it happen is a mystery to us, but it happens. Anyway, it means models are very good at looking after themselves and they'd probably be happy to have a would-be musical actress tagging along for a few days.

'I guess if I said I was staying with a friend . . . But Isabelle's so – you know – glamorous. Would she let me?' Jenny asks. She's not looking quite so devastated now. More thoughtful and almost eager. She blinks the last of her tears away and stares at me hopefully.

'Of course she would. She's practically my sister-in-law, after all.'

At this, Jenny looks astonished.

'WHAT?'

Oh yeah. I haven't mentioned that bit yet. So I tell her about the whole engagement thing, and her eyes grow brighter with every sentence.

'How romantic! And you really think she'd be OK about the flat?'

This is a flicker of the old Jenny. Two words for Harry and Isabelle, and she's off making plans for herself again. But right now, that's exactly what I need. People who have better things to think about than my brother's wedding arrangements.

'I'll call her now, if you like. At least, I'll call Harry, and Isabelle's practically glued to him these days.'

I call, and Isabelle is indeed standing next to Harry when he gets the call (or sitting in his lap or whatever) and she's delighted to help. She says she'll be in New York herself for some of the time, so she'll make sure Jenny is hooked up with 'some really cool people'.

Jenny's totally thrilled, and then suddenly horrified.

'Those assignments! I haven't even thought about them!'

We huddle round her computer and do the best we can for an hour, using Google and Wikipedia, Edie's tips, what we can remember from class, and our imaginations. We're probably not going to be A-grade students this time, but our English teacher is pretty used to that.

On the way out, I casually ask if Gloria's washing machine has broken down. Jenny looks at me dead-eyed.

'Not exactly. I'll get around to it. Just been busy worrying about New York. Until you came.'

At the door, she gives me a bear hug. I hear a door being closed in the corridor behind us.

'Give Gloria my love.'

She nods. 'Sure.'

For a second, her face flickers. Despite the workshop and Isabelle's flat, I'm not sure I've ever seen her look so sad.

Chapter 6

When I get back from Jenny's, Granny is waiting for me in the kitchen with Mum. Isabelle and Harry have gone off to some party to be congratulated by yet more friends.

Granny is wearing a coral pink suit she had made in India over Christmas and two strings of pearls. She's trying out a new hairstyle that makes her look like a 99 vanilla ice cream, without the flake. Her cheeks are flushed, her eyes are bright and her gin and tonic is at serious risk of spilling over as she rattles her glass to emphasise her Total Joy at the current situation.

'Isn't it FABULOUS? Nonie, you're a very lucky girl. They are the most wonderful family. Isabelle's father, Lucius, is the Earl of Arden. Absolutely charming. And her mother's brother made a fortune in plastic packaging in the 1980s and is simply rolling in the stuff. Lots of holidays in the Hamptons and I believe he has a rather nice yacht.'

'Mummy!'

Even my mother is shocked at this. Granny is many things, but subtle isn't one of them.

'Well, darling, these things are important. If Nonie wants to attract the right sort of person one day, she needs to show herself off. And there's nothing like diving from a relative's yacht to demonstrate good legs.'

I look down. My legs are currently encased in tartan tights and lace-up Doc Martens. I think they're too short to be good anyway. But I can't see myself diving off a relative's yacht any time in the near future to attract some nerdy trust-fund kid, so I'm not too worried.

'And of course there's always the wedding itself,' Granny goes on. 'I know it's a bit early for Nonie, but it will be full of prospects. You'll be a bridesmaid, I assume?'

I shrug. But by now Mum and Granny are back onto their favourite subject. Locations, guest lists, favoured relatives, banned relatives, hats . . .

A shudder of horror suddenly flickers over Granny's face.

'She is religious, isn't she? As far as weddings are concerned, I mean? I couldn't bear a two-minute ceremony in some register office. Buffy Peaswood's daughter did it in a concrete building in Swindon or something and held the reception on a bus. Buffy nearly died.'

Mum smiles. 'I don't know. We can ask her. Oh, sorry.' Mum's BlackBerry has started buzzing. She grabs it off the kitchen counter and pops outside to take the call. Granny immediately turns to me.

'This is so important for your mother, darling. You will help her out with it, won't you, when I'm not here? It's her first proper wedding. We haven't had one in the family since I married your grandpa. What with your Uncle Jack and . . . everything.'

My heart plummets. I nod. I'm suddenly feeling queasy. But there's something I've been wanting to ask for a while. Now seems as good a time as any.

'Er, Granny. About Vicente. Mum was really in love with him, wasn't she? Before she . . . had me.'

Granny gives me a sideways look. She pauses for a minute. Then she nods and looks nostalgic. 'They were a wonderful couple. He's so classically handsome. And my darling, the acres in Brazil. And he was so generous to your mother. Always. Even after . . . the complications. When I think that he just gave her this place for all of you to live in. But—' she takes a sharp breath, tangy with regret, '—life goes on. It wasn't to be.'

I nod again.

'Tell Mum I'm . . . in my room. I've got an assignment I need to finish. She knows all about it.'

'But darling, I've just got here!'

Granny looks appalled. She's not used to being abandoned in the kitchen while we get on with our lives. But I'm not up to entertaining her right now. I'm not up to anything right now.

I race to my room and close the door behind me. Then I slide down it and try to think about *King Lear*. As opposed to other tragedies, closer to home.

It's a simple story. Not very Shakespearean. Granny had two children and a practically religious desire to marry them off – ideally to people with yachts. However, Mum's brother, Uncle Jack, found drugs when he should have been finding a fiancée. It all went horribly wrong and he ended up in a caravan in East Anglia, where he works as an occasional mechanic and tries to cope with the fact that various bits of his body stopped working in the 1990s after he'd injected and sniffed too much gunk into them. Mum sends money and Granny donates food parcels from Harrods on a regular basis, but we don't really talk about him.

Mum, on the other hand, became a successful model in her teens and travelled the world. She met Vicente and had Harry after a whirlwind romance. They planned to get married and live on Vicente's estate in Brazil, but something went wrong between them and while she was modelling in Paris, she met my dad and accidentally had me. She obviously couldn't get back together again with Vicente after that. She couldn't marry my dad either. Mum and my dad have always made it clear that they would have been hopeless if they'd got married. The only things they really have in common are a love of art, and Paris. They manage to argue spectacularly whenever they meet. But, as Granny says, life goes on.

In Mum's case, life went on as a single mother with two children. She couldn't keep modelling with both of us in tow, so she set up as an art dealer. She was too busy with the new business for serious dating. She has been ever since.

As I say, it's a simple story and it shouldn't make me sit here shaking like this. But when I think about Mum and how beautiful she was (and still is – although a saggier, wrinklier version now, of course), it seems such a waste that she never got that wedding and that happy ever after.

Granny's right. I must be really supportive and excited about all the preparations. And I mustn't mind at all that Harry will be leaving home and it will just be Mum and me, rattling around this big house that Vicente gave us. And maybe one day I can leap off a relative's yacht and show off my 'good legs' to some appropriate fiancé-type and keep everyone happy. Then I can settle down with the appropriate fiancé-type in his overstuffed apartment somewhere suitable and read novels. Yaaay.

Chapter 7

To take my mind off things, I check my emails and Edie's website.

Edie's blog is full of news about her latest fundraising campaign to buy computers for the schools we support in Mumbai and Crow's village in Uganda. I say 'we'. Edie does most of the work, between orchestra practice, total school brilliance, debating and occasional five-minute breaks when her mother forces her to eat something.

There's an email from little Lakshmi, the girl I try and look after in India. Lakshmi is working hard to become a fashion designer, like Crow. The fact that she's a street child from Mumbai and has to sell books at the roadside to afford a roof over her head (she's nine) isn't holding her back for a second. She's online whenever she can persuade anyone to let her near a computer and type for her, and she already has her own opinions about the latest couture collections.

Another message, stiff and formal, turns out to be

from the matching overcoat men, asking for Crow's email address because 'they can't access it through the usual channels'. I don't know what the usual channels are, but I cheerfully inform them that Crow doesn't have an email address. Unlike Lakshmi, Crow hates computers and avoids them as much as possible. Same with phones, mostly. She uses me to manage communications, so they will have to talk to me if they want to ask her anything. Hah! I may have had cappuccino foam on my lip or whatever (maybe it was the kimono?), but they're stuck with me now.

I wish I'd paid more attention when they chatted to us in Paris. I'm sure they were explaining something really important, but the only words I can remember are 'investment vehicle', which after 'pension prospects' and 'tax liability' is the phrase most guaranteed to switch my brain off. Do they want to invest in Crow? Do they want her to design a vehicle? Do they realise that she mostly does mini-dresses? I'll have to wait for them to email back to find out.

I go downstairs to see if Crow is still working, so I can tell her about it. It's late by now. She ought to be at home in bed, but you never know. However, when I get to her workroom in the basement, the lights are off. The room is quiet. She must actually be getting some sleep for once.

I flick the switch – I can't help it – and the room is bathed in pools of light. It's impossible for me to enter this place and not check what Crow's been up to. Until last week, she was finishing off a couple of rock-chick outfits for her clients to wear to It girl parties. Now, though, the mannequins are bare. It isn't until I get to her worktable that I see what she's been concentrating on since we got back from Paris.

The desktop is covered in drawings of the same girl – with a halo of ringlets and grey-green eyes – wearing different variations of the same dress. The skirt is very full and mid-calf length. It's several skirts actually, made of lace or net by the look of them, and they're scattered with rosebuds, as is the bodice. It's the sort of thing Giselle or some other romantic ballet heroine might wear.

It's obvious that the girl is supposed to be Isabelle, but it's not until I focus on the small bouquet of roses she's holding that I realise what the design is for. It's a wedding dress. THE wedding dress. The dress that will mark the start of everything being different.

Has Crow really been asked to make it? Whatever Isabelle wears is going to make headlines and designers will be falling over themselves to do it. I've already read that Galliano offered on the spot. If Isabelle's asked Crow instead, why didn't Crow tell me?

Crow's design is beautiful, but it's not quite there yet. Actually, it's a bit sickly, to be honest. But no doubt Crow will jazz it up somehow when she gets back to it tomorrow. Isabelle will love it, I'm sure, when it's right. Mum will be over the moon about it. Granny will probably levitate with pleasure.

And here I am. Back to thinking about Granny, and weddings, and Mum.

I turn off the workroom lights and drag myself up to bed.

Chapter 8

'Oh, not you too?'

Next morning in school, Edie notices the grey shadows under my eyes.

'Lear,' I say ominously. 'And I don't mean the jets.'

Luckily, she believes me. Shakespeare has been known to make me look tragic.

Jenny, on the other hand, is perky. Jenny is wondering where exactly in SoHo Isabelle's flat might be, and what the movies will be on the plane to New York. Jenny is humming two of the latest songs she's been learning for the workshop. Jenny is looking like a girl who slept well last night and slightly ODd on the Coco Pops at breakfast.

She gives me another hug.

'Mum said yes, no problem with me going if Isabelle will be there. Nonie, you're a total star.'

I smile modestly. If being almost related to people with multiple mega-homes makes me a star, I'm happy to help.

Edie looks across at us and notices what we're wearing.

'Oh God. Keep your head down Friday?' she asks sympathetically.

We nod. We don't have a uniform at our school, so normally I'd be in some magic, knitted number of Crow's, my tartan tights and a pair of silver glitter Doc Martens or customised wellies, like Crow's. Jenny's developed a nice line in prom dresses and little cardigans, which I cheer up for her with felt flowers and an ever-expanding brooch collection. But today she's in jeans and a baggy navy-blue jumper, and I'm in a pleated grey skirt, white shirt, black tights and chequerboard Converse, which is about as conservative as I can physically get.

It all started in September, and it's got gradually worse ever since.

Jenny and I picked French for AS level this year. Then our headmistress had the genius idea of combining with a local state school, Wetherby, for French, so they can use our old teacher, Madame Stanley, who's a bit of an institution, and we can use their new language labs, which are bristling with the latest kit. Even when the genius idea was announced, we thought it sounded OK. A chance to meet some people our age. Now we'd have more people to go to the movies with, share essay crises with and generally hang out with. Including boys our age. Interesting. Fantastic if you go to an all-girls' school and have done since you were eleven.

But we didn't reckon on the Belles.

Annabelle Knechtli arrived at our school at the beginning of the year. At first, she was really excited to have a girl in the class – Jenny – who'd been in a movie and a West End play. Annabelle wants to go into TV when she leaves school and she was keen to hang out with Jenny, find out all about 'the business', be her BFF and totally monopolise her on Facebook. But Jenny already had two best friends – me and Edie – so things didn't really work out. Instead, Annabelle made friends with Maybelle, a girl from Wetherby, in French class and they formed the Belles. The Belles have two missions in life. To be really, *really* popular, especially with the boys. And to keep Jenny and me 'in our place'.

I'm still not exactly sure where 'our place' is, but I know it involves sitting at the back of the class and trying to avoid joining in conversations or plans, because we'll get frozen out. Lines like, 'Shouldn't you be at a premiere right now?' and 'I thought it was fashion week in Rio, DAH-LING,' tend to do it. To our faces, the Belles are always sort-of polite. But things tend to go wrong in class. Stuff gets lost, or knocked over, or scribbled on, or broken. Our bags often disappear. We try and stay out of things as much as possible, so they'll forget we're even there.

I could really do without Keep your head down Friday right now, but I don't have much choice. We join the other girls doing French and lug our books and files down the road to Wetherby's state-of-the-art Language Pod.

Jenny and I make our way to the back seats as usual. Jenny immediately gets out a map of New York, hides it in her text book and starts working out how to get to her top three sights, which are the Empire State Building, 42nd Street and Times Square. I do my usual thing, which is staring at the back of the boys' heads and working out, in order, which ones I'd like to go out with if only I could get close enough to talk to any of them.

At least four of them are delectable. I don't know what it is about this school, but it breeds gorgeous boys. Gorgeous, unattainable, fascinating boys. All of whom in this class, by definition, speak at least a bit of French. And there's nothing sexier than listening to a London boy struggle to do a decent French accent. I do find this class distracting. It's lucky my dad's French, or this would be yet another subject I'd be scraping through by the skin of my teeth.

I'm just in the process of ranking Ashley (blond hair, dirty jeans and a cheeky way with French vowels) above Liam (black curls, aquamarine eyes, hint of an Irish accent, permanent half-amused smile), when I notice more activity than usual around the Belles. Madame Stanley has, typically, forgotten something and needs to phone someone to bring it over. Meanwhile, the Belles are looking at something on their desk – a magazine, I think – and have got some of the nearest class members to cluster round. There is giggling from the girls and sniggering from the boys. There is also furtive glancing in our direction.

'Ignore them,' Jenny mutters under her breath.

I try.

A thought has occurred to me. A truly terrible, horrible thought. I push it to the back of my mind.

Madame Stanley dashes back in, looking stressed.

'Everyone back to your desks,' she says briskly. 'Headphones on.'

As they slowly disperse I catch sight of the magazine. It's open on a group photo. I recognise the group, even from several desks away. Annabelle catches my eye and grins delightedly.

I only catch one word as they settle back down. It's almost drowned by sniggering.

'Kimono.'

'Ignore them,' Jenny says more fiercely.

But I can't. It's my own fault. I knew it was a mistake at the time. I was just having a floral Japanese moment. Now it's in a weekly magazine, with commentary by the style queens with the sharpest tongues in the country.

A few faces look round, pityingly. This is the worst bit. One of them is Liam's. The boy with the black curls and blue, blue eyes. But no half-amused expression this time. In fact, he looks perplexed. Presumably he's wondering how any girl can wear a kimono in public outside Tokyo. As, at the moment, am I.

I shrug my shoulders back at him and try to imagine impressing him instead, by leaping off a relative's yacht. But to be honest, I think it would have the same effect. I am destined to perplex boys I like and attract weird and unreliable ones, like Alexander last year – the ballet dancer with the lowest kissing ability in London. Thank God Harry's getting married, because this is the nearest Mum's ever going to get to planning a wedding in our family.

Chapter 9

On Saturday Vicente arrives from Brazil, and Mum throws a party to celebrate.

Mum doesn't throw parties very often. When your house is mostly white, apart from the delicate artworks on the walls, which have been given to you by old friends and are extremely precious, you don't like the idea of filling it with dirty shoes and alcohol-filled glasses – or, as we would say, guests.

But to be fair, when Mum parties, she PARTIES. She's called some company that can do decorations and cock-tails in a hurry, and when I get home from school on Friday they're already busy hanging lanterns around the place and setting up a mini-disco in our sitting room. By Saturday morning, every surface in the kitchen is covered in boxes of glasses or canapé trays and I have to eat my toast on the stairs.

It's handy having a resident DJ. Harry's busy in his bedroom, making the playlist to end all playlists. This is only the second time he's had the chance to DJ in front of his dad. (The first time was during Rio Fashion Week last year, and no, I didn't tell The Belles he was working there.) You'd think, at twenty-three and running his own successful business, that he might have moved out by now, but it simply hasn't occurred to him. With his job, he's almost always travelling, so if he got a flat he'd hardly be in it. Plus he's usually going out with a supermodel, so if he needs to kip somewhere cool, he can do it at one of her places. Plus our house is really, really nice.

It's nice anyway, when it's just Mum, Harry, Crow and me, all quietly doing our thing in our different rooms and not talking to each other much. But the place is fantastic when it's all dressed up for a party. I wander around, checking out the lanterns, the glitter balls (there are several), the coloured lights and the flower arrangements. The place is suddenly full of white roses. Mum explains that Vicente has sent her a hundred of them – her favourite – as a sort of 'hello' present.

Crow arrives to start work on some new dresses. When she's not making them to order for clients, she makes them for a stall in the Portobello Road. People love wearing her experimental shapes and flattering styles. They love their friends saying, 'Oh my GOD! You look incredible! Where did you get that?' Which happens a lot when you're wearing Crow's handmade masterpieces. The stallholder is always asking her for more dresses to sell.

Meanwhile, I take the chance to have another look at the sketches she did for Isabelle.

'Is this the wedding dress?' I ask. 'It looks, er, great.'

Crow comes over. 'Oh, those are just doodles. I wasn't sure about them. They're wrong for her, aren't they? I was aiming for romantic, but I think I went too far.'

'So you're definitely doing the dress?' I check. 'Isabelle asked you?'

Crow nods. 'On the way back from Paris. Didn't I tell you? She wants to have three dresses for different bits of the day, but she wants me to do one of them.'

'No, you didn't tell me. But yaaay.'

Why can't I sound enthusiastic when I talk about Harry's wedding? What's wrong with me? And why do I feel the need to change the subject?

'Those men were back in touch,' I add. 'The matching overcoat ones.'

'Oh,' Crow says. 'What did they want?'

'Your email address.'

She grins. She likes not having one. If she did, she might end up having conversations about investment vehicles. Instead, two minutes later, she's busy at her desk, working on a new design for Isabelle.

I leave her to it. I have a bit of a wardrobe crisis to resolve. I need to impress Mum's and Harry's friends with my amazing style savvy this evening. More of them than I care to imagine will have seen the kimono moment in that magazine and I have lots of catching up to do. I try not to think about the fact that Isabelle's friends will be there too, and ninety per cent of them are models. Even in the normal world, I am short, flat-faced and cursed with wonky dark hair. Tonight, I will look positively deformed beside the average guest. But, to quote Granny again, life goes on.

I reject the brief idea of a burka, and consider my more serious options.

Chapter 10

'Doesn't she look beautiful?'

Vicente has slipped in beside me at the party and we're both admiring Mum as she chats to some of her arty friends. I nod in agreement. Mum's in a vintage floor-length Halston dress she's had since her modelling days, and a long gold necklace with a large topaz rock at the bottom of it. Even without much makeup – she never wears more than lipgloss nowadays – she's still pretty stunning. The soft light helps, of course. I enjoy teasing Mum about her age, but actually, it doesn't bother her. She says she's having more fun now than she did when she was modelling. This can't be possible, of course. She just sits around working most of the time. But at least she doesn't complain about it.

Vicente is not bad himself. Jet-black hair. Angular face. Granny wasn't joking when she called him classically handsome. But more than that, he is totally charming. He's been charming all evening and he keeps it up as he guides me onto the dance floor and makes a decent job of grooving on down to some Rolling Stones that Harry has put on in his honour.

'Mum loved the roses,' I shout across at him. Harry is not shy about loud music. The neighbours have been round to complain twice already. I think even the walls are rattling.

'Good to hear it,' Vicente shouts back. 'That reminds me . . . do you mind?'

He eases his way across the dance floor and invites Mum onto it. I don't mind, really. They make such a good couple.

Crow and Jenny are clustered in a corner. I go and join them and we all watch Mum and Vicente doing their thing.

'They're naturals, aren't they?' Jenny shouts across at me.

I nod.

'You'd think they'd been together for the last twenty years.'

I nod again, hoping that my sudden blurry vision is due to standing too close to a speaker, and nothing else.

'Why didn't they stay together, anyway?' Jenny asks.

I want to say something, but I'm still trying to find the words when a red-faced man suddenly appears in the middle of the dance floor, shouting and waving his arms around in an extremely unfunky way.

Harry, shocked, turns the music off.

'I SAID,' the man bellows, going a dangerous shade of maroon, 'TURN THE BLOODY MUSIC DOWN OR I WILL SUE!'

As the room is actually totally quiet by now, apart from him, he surprises even himself with his personal volume. Fifty pairs of eyes are looking at him. He coughs.

'I'm sorry,' he says. 'Let me rephrase. Thank you very much for turning the music down. Now, if you'll excuse me, I'll get back to my dinner party.'

'Oh!' Mum exclaims, her hand going to her mouth. 'You were having a dinner party? I'm so sorry. I had no idea. What can we do?'

'Nothing,' the man says flatly. I recognise him as our next-door neighbour, the grumpy guy who moved in last year. 'My more sensitive guests have gone home. The others are nursing Nurofen in a darkened room. I should get back to them. Oh, congratulations, by the way.' He says this to Harry. 'I heard the news. Hard to miss it. I assume this means you'll be moving out?'

Harry grins, looks sheepish and nods.

The man smiles with grim satisfaction and disappears. Harry turns the music back up to half its original volume.

Jenny, thank goodness, forgets what she was talking about and instead goes back to complaining about how Edie (not here – debating rehearsal) never has any fun any more, and how amazing the latest styles look on all the passing models.

'By the way, I like your outfit,' she says to me eventually, as an afterthought.

I know she's being polite. I'm in a black knitted dress I've borrowed from Mum. It's skin-tight Azzedine Alaïa and totally fashion-safe. But it was made for a taller person than me and, bizarrely, makes me look like a slightly fashion-conscious nun. Better than the kimono, but not one of my greatest moments.

'Doesn't Isabelle look incredible?' Jenny adds.

This is easy to agree with. My future sister-in-law has turned up in an oversize white cotton shirt worn as a dress, with a seashell necklace and a dog lead worn as a belt. Oh, and a pair of sculpture ankle boots borrowed from the Dior couture collection, to show she's making an effort.

Me, Azzedine Alaïa – nun. Isabelle, white cotton shirt – sex goddess.

I love Harry, and Isabelle's adorable, but couldn't he have gone out with a normal human, just for once?

Chapter 11

I wonder whether to try and adapt the Alaïa for Keep your head down Friday, but decide against it. Even though – with a bit of customising and a black cardigan – it would make me practically invisible, I don't think Mum would appreciate me taking my scissors to her vintage wardrobe.

Luckily, Maybelle was in the audience for a quiz show that will be on TV tomorrow, so most of French class is talking about that. Madame Stanley is struggling to make them at least do it in French, but as none of us know the words for quiz master, studio, retakes or broadcast, it's a painful process.

I'm sitting with my head practically between my knees, secretly checking my phone for messages. I'm expecting something from Jenny any minute. We're not technically allowed our phones in class. We're DEFI-NITELY not allowed to check them. But I've known people start and end whole relationships by text in the course of a single lesson. My phone, though, stays dark and silent the whole time.

Jenny's been in New York for five days. She hasn't been in touch since Tuesday, when she rang to say that Isabelle's flat was gorgeous and she was sitting in it, eating fries and watching *American Idol* on Isabelle's outsize plasma screen TV. As it was three o'clock in the morning in London when I got the call, I wasn't as thrilled for her as I might have been. Since then, everything's gone quiet.

Jenny has a habit of getting into trouble when she's off doing her drama thing. Sometimes it's boy trouble (being kissed by the two-timing Teenage Sex God while making her movie). Sometimes it's girl trouble (being upstaged, for a while at least, by the girl the sex god two-timed her with). Sometimes it's critic trouble (being compared to dining furniture for her wooden performance in the movie). This is the first time she's had to perform in a foreign city all by herself, without even her mother for support. Her silence is worrying me.

It's not helped by Maybelle and her friends whispering things like, 'So where's Sandra Bullock Junior then? Gone to the Oscars, has she? Hahahaha. Maybe Miley Cyrus needs her for a co-star.'

'She's off sick,' I mutter. I can't believe that Miley Cyrus had to put up with this. Except I'm sure I read somewhere that she did. She must have had lots of days 'off sick', I suppose.

I tell Edie about the lack of contact over lunch. She looks as worried as me.

'Have you heard from Phil, by the way?' I ask, while we're on the subject of people we like who happen to be in America right now.

'Yeah,' she sighs. 'He says I'm working too hard. He says when he was at high school, he was out surfing most afternoons.'

'The web?'

'No. The Pacific.'

'Oh. Huh. That's kind of him, rubbing it in.'

Edie sighs again. I'm sure there are many things she'd like Hot Phil to rub in, but references to surfing aren't one of them.

'He says I really need to go over there and he'll take me out and show me the coast and give me a chance to chill out.'

This sounds pretty good to me, but I can tell from Edie's expression that, even though she spent Christmas with her face glued to his, she thinks it's the stupidest idea she's ever heard.

'He just doesn't have a clue,' she says. 'This is the biggest exam year of my life. Apart from next year. And I need the holidays for music practice. And to revise for SATs and rehearse my interview techniques. Plus I need to keep my website up to speed. If it doesn't constantly have new stuff on it, people will stop looking at it.'

She makes the whole experience sound such fun. Not. I know what I'm about to say will be wrong for some reason, but I say it anyway.

'But does it really matter how many people look at your website? I mean, I know it's an amazingly large number, but can't it dip for a while?'

She looks at me, horrified.

'No, it can't! It's part of my personal statement for Harvard that I run the site and it's got this many visitors a week and we're raising enough money to buy those computers next year. Remember?' She sees my expression. 'What?'

I can't really tell her what I'm thinking. Because I'm thinking that this isn't exactly Edie at her best. Normal Edie wants to buy those computers for the schools we support because the children need them. Not because it will make her look good in front of a bunch of professors at Harvard. Maybe Hot Phil's right. Maybe she should do a bit less stressing out and a bit more surfing.

'I'm thinking about Jenny,' I lie. 'You know, hoping she hasn't lost her voice or anything.'

'Oh, great. Thanks for all your support,' Edie says with maximum sarcasm. But I still think the Jenny answer was better than the 'you're turning into a self-centred exam freak' answer.

Despite that, Edie doesn't talk to me for the rest of the afternoon.

As soon as Jenny gets back, I check anxiously for disasters. It turns out that I was wrong to worry, though.

She arrives at school on Monday morning with a song on her lips. A loud, bouncy one from *Mamma Mia*. And a big smile. In reply to my questions, she assures me that she didn't lose her voice, or get kissed by anyone unsuitable or upstaged by anyone more talented. Bill was thrilled with the way she did the songs and said so. So did the composer, Jackson Ward, who it turns out is one of the most famous men on Broadway and The Kind Of Person You Want To Impress.

'He was so lovely,' Jenny sighs dreamily, as she's telling me all about it for the fourth time. 'He said he loved my "perky personality" and he just wanted to adopt me. His daughter's nineteen and we hung out a lot together. She's called Charlotte and she's really cool. She goes to Juilliard. You know . . . the music school.'

Jenny actually has a slight American accent as she says this. She's still mentally on 42nd Street and clearly it is for her what Oxford Street and the V&A are for me. But I'm still nervous. I check whether Isabelle's flat was really OK, whether Jenny was approached by any pervy men (I remember Mum's modelling stories), whether she was bored or lonely or intimidated by all the amazing musical people she met. But no.

'I didn't get the chance to hang out with Isabelle's friends. Charlotte Ward and the guys from the workshop looked after me, like, the whole time,' she says, with her new transatlantic twang. 'We went out together, we did crazy karaoke together. They told me all their stories about the shows they've done, the tours they've been on . . . And the singing was awesome. Even better than acting. It was . . .' she pauses, searching for the right word, '. . . it was natural, Nonie. I mean, it was hard to nail the songs in the first place, but once I did, it was like I'd done it all my life. Except, of course, I never have. Not at that level.' She sounds wistful.

'One day you will,' I reassure her. 'You'll go to drama school and get some amazing theatre role and they'll be begging you to go to America. And I'll be helping Crow and she'll be designing in some incredible studio in Paris . . .'

I wait for Jenny to ask me more about the incredible studio in Paris. I've been picturing this for a while now. Crow with her own fashion house (we'll be about thirty by then) and me running it for her. I've even worked out what colour we'll paint the walls – sky blue – and what the logo might look like.

But instead Jenny asks, 'Did you know the Queen was only twenty-five when she became Queen?'

'Yes, I think so,' I say, hoping this will satisfy her so we can get back to Paris.

'There she was, madly in love, new husband, two little children. She just wanted to have a nice family life and ride horses, and suddenly she had to run a country. Not just a country. An empire.'

'Mm hmm.'

'Princess Margaret had a great life, though. Dancing. Cocktails. Friends. And she went to the ballet a lot and hung around with artists. And wore the most beautiful clothes.'

'Mm hmm.'

I say this in my most uninterested voice, but Jenny still doesn't get the message.

'Alanna – the girl who was singing Margaret – was absolutely awesome. She's been in musicals since she was six. If the show ever goes to Broadway and she gets the part, I'm definitely going to watch her do it.'

'Mm hmm.'

Jenny finally looks at me, surprised.

'You're not listening, are you?'

'Well, I wasn't there. I'm thrilled, though. Honestly.'

She sighs.

'So, did anything happen while I was away?'

'Well, Hot Phil thinks Edie's working too hard and he wants her to go surfing . . .'

'Mm hmm.'

Jenny is not riveted by the Hot Phil relationship, I can tell.

'Oh, and they've been in touch about *Vogue* next month.'

'Oh, have they?' she asks. Her voice is tiny. We're both glad the Belles aren't here to listen to this conversation.

'The photographer's fixed, and the studio,' I say. 'You

need to have your hair cut and coloured next week, but they're sorting that too.'

'Mm hmm.'

But this isn't a bored 'mm hmm'. This is an old-Jenny, super-nervous 'mm hmm'.

'You'll be fabulous,' I assure her.

'Mm hmm?'

She looks at me as if I've signed her up to star at the Coliseum. Facing the lions.

Chapter 12

We're not talking about buying *Vogue* here, or even visiting their offices. We're not talking about Isabelle being in *Vogue* (which she is, of course, on a regular basis). We're talking about Jenny being in the June issue. And on it. On the cover. And as far as Jenny's concerned, it's all my fault.

It's not actually my fault – it's Crow's. Two Christmases ago, Crow launched her first high-street collection for Miss Teen. Just a few pieces. Jewel-coloured party dresses, skirts and crystal embroidered tee-shirts, mostly. Finally it meant that thousands of girls could wear her stuff, instead of just a lucky few. The collection sold out almost overnight. So naturally, they asked her to design another one. This time it's a summer one – all white cotton, layering and clever cutting. It'll be launched in May, but they're already busy on the publicity for it.

Making Jenny the face of the new collection was, admittedly, my idea. Jenny is curvy and gorgeous and looks fabulous in Crow's clothes. When the news first started to leak out about how good this collection was going to be, the editor of British *Vogue* decided to stick her neck out and put Jenny on the cover in one of Crow's new designs, despite the fact that she's a size 14 and isn't exactly super-famous, having been in one school musical, one film and one play. At first Jenny was thrilled, but the closer the shoot gets, the more she's changing her mind about me being a fashion genius and deciding that I am, instead, DELUDED AND CRUEL.

But that's just nerves, as I keep telling her. She looks great, in her redheaded, bouncy, bubbly way. And even if she gets the zit outbreak to end all zit outbreaks, they can just airbrush it out. All she has to do is smile. She's an actress. Can't be that difficult.

You'd think.

Jenny's seventeenth birthday is coming up soon and in the past few years she has learned many things. One is that you can't trust a Hollywood Teenage Sex God as far as you can throw him. Another is that yellow trouser suits (Tokyo premiere for the movie three years ago) are a no-no. And finally, if you're not super-confident about the way you look, don't get your best friend to sign you up for the cover of *Vogue*. But if it's too late to back out, blame her and look at her accusingly whenever you get the chance.

When the day of the photo shoot comes, Jenny sits in front of the wall-size mirror at the studio, having her newly-coloured hair done and looking like she's about to be shot by a firing squad, instead of Ted Regent – otherwise known as 'the new David Bailey' or 'the man who makes cool hot'. The expression in her eyes flits between terror, whenever she catches sight of herself in her cover-ready makeup, and fury, whenever she catches sight of me, bobbing around behind her.

They're going for a sort of 'visiting alien' look. Jenny's wearing super-pale foundation (unnecessary, given how white her face looks already), loads of multicoloured eyeshadow, feathery false eyelashes in peacock colours and silver lipstick. She'll be almost unrecognisable, I assure her.

'They'll recognise my boobs though,' she says miserably. 'Even under all the clothes. And my fat shoulders.'

'They're not fat. They're curvy.' How often do I have to tell this girl?

'And my fat arms.'

I sigh and give up. Luckily the hairdresser takes over. He seems to be used to reassuring nervous models before a big shoot.

'You've got gorgeous, delicate wrists. I've been admiring. And your hair is to die for, girl! The shade! That colour's taken like a total dream. Everyone will want Jenny Burnt Orange by the time you're done. E-ver-y-one. Trust me.'

Eventually, when hair and makeup and wardrobe and nails and the fashion editor from *Vogue* and Crow and

Amanda Elat, who runs Miss Teen, are satisfied, Jenny shuffles out to pose for Ted Regent. We're in a studio in Shoreditch that used to be a workshop or a storage area, I'm guessing. All white-painted brick, with a glitter ball in the centre and a large white background for Jenny to pose against.

'I could picture doing a show here,' Crow says happily.

I agree. It would be perfect for a little catwalk show. Atmospheric and exciting, especially with Lady Gaga playing at full volume on the sound system, like she is now. I imagine where I'd seat the photographers and the audience, and how I'd organise the models coming out and what I'd do with the cute little gallery upstairs . . .

In front of the white background, Ted Regent is arranging Jenny on a chair. He looks like a model himself – all skinny jeans and designer stubble. He seems to have the energy of a hyperactive four-year-old. One minute he's on his knees, adjusting Jenny's ankle. Then he's back on his feet, changing the angle of her head. Then he's dancing around, calling out emotions for Jenny to act and singing along to snatches of Poker Face. Jenny, on the other hand, looks like she's taken the song literally: her features are set rigid and it's impossible to tell what's going on behind her eyes. I bet it isn't like this when Isabelle's in front of the lights.

There's a break, while everyone who can clusters round a laptop to look at what they've done so far. They tweak the clothes, try another few poses, cluster round the computer again and then Jenny's taken off to put on outfit number two. Meanwhile, Crow and I stare at each other. She's done a beautiful job with this collection and personally I can't wait to wear it. This is the moment when it should all come to life. It's about to get the biggest splash of publicity we could ever imagine. But so far, our model looks more like something out of a wanted poster. My mistake, of course, but Crow's too nice to say so out loud. Instead, she gives me a wonky smile.

Jenny comes back in a tunic and leggings, accessorised with a big scarf and chunky jewellery. She tries out a few more poses. Increasingly, Ted gets her to turn away from the camera and shoots the back of her head. Understandably. It's the most animated part of her.

It's early evening before we get to go home.

'God, I'm glad that's over!' Jenny says, slumping into a taxi beside us in jeans and a puffa jacket. Oh, and still wearing the feathery eyelashes. She wants to show them to Gloria before she takes them off. Then she's going to give them to Stella, the cat, as a present. Stella will love chasing and killing them.

She rootles through her handbag for her phone, to tell Gloria she's on her way. When she pulls it out, she looks surprised.

'Ooh, a text. From Jackson Ward. You know, the composer.' She frowns. 'Oh, he sent it ages ago. Damn.'

She checks her watch. But as I vividly remember from

her call, New York is five hours behind. Although it's quite late in London, it's still a perfectly reasonable time of day over there. She calls him back.

'Hi! Jackson? It's Jenny Merritt. You called me?'

And from that moment on, her face gradually transforms. By the end of the call, she's glowing. If Ted Regent could have got that out of her for even a couple of frames, he'd be going home a happy man.

'What is it?' Crow asks, as Jenny stuffs her phone back into her bag.

'Jackson wants me,' she says. 'A couple of the producers who saw the first workshop are interested in staging the show. They want to do another workshop and make some tweaks.'

'With you? Again?' I say, to be sure.

Jenny gives me a hurt look for ever doubting her. 'Jackson says, as far as he's concerned, he's found his princess. Bill agrees. I just have to convince these producers. Jackson said, "You're my Elizabeth, Jenny." Imagine!' Her eyes sparkle.

This is fantastic, of course. A tiny part of me wishes that she could have received this call about four hours ago, when we really needed it, but hey – it was only a *Vogue* cover shoot. What's to stress about?

Amanda Elat calls from Miss Teen next morning. *Vogue* liked the editorial shots of Jenny for the six-page spread inside, but they've decided to use Kate Moss on the cover.

I'm not surprised.

Crow finally admitted it, after we'd dropped Jenny off at her flat.

'I love her and everything. I mean, she's really special and great. But next time, shall we use a professional?'

And, despite the fact that Jenny is my best friend from primary school, and my favourite person to look at in Crow's clothes, and using her was my idea, I said, 'Absolutely.'

Chapter 13

'Blimey, girls, what a disaster. I should never have listened to you. We should have used a professional.'

'It's not a disaster at all. Jenny was fantastic!' I say hotly.

Crow and I are in the boardroom of Miss Teen. It's a week later and we're discussing the PR campaign for the launch of Crow's collection. The centrepiece of this campaign, naturally, was going to be the *Vogue* cover. Now it's not. Oops. But it's one thing for Crow and me to point out Jenny's less-than-perfect modelling ability, and quite another for elderly adults to do it. Especially as Andy Elat, Amanda's father and the man who owns Miss Teen, is hardly a cover girl himself.

'Oh?' he says, looking at me sceptically. 'Fantastic? Explain.'

Hmm. This is tricky. How do I explain that what happened on the shoot was a triumph? However, I've started so I'd better finish.

'Well,' I say, trying to squash the rising waves of panic and defend my friend, 'Jenny was amazing in the editorial shots. Six pages of them. She's got a very different look from all the super-skinny supermodels.' Gradually, I start to remember why I wanted Jenny in the first place. 'And the way she wears the clothes, girls will be able to imagine looking good in them too, because she's one of them. And it was *because* she wasn't a professional model that *Vogue* found her so interesting. So without her, we might not have got to shoot the collection for them at all.'

I sit back, panting slightly, and hide it by taking a sip of water. There are a few nervous faces around the table. But a few nods too.

'Fair point,' someone mutters.

Andy Elat smiles very slightly and is about to move on when Crow jabs me, hard, in the ribs with her elbow and I remember the other thing I was supposed to say about Jenny. This time, it's a bit easier because we've been practising. I take another quick sip of water.

'Oh and by the way,' I say as casually as I can, 'it's thanks to Jenny that we'll be getting some extra coverage. She's going to the Met Ball in May, just before the launch, and she's wearing a ballgown of Crow's to it. She's going with Isabelle Carruthers, so we should get quite a lot of publicity from that too, I guess.'

The reaction around the room is everything we'd hoped for. Spilt coffee. Impressed swear words. A moment of stunned silence. And then a babble of conversation. Crow and I look nonchalant throughout the whole thing. We rehearsed it in the mirror last night, so we know we've got nonchalance sussed.

After that, the meeting goes much better.

Andy Elat catches me as I'm leaving the boardroom at the end and gives me a grin.

'Nicely played, Nonie,' he says. 'Some people get overwhelmed by these meetings but you've got . . .' He searches for a word suitable for my delicate teenage ears. 'Chutzpah. I like your style, kid. And you know your stuff.'

Crow tucks her arm into mine as we make our way downstairs. She helps anchor me, as otherwise I'd probably float out of the building and off down Oxford Street. I love these moments. They're the ones I live for: sharing Crow's vision, persuading people to be on our side, turning things around . . .

'It worked!' Crow says. 'You were sweet about Jenny. And you really sounded like we planned all that Met Ball stuff.'

'I know!' I giggle. 'Do you remember my face when Isabelle first mentioned it?'

She does.

The day after the *Vogue* shoot, Jenny got a call from New York to give her the dates of the new workshop. Crow was there when we rang Isabelle to ask about Jenny using her apartment again. Isabelle said 'Sure! First week in May, did you say? Oh, I'm going to the Met Ball that week. Would Jenny like to come?'

Me: 'Hahahahah!'

Jenny: 'Why are you laughing, Nonie? What did she say?'

Me: 'She said would you like to go to the Met Ball?'

Jenny: 'What's the Met Ball?'

Me: 'WHAT?'

Jenny: 'Don't look at me like that! I've never heard of it. What is it?'

Me: long sigh. And then, to Isabelle, 'I'll call you back, if that's OK. But . . . hahahahaha.'

Jenny: 'Stop giggling and tell me.'

So I told her. Crow helped.

The Met Ball is THE fashion party of the year. The biggest, the glitziest and the best. It's the gala held at the Metropolitan Museum of Art in New York to launch their annual Costume Institute exhibition, and it's attended by anyone who is anyone in fashion. It's where Tom Ford will be queuing up for drinks behind Marc Jacobs. Well, probably not queuing, but whatever they do. And Anna Wintour will be wafting around, impressing people with her amazing haircut and the fact that she knows EVERY-BODY, while Gwen Stefani chats to Claudia Schiffer in a corner and John Galliano struts about in his cloak. Film stars – major film stars – will be BEGGING to go along. And every fashion editor in existence will be aching to see what they wear, so they can publicise it to the world.

That's the Met Ball. The chances of them wanting a seventeen-year-old schoolgirl actress and wannabe musical star on their guest list are minimal. But by the time I'd finished describing the event to Jenny, she badly wanted to go.

So I called Isabelle back and said, 'Look, I know it's practically impossible, but if you can make a miracle happen, that would be amazing.'

Isabelle said, 'Jenny's just done a *Vogue* shoot, hasn't she? And I keep meeting people in New York who are talking about her. Jackson Ward's a big fan, apparently. Don't worry, I'm sure I'll get her in.'

Being Isabelle, she did.

When she called back, Crow and Jenny were still in my room. We did a sort of Indian war dance around the room, whooping and hollering and laughing. Jenny suddenly stopped and said, 'Oh my God. Who's going to make my dress?'

Crow and I looked shocked and hurt and stopped dancing. Jenny laughed and said, 'Got you!' Crow grinned too and instantly sat down and started designing something. On what happened to be the cover of my Business Studies workbook, which is now decorated with sketches of full-skirted ballgowns, evening coats and Crow's attempts at Christian Louboutin shoes.

We celebrated with hot chocolate and popcorn. Then we called Edie to tell her, and even Edie was pleased. Then we started practising our nonchalant expressions for today's meeting. They took a lot of practising, because we kept bursting into fits of giggles. But practice makes perfect, as I have just proved. It's a chutzpah thing.

Chapter 14

The next few weeks are packed with activity. School gives way to the Easter holidays, thank goodness, because I have better things to do than endless assignments and organising Keep your head down Friday outfits. Finally, I can concentrate on checking Jenny's *Vogue* interview to go with the photos (it's great) and discussing launch events with Miss Teen. In fact, if I had to describe my life right now, I would have to admit it feels glamorous. Like somebody else's life – not the sort of girl who still has the butterfly duvet cover from when she was ten, but the sort of girl who knows people who do photo shoots and design collections. The sort of girl the Belles would really *hate*, if they knew. Another good reason it's the holidays.

Crow, meanwhile, is happily designing the perfect ballgown for Jenny, using every spare minute to get the right white satin, the right black velvet and the perfect fit. Her original sketch has been refined into something simple and dramatic: a bit Audrey Hepburn, a bit Grace Kelly, and – to Jenny's delight – a bit the young Queen Elizabeth, when she looked like a film star herself, before she hit her matching-hat-and-coat phase.

There is one slight complication, which Edie is the first to notice when we get back to school. Jenny will have to miss two AS papers while she's in New York. Our head has this thing about missing exams. She doesn't like it. Which is why we leave it until the last possible minute to tell her. Alarmingly, she seems to be on the brink of saying no. Then, three days before Jenny's due to fly, the head summons her to her office. We meet her in the cafeteria afterwards, to find out the decision.

'How did it go?' Edie asks. She's got a SAT test this afternoon, so her eyes are glassy and her cheeks look drawn with nerves, but she's doing her best to pay attention.

'Well, you'll never guess—' Jenny says breathily.

'No,' Edie interrupts, 'we won't. Tell us.'

'OK. Well, apparently Jackson Ward rang her yesterday and kind of begged,' Jenny grins. 'It was great. He said he had to be quick, because Shirley Bassey needed to call him about something and he had to keep the line clear. She loved it! Plus she looked him up afterwards and found out all about his Tonys and Oscars . . .'

'*Oscars?*' I ask.

'Yup. He has two. For film scores. He's really good. I

keep telling you. Anyway, he explained that the workshop wouldn't be the same without me. How could she say no? As long as I take my books with me and revise blah blah blah. There's just one thing, though,' she adds, fiddling about with Edie's discarded paper napkin and avoiding our eyes.

'What?'

'Could one of you look after Stella while I'm away? Her kittens are due soon and I'd hate nobody to be there when they come. She'll need help.'

Edie and I look a bit confused. Not because Jenny's cat is pregnant. That's been a big topic of conversation recently. But it's surprising that she'll need help.

'What about your mum?' I ask. 'Can't she do it?'

There's a long pause. Jenny twists the napkin so much it breaks in half. She smoothes the pieces out on the table.

'She's not well. I don't think she's up to managing kittens on top of . . . stuff.'

'Oh, poor Gloria!' Edie, suddenly perks up, looks concerned and reaches out for Jenny's hand. 'What's the matter?'

Jenny shrugs. 'Just something she's had for a long time. She'll be fine. Eventually. But she's not good right now. Will you go?'

'Of course!' Edie says. 'I've always wanted a cat . . .'

Jenny reaches down for her bag, scrabbles around in it and, hesitating slightly, hands over a key with a mini Statue of Liberty attached to the keyring.

'It's my spare. Use it to let yourself in.'

Edie takes the key and nods.

Jenny smiles and shudders slightly, as if to shake off that part of the conversation. 'Anyway,' she says, turning to me, 'when shall I pick up the dress?'

'You can come round tonight, if you like,' I tell her, picturing the ballgown already neatly boxed up in our front hall and ready to fly to America, where it will be worn with a diamond bracelet that Isabelle's arranged for Jenny to borrow.

Edie gets up and gives both of us a strained smile. 'I'd better be going. See you later.'

We watch her head off to prepare for her test, while Jenny plans her ballgown and diamonds. We both know who we'd rather be.

Chapter 15

I should be jealous, but I'm not. I have fun stuff of my own to think about. Andy Elat has arranged a preview party to show Crow's new Miss Teen collection to influential people on the London fashion scene. We're off to the Tate Modern gallery, which is an ex-power station with enormous industrial spaces that are now full of modern art. And also, tonight, full of waiters with canapés and models in Crow's pared-back, white, layered clothes, which will look appropriately minimalist and artistic.

I've been planning my outfit for this event for weeks. I'm now on version twenty-seven, which is a chain-mail tunic over two dresses and some leggings from the collection, and a borrowed pair of plastic Vivienne Westwood platforms. Crow, being Crow, started to think about her outfit at about half-past three. When she shows up at the Tate Modern, it's in patchwork dungarees, her gold wellies and the origami headdress that John

Galliano gave her in January, and which she's kept like a religious relic ever since.

Edie is here with her mum, both wearing jackets and skirts that make them look like air hostesses for rival airlines. However, what they lack in fashion fabulousness, they make up for in friendliness. They've wordlessly adopted Jenny for the evening, not mentioning Gloria's absence. Edie's mum beckons me over with a smile and a wave.

'Nonie! At last someone I recognise! I mean, goodness, there are so many faces here that look familiar from magazines, but you're someone I actually know. How are you?'

As she says this, her face adopts a concerned, motherly look. She is, after all, the parent of one of the school's resident geniuses, so as far as she knows our lives are wall-to-wall exams and clarinet practice at the moment, when we're not volunteering and getting other brownie points for our CVs.

I'm about to tell her I am absolutely fine, but then I wonder if that will make me look a bit too laid-back.

'Oh, you know, coping,' I say.

'My poor girl. All of this . . .' she gestures around the Tate Modern at the models and fashion editors, celebrities and canapés, '. . . and end-of-year exams. I don't know how you do it. I keep telling Edie to slow down, but she won't hear of it. You're all such high achievers these days.'

I like Edie's mum. I like being bundled in the 'high achiever' category with her frankly quite scary daughter. I like the way she feels sorry for me for being surrounded by fashion editors on a Friday night after school. I don't agree with her, but I love her natural kindness. It's easy to see where Edie gets it from.

'Well, some of it's not too bad,' I say, catching sight of the editor of *Grazia*.

'You're so brave,' Edie's mum says. 'And busy, I imagine. I'll leave you to it.'

By now Crow, Edie and Jenny have moved to the other side of the room. She goes off to join them and I glance around me to see who I should talk to. Then I realise I'm standing next to a smart, grey-haired lady, about Granny's age, wearing a cashmere sweater and tailored trousers. Even now, she has cheekbones to die for and a lively gleam in her eyes.

My heart goes fluttery. I realise I'm within touching distance of a fashion legend. The legend who discovered Alexander McQueen and bought up John Galliano's first collection and put it in the window of her shop in South Molton Street. I turn to her, not sure what to say. I need to let her know how amazing I think she is.

'Mrs Burstein,' I cough, 'you don't know me, but I just wanted to tell you how much I love Browns. I think you're incredible.'

She looks at me and smiles. 'Thank you. It's Nonie

Chatham, isn't it? Actually, I do know you. I've been following your progress recently – well, your friend Crow, anyway. She has a very unusual eye. Will she do her own label one day?'

'I guess she'd love to,' I say, once I've got my voice working properly. The first two attempts are so squeaky only dogs could hear them. 'Miss Teen has kept us busy so far. And school. And her dresses for clients.'

Joan Burstein nods, as if this is familiar news. 'Every time someone appears in one of her dresses my daughter says we get people coming into the shop asking if we stock Crow. And of course we don't, but the staff keep telling me how much they'd love to.'

'Oh!' I squeak. 'Really?' I sound as if I'm on helium.

She smiles at me in a sympathetic way. I assume she thinks I have some kind of awful vocal condition. Then she spots someone she knows and heads off into the crowd.

Did that really just happen? Did the woman who discovered John Galliano just practically OFFER to stock Crow's stuff?

'What's the matter?' asks a voice.

I shake myself and focus. It's Crow. She looks worried about me.

'Joan Burstein,' I croak. 'Browns. Offer. Label. Stock. Shop.'

'Really?' Crow asks, just as I did.

I nod. My voice has completely given up now.

Crow smiles. 'Cool.'

I shake my head. This is not cool. This is beyond cool. This is the woman who started the coolest fashion boutique in the world saying she and her staff could sell your clothes to the coolest customers in the world. This would be so different from Miss Teen. Designing a high street collection was great, but for a ready-to-wear collection Crow could use more luxurious fabrics and trimmings, and more intricate sewing techniques. The dresses would be more expensive, but they would also be BE-AUTIFUL, and exactly the way Crow wanted them. It's like being asked to design a Porsche instead of a VW. But with sequins instead of headlights. You know what I mean.

Crow's smile turns into a grin. 'She had quite an effect on you, didn't she?'

She laughs. At this point, Andy Elat joins us.

'I saw you chatting,' he says to me. 'Do you know who that was?'

I nod.

'Nonie's in shock,' Crow says. 'Apparently, Mrs B's interested in my dresses.'

Andy's eyebrows shoot up towards his hairline. A couple of words slip out that shouldn't. I gibber for a while, giving a rough idea of the conversation.

'And are you?' Andy asks Crow. 'Thinking of doing your own label?'

Crow looks at me. 'We haven't really got that far. I just

make things for people who ask me. You know, with school and everything. But one day . . .'

Andy looks from her to me and back again. 'Well, I don't say this to many people. In fact, I spend most of my life saying the exact opposite, but you should think about it. You've got the talent. You've got an unbelievable knack for publicity. I've always thought of Miss Teen as just a stepping stone for you.'

Crow looks uncertain.

'I mean it,' he says. 'You're hot property. This is your moment, kid. Anyway, think about it. Call me.'

He spots someone important waving at him and heads back into the crowd. Crow stares after him, her eyes round as saucers.

My imagination starts to go into overdrive. Crow has done one catwalk show before, but that was just twelve pieces. A label means designing regular collections and buyers ordering them for shops around the world. Maybe there will be handbags one day, and shoes. And maybe a line of pencil cases . . . OK, maybe not pencil cases, but cute stuff anyway. Lots of cute stuff. And there'll be advertising campaigns, and more catwalk shows. We'll walk into cool boutiques around the world and see Crow's dresses on little racks of adorableness . . .

'Nonie? Nonie?'

'What?'

Crow's grinning at me now. 'You're wanted.'

It's the journalist who interviewed Jenny for *Vogue*, coming over to say hi. It's great to see her, but I'm almost smiling too much to talk.

Chapter 16

Next day, I'm still on a high from the party and my mood is enhanced by a series of delicious smells coming from the kitchen. Mum's cooking. Family dinners are rare, as Mum's generally exhausted from reassuring artists all day about how deeply talented they are, and how their next exhibition is going to be a record-breaking success. But Granny's in town again, and Isabelle's spending the night here before flying back to New York with Jenny, so Mum's making an effort.

With Isabelle around, the main topic of conversation over dinner is, naturally, weddings.

'So tell me,' Granny says, 'have you had any thoughts about the actual ceremony? Are you a register office girl?'

'Oh *no*!' Isabelle says with a laugh. 'I've been planning this all my life. There's a little church on my dad's estate. More of a chapel, really. It only holds about sixty people, but it's so romantic. I picture it lit by candles, with rose petals scattered down the aisle . . .'

Granny catches Mum's eye and beams with satisfaction. Meanwhile, Isabelle seems keen to draw me into the conversation.

'So, Nonie. How did it go last night? I hear the collection's going to be huge.'

'It is', I say. 'And the best thing is, we've decided what we're doing next. Crow's going to do her own ready-to-wear label. And we're going to sell her stuff to Browns and cool boutiques—'

'And pigs might fly,' Mum interrupts with a smile. 'It's not the sort of thing you can fit in after school, Nonie. Anyway, Isabelle – after the wedding – what are your plans?'

Isabelle gives me an apologetic look and shrugs. I shrug back. After all, it's only my career we're talking about here. Only all my hopes and dreams.

'Well,' Isabelle replies, anxious to be polite to Mum, 'it won't be for a year anyway. We can't fit the wedding in till next summer. Then I need to be in New York for work, so we'll have to find somewhere over there to make our base. And I haven't told anyone this before, but there's this heavenly apartment block in the East Village. It used to be artists' studios, but it's been turned into warehouse-style accommodation with huge rooms, fabulous views . . . I really want to show Harry when we go next time.'

She looks at him with an uncertain smile and Harry smiles back at her, but he seems uncertain too. Perhaps

88

he's not so sure about New York. Perhaps he doesn't like the East Village. Maybe that's why he's looking so uncomfortable.

'Oh, how gorgeous,' Granny chimes in, oblivious. 'Not too far from Central Park, I hope. I can't wait to stay in the Plaza and take my great-grandchildren to play in the park. I shall, of course, be the world's chicest great-grandma.'

'Mummy!' Mum scolds her. Granny's done it again. We all look at Isabelle nervously, but actually she looks radiant. It seems she's had the children/Central Park/great-grandma vision too.

'Well, darling, it looks like that's sorted,' Mum teases Harry. He smiles back, embarrassed. I'm not sure he's quite so keen on having his future flat or his future kids discussed in public.

'Oh, and Crow mentioned you're thinking of having three wedding dresses by different designers. Is that right?' I ask. I'm keen to rescue Harry from the whole Central Park thing, but I've realised that unless we talk about weddings in some way, that isn't going to happen.

So Isabelle explains about her dress for the ceremony (white, romantic – Crow's one), and dress for the reception (white, but a bit more edgy – Galliano) and her dress for the late-night dancing (anything goes – designer undecided). In a fashion-conscious household, talking to a supermodel about the most important dresses she'll ever wear in her life is the kind of thing that can take a whole evening if you let it. Isabelle and Mum are still discussing the merits of vintage Lacroix over Vera Wang and Valentino as I go up to bed.

As I'm brushing my teeth, I notice that there's a note in biro on my hand, now faded. I try to remember what it was about. Oh yes. *The Canterbury Tales*. Now overdue. English teacher not happy. But it's too late to do anything about it now. And you don't need to be an expert on Chaucer to work for a major fashion label.

I decide I'll quickly run something off in bullet points again before school tomorrow. Five minutes later, I'm asleep.

Chapter 17

This time, Jenny doesn't maintain radio silence from New York. In fact, she calls several times to tell me how the new workshop rehearsals are going – which is well – and how the casting has changed. Her friend Alanna hasn't been invited back to play Princess Margaret after all. Instead, they now have an even bigger Broadway star called Carmen Candy, who Jenny says – breathlessly – is 'the most talented and incredible artist' she's ever worked with. I think I'm going to make her pay me a pound for every time she says 'talented' and 'artist'. I'll end up with a fortune.

Meanwhile, I have AS papers looming and enough revision notes to line every wall in the house. However, I somehow manage to get food poisoning on Thursday night, or so I tell Mum, which sadly means I can't make it into school for the last Keep your head down Friday before exams. Poor me. Last week Jenny's *Vogue* hit the magazine shelves – and also the desk of every girl and boy in French class, with added moustache, beard and other amendments by the Belles. I really don't think I can face that again right now.

However, unfortunately Mum has noticed about Keep your head down Friday and doesn't believe me about the food poisoning.

'You've got French today, haven't you?' she asks.

I nod miserably.

'Well, that's the one paper you stand some chance of passing, isn't it? For goodness' sake, don't mess that up, darling. Off you go.'

Good to see that my parent has total confidence in my ability, combined with a keen insight into my social problems. Not.

I sit in my usual place at the back, waiting for it all to start. The Belles do their standard giggling and pointing, but a couple of the boys (actually the cute ones – Ashley and Liam) tell them to give it a rest.

'We've got exams, in case you hadn't noticed,' Ashley says. 'And you're kind of stuck on repeat, guys.'

The Belles look shocked. So shocked that they concentrate for the rest of the lesson. When it's over, I give Ashley and Liam a big smile that I hope says 'Thank you so much for being real gentlemen, I appreciate it,' and not 'God, I really fancy both of you'. They smile back in a 'Don't mention it' way, which I assume means they got the 'thank you' message, not the 'fancy you' message, which is a relief.

On the way home, I notice Jenny on an advertising hoarding, and nearly fall over. I'd forgotten about this. Thank goodness Jenny's not here. Miss Teen is going into overdrive about the launch of Crow's collection. They've done a massive advert using a picture we took during a shoot in India at Christmas. Mind you, Jenny likes this picture, because it also includes an elephant, a painted backdrop of the Taj Mahal and several Bollywood dancers.

'I look quite tiny among that lot,' she said, when we first saw it. 'Perfect.'

Her obsession with her weight in photos worries me. Because Crow and I really need her to pose on the steps of the Met when she goes to the Ball with Isabelle. I'm nervous that she'll just jog past the photographers, anxious to be out of their way. Or, worse, try and hide behind someone. That never works. We've promised Andy Elat publicity and I'm hoping that my chutzpah will pay off.

The day after the Ball, I scan the web for photos. Not hard. It's on every fashion blog, online magazine and news site. Most of them cheerfully gush about how it was one of the best for several years. There are loads of pictures of Isabelle in her shocking pink Dior bustle, looking like a sexy Victorian countess. And there's general agreement that the whole event had a sort of vintage, old-fashioned feel about it. Another girl who best captured that was the girl with the cropped red hair. The one who arrived with Isabelle, in an exquisite black velvet ballgown with a white satin halter-neck panel. Jenny Merritt, the actress, who recently posed for *Vogue*. And whose ballgown, though it looked vintage, was actually by the 'Oscar designer' Crow Lamogi, whose new high street collection is about to hit the shops in the UK . . .

I'm so grateful I could cry.

The timing is perfect. The official launch is two days later and once again, girls are queuing round the block to get their hands on Crow's designs. Luckily, this time the shops won't sell out so fast, but only because Miss Teen have made enough to clothe practically every girl in England.

I love this part. Crow and I meet after school and wander round Kensington, each trying to be first to spot one of the new pieces on a real person. Gradually, we start seeing them all over the place: in the street, in parks, on buses, on Saturday morning TV presenters. It's fascinating to see how they mix Crow's designs with stuff from Topshop, New Look or wherever else they happen to shop. The really trendy ones play about with them in ways we wouldn't have imagined. Leggings worn as scarves. Tunics worn as mini-dresses with coloured tights. Longer dresses worn like petticoats, under something ruffled and pretty from H&M. Lakshmi emails me from India to say that rip-offs are already appearing in Mumbai shops, which is flattering.

We're also busy talking about what to do next. Crow has so many ideas she can hardly choose. She'd like to do more designs inspired by the 1950s, with full skirts and nipped-in waists. I think she should experiment with modern fabrics and techniques, like neoprene and laser-cutting. Edie suggests creating an ethical range, using Fair Trade cotton from Uganda. Crow likes that idea too. It's just a question of choosing the best one and contacting Andy Elat to discuss the next step towards setting up our ready-to-wear label.

This is not a good time to be doing exams. It's almost impossible to concentrate, but I do what I can. Mum has promised me a new laptop if I do well this year. I really need it, because I spilled smoothie on the keyboard of my old one and it hasn't been the same since.

Chapter 18

I'm supposed to be revising for Business Studies when Jenny announces that she's back from New York and do we want to meet up? Well, of course we do. We agree to go out for pizza together. I even persuade Edie and Crow to come along.

We spend ages agreeing how good Jenny looked in her ballgown and diamonds. Even now, she still looks radiant, in a jet-lagged sort of way.

'So?' I tease her. 'Who's the lucky boy?'

'Which lucky boy?'

'The bloggers all said you must be in love, you looked so happy.'

'Oh, *that*,' she says. She shrugs. 'No lucky boy. I was just having a good time.'

'Was it meeting Tom Ford?' I ask.

She looks apologetic. 'Didn't even see him. Sorry.'

'Was it wearing all those diamonds?' Edie asks. 'I hope they were ethically sourced, by the way.'

Jenny sighs. 'I knew you'd ask, and yes they were. But I don't think it was the diamonds. I was more worried about losing them.'

'What then?'

'Was it singing?' Crow asks.

Jenny grins at her. 'Yes! Yes, you're right. It was. We'd just nailed a couple of songs in the workshop. It was incredible. How did you know?'

Crow smiles. 'When you've made something . . . right. The way you wanted it. I feel like that, sometimes.'

Jenny nods. 'Oh, and I forgot to say, thanks for looking after Stella, Edie. The kittens are so cute.'

I whip my attention from the Met Ball to Jenny's kittens. Meanwhile, Edie looks uncomfortable and stares at her plate.

'Oh, you did go round, didn't you?' Jenny moans.

'Yes I did!' Edie snaps. 'I went round twice. Stella was fine. She hadn't had them yet, but she'd made a little sort of nest in your wardrobe.' Then she hesitates. '. . . Jenny, you know you said your mum wasn't well? Well, is she stuck in bed or something?'

Jenny's face clouds over. 'No. Sometimes there are days she doesn't get out of it. But she could. It's not as if she can't walk or anything.'

'But the place was really untidy, Jenny. Not just untidy, but *smelly*. And I didn't actually see Gloria, but I got the impression she was following me. It was creepy.'

Jenny's lip trembles. 'Thanks,' she says, offended. 'It's great to know my mum is *creepy*.'

Edie looks embarrassed. 'Sorry. I was just worried about her.'

'Well, I'm home now,' Jenny says. 'So that's fine.'

Crow and I look at each other. We're not sure what happened. One minute we're talking about diamonds and kittens, and the next, Jenny and Edie are having a fight. I put it down to the stress of exams and jet lag. The only solution is ice-cream sundaes for pudding. Large ones. I order them for all of us. We were supposed to grow out of them years ago, but luckily we didn't. There are times when a teeny-weeny grown-up coffee and a biscuit just won't do.

At home, things are back to normal. Granny's gone. Isabelle's still in New York and Harry's staying with her. Mum and I are alone, and instead of home-cooked casserole, evening meals tend to be a snack whenever we think of it.

Business Studies revision requires serious quantities of popcorn and after I've ruined two expensive pans trying to make it, Mum has kindly offered to do it for me. We sit in the kitchen, waiting to hear the first popping sounds from pan number three.

Mum looks like she's about to say something, but I interrupt her.

'You know Gloria Merritt . . .'

'Yes,' she says, with a wary expression.

'Yeah. Well, you've known her for a long time, haven't you? D'you know what's the matter with her? She's been acting strange recently.'

'Strange, how?'

'Well, letting the flat get into a state. And not going to New York with Jenny.'

'God. Gloria,' Mum says. 'She always was unreliable. When you were younger, the number of times I'd get a call asking if I could pick you both up because she was late for Jenny. I always used to wonder if there was something going on there. I didn't like to ask. I thought she'd been better the last few years, though. Mind you, do you remember how she knocked back the drinks at Jenny's opening night last summer?'

'Oh!'

Goodness. Does Gloria have bottles of vodka secretly stashed round the flat? Is she lying comatose somewhere, while Jenny cleans up the mess? That would be completely terrible. When I think how I sometimes worry about Mum's Chardonnay consumption. This is in a different league.

'What should we do?' I ask.

'What can we do?' Mum sighs. 'Be nice to Jenny, I suppose. Make sure she's OK. She is OK at the moment, isn't she?'

'She seems really happy, most of the time.'

'Well, there you go.'

'Edie went round to check on her kittens,' I add.

'That's nice of her.' Mum smiles. She's always approved of Edie. Sensible, skirt-to-the-knee clothes, super-kindness and straight As. Mum's template for the perfect teenager.

The popcorn starts popping. Once I have a yummy bowl of it in front of me, Mum sits down opposite me again with a strange expression in her eyes.

'Nonie, I've been thinking,' she starts.

This suddenly doesn't feel good. I don't say anything. My mouth has gone dry. Not ideal when you're trying to eat a bowl of popcorn.

'About this house. It's a bit huge, isn't it?'

'Is it?' I ask. I would have said it was about the perfect size, personally.

'We'll be a bit lost in it when Harry's gone, won't we?'

'Will we?'

Mum changes tack. 'Don't you think a flat somewhere trendy would be good once you've finished your A levels? You'll be at college somewhere and it'll be just me, really. Somewhere in the East End, where the creative energy is. I was thinking about that apartment in New York Isabelle was describing, and how perfect it sounded. A part of me has always been a converted warehouse girl at heart.'

Really? This is news to me. Certainly no part of me has ever been a converted warehouse girl. Or an East End girl. I'm a house in Kensington girl. I'm a Number 14 bus to the V&A girl. A ten minutes to Oxford Street for shopping girl. And a my-room-is-perfect-and-I-don't-want-to-change-any-of-it-ever girl.

'Have you?' I ask. It's all I can manage.

'Mmm,' Mum says. 'Actually, I was going to get some estate agents round and get the place valued. It would be interesting to know how much it's worth. Of course, we'd have to pay Vicente back, which would be a lot, but we'd have enough left over to get somewhere nice for ourselves. Are you OK?'

I nod. I'm not, but I nod anyway.

'What about my room?' I ask in a little voice.

'You can take it with you. Lock, stock and barrel, if you like. All your posters and furniture. But honestly, darling, you've had it like that since you were about nine. It could do with a bit of updating. We could get you new stuff. One of those mirrored wardrobes you've been going on about. A four-poster . . .'

I nod again and feel sick. It's true, I've been pestering Mum for months – probably years – to upgrade my wardrobe to something cool with mirrored doors and lots of extra storage. And I've wanted a four-poster bed since I was tiny and she's always said no. I thought it was one of the most incredible things I could ever possibly own, but now that I'm actually being offered one, it suddenly doesn't matter.

Mum's BlackBerry goes off. She looks sorry, but I tell her to take it. I'm grateful that this conversation is over. I take my popcorn up to my room and sit at my desk, in front of my dodgy laptop with the sticky keyboard. I'm determined not to be upset. I'm busy. I have my career to plan and lots of revision to do. People move all the time. I'll just have to get used to it.

Besides, waiting in my inbox is an email from the men in matching overcoats – or MIMOs, as I like to think of them – reminding me about meeting us in Paris, and saying how impressed they were with the 'saturated coverage of your actress friend at the Met Ball' and the 'commercial appeal' of the new Miss Teen collection.

'We're interested in exploring avenues with rising talent relating to a prospective opportunity to establish a teen brand,' it continues. 'Please contact us to discuss, and to share perspectives on potential creative directions.'

I read it four times. I'm still not quite sure what it means. I wish I was better at English, and that they'd used a bit more punctuation. Or actual words I can under-stand. However, I think the gist of it is that they like Crow's designs and they want to talk to her about a job. An actual designer job, working for a big new fashion house called Alphia. With a salary and an office and rooms full of people to make the clothes. Do they know she's only sixteen next January? It sounds a bit high-powered for a teenager, but they've met her, so I suppose they think she'll cope. What would they do about me? The email doesn't mention me. I'd have to explain that I'm the chutzpah girl. But it feels like a dream anyway. Something crazy to tell Crow about and watch her eyes go wide.

Mum pops her head round the door with a mug of hot chocolate and a sort of 'sorry I'm selling the house' expression. She asks what I'm up to and I tell her it's French.

'Good girl,' she says, giving my hair a stroke. 'I thought that new laptop might be a good incentive.'

'Oh, it is,' I agree.

A nice new laptop to go in my nice new bedroom in my nice new warehouse apartment in East London, away from all my friends and, now that I think of it, without any space for Crow to work, either. But that's fine, because by then she'll be in her own studio, or maybe even in New York, working on a mega-label. She'll be fine. Absolutely fine.

A tear hits my keyboard, which is a surprise. But maybe it's a good thing. It might make the keys less sticky.

Chapter 19

'I couldn't imagine my mum selling this place,' Jenny says, sighing deeply on my behalf.

We're sitting in her kitchen, where there's a round, wooden table and an assortment of chairs that sort of go together, but look as though they've led very different lives. Gloria Merritt likes 'eclectic'. Mum calls it 'junk', but it creates a cosy atmosphere.

I don't reply. I'm glad that Jenny's being so sympathetic, of course, but she's been doing this for a month now, and I'd rather she didn't. I want to forget about my house. I'd rather be talking about Stella's three kittens, who are completely ADORABLE, and are nestled with their mother in a basket in the corner.

I was hoping I'd get to name them again, like I did with Stella herself, and I was going to call them Jean, Paul and Gaultier, but Jenny refused. She's thinking along a musical theme, of course. I suggested Andrew, Lloyd and Webber, but she told me to grow up. (It doesn't help that one of them's a girl.) Edie thought of Macavity, Gus and Jemima, because they're from *Cats* (musical), but invented by TS Eliot (poet, and therefore seriously good at thinking of names). Jenny said no: too obvious. Instead, she's suggested a dozen names from 1950s musicals that we've never heard of. Right now we're stuck.

Crow has stayed out of the whole naming issue, which is very wise. She's restricted herself to making pom-poms for them to play with. She's sitting on the floor next to them, happily winding pink wool around a piece of card like I used to do when I was six. For the moment, I think she's forgotten she's a Serious Fashion Designer. In fact, we haven't talked Serious Fashion since I told her about the MIMO email and her eyes practically filled her face, they were so huge. Since then, it's mostly been exams and panicking. Right now, she's just a girl who's got a friend with cute kittens, and who likes playing with wool. She's already wearing a pom-pom necklace and I have to admit, I'm thinking of asking her to make one for me.

'I must say, this place is looking a lot better,' Edie says. I think she can sense I don't want to talk about my room any more. She doesn't always say the right thing, but she certainly tries.

'Thanks,' Jenny mutters. 'Wasn't that difficult.'

It's true. The flat isn't a rubbish tip now. It's clean and bright and the perfect place to bring up kittens. Either Gloria's feeling better, or Jenny's been working hard on it in between exams. Which, thank God, are finally over. It gives us lots of time to sit in each other's kitchens, wondering what to do with ourselves.

Gloria still seems to be avoiding us though. I can't help scanning the cupboards, wondering if there are any vodka bottles stashed inside them. Does Jenny know? Does she look?

We all sit around in silence for a while, lost in our different thoughts.

'Any more news from Jackson Ward?' I ask, for the sake of something to say.

Jenny grins and goes pink.

'Yes, actually,' she says. I can tell she's really excited but she's trying to play it cool. 'I heard yesterday. The producers have managed to get a theatre in Chicago. The show's going to open in November. For six weeks. They've got this mega-incredible new director. And the cast is *amazing*.'

'Including you?' I check.

'Including me!'

Edie and Crow both look up sharply. Even one of the kittens opens a sleepy eye.

Jenny continues, happily. 'The workshop worked. They've got Carmen Candy as the star, so they can afford to have an igloo. Nope. Ingenius? Ingénue, that's it. The new girl. Plus I *was* in that movie, so people have kind of heard of me.'

'Wow!' Crow says, at the same time as me.

Edie's speechless for a bit longer, but eventually she says, 'SIX WEEKS?'

Jenny nods, excited.

Edie's still shocked. 'SIX WEEKS? In November? What about your A levels?'

Jenny shrugs. 'They'll give me a tutor. But I'll put exams on hold for a year. It's the only way, really.'

Edie sits there, stunned. 'Seriously?'

'I think you mean congratulations,' I prompt.

'I certainly don't,' Edie says. 'How will you get a work permit?'

'Born there,' Jenny says. 'Remember? Dad was on tour, so I have a US passport. It's the one thing I can be grateful to him for.'

'Oh my God,' Edie rushes on. 'And what about Stella and the kittens? Is your mum OK to look after them for six weeks?'

Jenny looks embarrassed. 'Actually, it's more than that. We *perform* for six weeks. But there's rehearsals too. And Jackson wants me to go back to New York first and work on my voice with a singing coach he knows, so I can handle so many performances. And learn the dance routines, because I'll need more time on those than most people.'

I feel dizzy. It sounds as though everything's organised and I can hardly get my head around it.

'So when do you start?'

'Any time I like,' Jenny says. 'Jackson says the more

time we spend together the better. I can stay with him. And don't worry, he's not some pervy old man. He's married to this amazing sculptress who's famous too, and there's Charlotte, his daughter – remember? She can't wait to show me more of New York. He just wants to help me out.'

Edie looks as shocked as me. Crow's got her head down, avoiding the conversation. I don't blame her. 'When exactly?' I ask.

Jenny tosses her red curls. 'In a couple of weeks. He's got this to-die-for house. I'm sure you could come and stay too for a bit, if you wanted to.'

Edie keeps her voice quiet, but she sounds super-unimpressed. 'I'm busy. I still have my personal statement to prepare for Harvard, remember? And essays. And more SATs. And my summer job. And it looks as though I'll have to come over here to keep an eye on your *kittens*.'

'Oh!' Jenny says. '*Would* you?'

I don't know if she's deliberately ignoring the sarcasm in Edie's voice, or if she hasn't noticed. But she seems thrilled to think that someone's going to look after the cats.

Edie says nothing. You could make the atmosphere into a thick blanket. I look across at Crow and laugh lightly. At least, that's how it's supposed to sound.

'Well, it looks like I'm going to have one friend in America and another in the library all summer. Thank goodness I've got you, hey?'

Crow puts her pom-pom down carefully and tilts her face to look at me. Her expression is not promising.

'My dad wrote to me last week. He's worried about how I'm doing at school. And the family's missing me. They want me to spend the summer with them in Uganda.'

I'm stunned. Crow's known this for a week and she hasn't told me until now. She is rubbish with important news. I do wish the girl would *talk* more occasionally. Well, sometimes her silences are lovely, but not *all* the time.

The kittens choose this moment to wake up properly and start crawling around, mewing gently.

Jenny, Edie and I use the excuse to grab one each and stroke them. We don't talk to each other. We don't look at each other.

My lovely, lovely, fashion-planning, friend-filled, exam-free summer is turning into a nightmare. And then my phone goes. It's a text from Mum.

'Just got your report. Come home now. Need to talk.'

The nightmare has just begun.

Chapter 20

Mum's sitting at the kitchen table (white marble, matching chairs, spill-phobic), with my report open in front of her and a very strong cup of coffee beside her. And the worst thing is, she doesn't even look angry. She just looks helpless and sad.

'What am I supposed to do, Nonie?' she asks.

This is a trick question. I bite my lip.

'I mean, I send you to that expensive school. I spend hours helping you choose your options. I tell you over and over again about the importance of exams, and college, and preparing for your future. But if none of it goes in, what can I do?'

'It wasn't good, then?' I ask. I might as well get the basics over with first.

She sighs. 'No. It wasn't good.'

She slides the report over the table to me. It skids across the marble. But I have no great desire to read it.

'But it's only my first year of sixth form, right? I mean, it's next year that counts,' I say hopefully.

'If you carry on like this, you won't last through next year,' Mum says. 'They're not just disappointed in you, Nonie. They're worried about you.'

'Oh.' Maybe all those bullet-point essays didn't have quite the effect I hoped for. However, I'm determined to keep looking on the bright side. 'But Mum, it's not as if I really need loads of A levels anyway. I know you keep saying about college and everything, but if Crow does her own label, she'll need me to run it for her, and if she doesn't, there's this big fashion house that could hire us. It's kind of happening already.'

I try not to sound smug or anything, but basically I am pretty smug, to be honest. I've helped Crow produce three collections and if Andy Elat's right – which he always is – she's about to go stratospheric. I have a career! Yay! And I didn't even need to leave school to get it!

'Oh, Nonie,' Mum sighs again. 'You're so naïve, darling. You have no idea, do you?'

OK, I'm not smug now, I'm cross. No idea? NO IDEA? Haven't I produced a catwalk show at London Fashion Week? Haven't I just helped to launch a high street collection and chatted to Joan Burstein? What kind of an idea do I need?

'Look, sit down,' Mum says.

I'm so wound-up I hadn't even realised I was still standing up. I slide into a chair and half-perch on the edge of it. Mum tries to reach out for my hand, but 'the girl with no idea' doesn't feel like holding hands right now.

'Think about it, darling. Crow is the designer. She's the name. She's the one people want. What would you do?'

'What I've always done,' I say. 'Help her.'

'How?'

'I don't know . . .' I stumble, grappling for ideas. I haven't thought this through, because it seemed so obvious. 'Make decisions, you know – talk to people. Make her designs come true.'

Mum sighs. 'But running a label is a serious business.'

'I know that.'

'It takes a lot of money.'

'Yes, but . . .'

'And that money has to be managed by someone who knows what she's doing. Someone who understands about cash flow and market research and sales projections. Do you actually *want* to know all that stuff, Nonie?'

'Of course I do,' I say.

I mean, obviously I don't want to become an expert in cash flow, exactly. Or sales projections, whatever they are. Did we do something about them in Business Studies? I think I was mentally working out a party outfit that day.

'Well, maybe I wouldn't *run* the label,' I admit. 'I'd do something . . . helpful.'

'Like what?'

There's a silence.

'And anyway,' Mum goes on, 'how can you help if you produce "the worst performance of a promising student" that your Business Studies teacher has seen in the last ten years?' She is seriously rubbing it in. What is her problem? Andy Elat said this was Crow's moment. I want it to be mine, too.

'If I need to, I'll go to college and learn . . . whatever,' I say, to keep Mum happy. I haven't stopped being promising, have I?

'But you can't!' Mum practically wails. 'You're not good enough. You haven't worked hard enough. You wouldn't get in. You're throwing your life away, Nonie. How can I make you see?'

Well, I can't see a thing right now. I'm trying to focus through a wall of tears. It's pointless trying to talk. My voice won't work. We sit there for ages, not saying anything. What I'm thinking is, 'Why couldn't I have been Joan Burstein's daughter?' But I guess Mum would be offended if I said it out loud. Goodness knows what she's thinking, but it's probably about my A-level predictions, and it's probably not good.

Up in my room, I stay sitting in the middle of my floor, not touching anything, not moving, as the light gradually fades from the day and the evening takes over. I wait for Mum to knock on the door and invite me down to supper, but she doesn't. Harry's working away from home, so his room is silent too.

Eventually, as darkness properly falls, I hear the front door open and shut and I creep downstairs to see if Crow's arrived. She has. She looks up at me with a shocked expression.

'What happened?'

I run a hand through my hair. I probably look a bit of a state right now.

'School report,' I explain. 'You OK?'

Crow nods, and holds out her hand to me.

We go down to her workroom together. It's full of paper flowers. Her latest idea for Isabelle's dress is a skirt covered in silk blooms and she's practising with paper, to see how it would look.

It's so beautiful. A sea of flowers on the carpet. So unexpected, but so typical of Crow. How will I live without this room, and without her in it?

I start crying again. Crow puts a friendly arm around me and doesn't ask me why. This is a good silence. But eventually I break it.

'So you're going to Uganda?'

'Yes.'

'I guess Victoria will be thrilled to see you.'

Victoria is Crow's little sister, and they've only seen each other twice since Crow came to England to get a good education when she was eight. Since then, things have improved at home and Victoria is getting a good education of her own, in a school that Edie helped raise money to build. Victoria loves hearing what Crow's up to and I can only imagine how happy she'll be to have her big sister home again, even if it's just for a few weeks.

Crow grins and her face lights up. I suddenly realise that she's just as happy to be going. I'd sort of assumed she'd be as annoyed about it as me, but of course she's looking forward to seeing her family. She loves them very much and although she doesn't talk about it, she misses them.

'What about Henry? Is he going too?' I ask.

'He is,' she grins. 'He wants to train to be a teacher, like Dad. So he's going to get a bit of practice. And I'm going to go and help. Dad says I need to concentrate more on my learning.'

Crow's dad and my mum should get together. They'd have a ball.

'You're fine at school, though, aren't you?' I ask.

'Not really,' she says, with a sheepish grin. 'I get too carried away with the clothes sometimes. They say I might not get my GCSEs next year.'

'Well, I know how that feels,' I assure her.

I realise that suddenly we hardly have any time for all those fashion discussions we need to have.

'What about the label?' I ask. 'Do you still want to do it?'

Crow shrugs. 'I'll think about it when I'm back from Uganda.'

'Mum said I'd be rubbish at running it because I don't know about cash flow.'

I wait for her to look horrified and say something to defend me. But she doesn't. This time she doesn't even bother to reply. Her mind is already back in her village with her family.

'Right. Well. We'll talk about it when you get back.'

She smiles absent-mindedly. 'Sure.'

'Great.'

I tiptoe carefully back through the sea of paper flowers and try not to cry again, but it doesn't really work. I decide I need a plan. Something to fill the summer and take my mind off Mum, and the house, and missing everybody. I'm seventeen, for goodness' sake, and living in London and I was nearly glamorous for five minutes at Easter. I'm sure I'm supposed to feel happier than this.

Chapter 21

Crow and Henry are the first ones to leave, on a flight to Kampala. A few days later, Edie comes with me to see Jenny off to New York. As Jenny's heading for the security queue at Heathrow, Edie gives her the most penetrating, accusatory stare I've ever seen. Jenny doesn't seem to notice.

'Have a great summer without me, guys,' she says cheerfully. 'See you at Christmas!'

'Anyone would think she was glad to be going,' Edie mutters.

'But she is!' I point out.

'She'll regret it,' Edie says. 'She'll miss London. The museums. The shops. Home. Us.'

'Don't forget you're going there yourself next year,' I point out. 'Harvard isn't exactly down the road.'

'Hmm.' Edie gives me an odd look, as if she hadn't thought of this. Honestly! The place is in Boston, up the coast from New York. She's not stupid. Surely she's pictured herself there a million times?

'And why aren't you going over to California, while I think of it? Or is Hot Phil coming here?' I ask.

She shrugs. 'Phil's trying to be nice, I suppose. He said I'm welcome to go and visit him and take advantage of the sun and everything. But he's not going to come to London and watch me work all summer. He says I seriously need a break.'

'He's right.'

She sighs. 'I know. But I've got my summer job working at the library. And so much reading to do. It's better if I just stay at home and work my way through it. And my parents are taking us camping for a week. That'll be good.'

She makes it sound amazing. Not.

'How about you?' she asks. 'Has your mum seriously stopped your allowance?'

'Yeah,' I admit. It's the thing parents try just before they say, 'I don't know what else to do', and throw their hands up and look at you as though you're some sort of unsolvable Sudoku.

'I can probably lend you some money,' Edie adds doubtfully. It's really sweet of her to offer, but I know she doesn't have much to spare. And besides, I won't need it anyway.

'Thanks, but no thanks,' I say. 'I have a plan.'

'Oooh!' Edie says, brightening up. 'I love it when you have a plan. What's this one?'

'It's brilliant. I thought of it last week. It kills lots of birds with one stone. I get money. I get to do something I love. I show Mum how capable I am of sorting out my own career. And I find my perfect job in fashion.'

'And?' Edie asks.

'And what?'

'What's the actual plan?'

'Oh, right. I've got an internship at Miss Teen. I begged and pleaded. They'd given all the proper ones away ages ago, of course, but they squeezed me in. I already know lots of people there, and what they do, so they won't have to spend too much time training me. And I work really hard. They know I do.' I pause for breath.

'And they're paying you?' Edie asks, surprised. Interns aren't exactly showered with cash, as we know from friends who've practically had to pay to do their jobs.

'A bit. Not much. Travel and lunch money, basically, but it's better than nothing. Anyway, I'm really looking forward to it. I just wish . . .'

'What?'

'I just wish Jenny and Crow were around so we could all get together in the evenings and I could tell you how great it is.'

Edie smiles. 'I'll be around some of the time. You can tell me.'

I smile back. I don't say that, much as I love her, telling a girl who wears MATCHING TWINSETS and BEIGE CULOTTES about my time at Miss Teen might be slightly pointless. I look at her now. She's in slacks. There's no other word for them. Actual slacks. And a brown jacket that has been instructed not to approach the body under any circumstances. Edie and fashion are distant acquaintances. Still, it's sweet of her to try and take an interest.

I was expecting Mum to be appalled when I told her about the internship. After all, it's me trying to pursue my 'flying pig' career in fashion. But instead, she seemed thrilled.

'Well done, darling. That should keep you out of trouble. I'm sure you'll learn loads.'

I nod wisely. Indeed I will. About how to help Crow run her label. Which is what we're going to be doing next year, after we've done our exams. I say this bit in my head, though. Not out loud. Despite the job, I really need Mum to change her mind about my allowance if I'm going to have any fun this summer.

I'm talking a lot in my head at the moment. Mum and I don't have too much to say to each other. After the whole 'You're not good enough,' 'I just don't know what to do with you,' 'I'm stopping your allowance' scenario, I think she's said most of it already.

Chapter 22

I've often wondered what interns do. And now I know.

They make a LOT of tea. And coffee. Plenty of coffee. They are experts at packing and unpacking clothes samples, getting the photocopier to work and asking people if they need help, which generally they don't. Senior managers DO NOT come up to them and say, 'Our top designer's off sick today – can you run off a quick collection and have it in by teatime?' Although interns spend a lot of their time daydreaming that this will happen. Usually while waiting for the coffee machine to percolate.

This is fine, though. My original dream was to make the tea for a big designer. Even though my dreams have grown a bit since then, I'm still happy to produce hot refreshments for major fashion retailers while I'm learning.

It's lovely being back at Miss Teen's headquarters, which are just off Oxford Street and basically in Fashion

Central. Whenever I've been here before, it's been with Crow for a meeting to talk about her designs. That was exciting, but stressful, especially if it involved the board-room and Andy Elat being upset about something. Now I get to mix with all the people who make the high street collections happen and watch what they do, but the only stressful thing I have to worry about is who wants which sandwiches for lunch.

That, and wondering what to wear every morning. Miss Teen girls and boys are fashion forward. They don't wear the current favourite looks, but what's going to be cool in a few weeks, or a few months. They even have fashion forward hair. I would join in, but next season apparently, is going to be all about a major goth revival and I can't bring myself to wear black velvet and lacy gloves at the height of summer.

Instead, I wear things to cheer myself up. Things I'm quite sure Mum wouldn't approve of. Colourful, silly things from around the house that will probably rip or tear and are quite often not entirely clean, but make me smile when I put them on. Things that Crow has made for me over the years, that don't necessarily fit me any more, but work in an ironic, babydoll way. I hope.

I'm in one of these outfits when a Senior Buyer comes into the room where I'm having a quiet argument with the photocopier and asks me to get her a coffee.

'I'm sorry to be such a pest,' she says. (She is a very nice, polite Senior Buyer, which is a rare species.) 'But I'm on a deadline and I need caffeine. A Starbucks triple shot latte, basically. It's the only thing that works. Here's a fiver.'

She hands me a note and looks apologetic. I grab it cheerfully. I *am* Anne Hathaway in *The Devil Wears Prada*. I'm getting coffee for a Serious Fashion Person and the fact that I'm not doing it in a teeny-weeny little print shift by Marc Jacobs and vertiginous heels doesn't matter.

'No problem,' I say. 'Sugar?'

She looks at me as if I'm talking a foreign language. Then I remember. Serious Fashion People don't do sugar.

'I mean, skinny milk?' I correct myself.

She nods gratefully and I dash across the road on my mission of mercy.

And straight into Keep your head down Friday.

When I get to the front of the queue, a familiar pair of aquamarine eyes meets mine and widens with surprise. It's Liam. My second-favourite unattainable boy from French class. The one (actually, one of the many) who saw that picture of me in the kimono and wondered what possessed me. And didn't seem to mind too much when I smiled at him in class.

'Hi,' he says. There's a question in his eyes. I'm lost and confused. It takes me a while to remember that I'm in a Starbucks, and he's behind the counter, and I'm supposed to tell him some sort of coffee order. I know I had one. I just can't remember what it was.

'Cappuccino,' I say without thinking. 'To go.'

He marks it down on a cup and passes it down the line.

'Anything else?'

He gives me his half-amused smile. Seeing it close-to, and in the context of Starbucks, not French class, I suddenly realise what an impressive smile it is. I think he's quickly becoming my joint-favourite unattainable boy. He's still looking at me. I realise I haven't answered his next question. And then I remember what I really came for.

'I mean, no – sorry. It was supposed to be a triple shot latte. With skinny milk. Oops.'

The half-amused smile becomes fully amused. Liam glances down the line, where my original cappuccino order is being dutifully made by one of his colleagues.

'Don't worry, I'll sort it,' he says. Then, 'Triple shot? That's a bit much, isn't it?'

'Oh, it's not for me,' I assure him. I'd be high as a kite after a triple shot. I wouldn't be able to sleep for days. I'd be tossing and turning . . .

Oh my God. I'm thinking about my bedroom, sort of, and that's embarrassing, sort of. He's staring at me oddly. But not at my face (luckily – it's burning). At my outfit.

Oh no.

I pay him for the latte and head for the pick-up point without another word.

Apart from the one kimono incident, he knows me as

the safely dressed, white-shirted girl from Keep your head down Friday. Today I'm in a skirt made out of an embroidered, fringed tablecloth of Mum's, a tie-dyed top that Crow did for me a while ago, a bag I made out of old CDs of Harry's and, to top it all off, a belt made from Harry's bicycle chain.

I can almost hear the Belles laughing in the background. If ever Liam needed proof that I really am a mad, style-challenged freak, this is it. No wonder he was staring at me. I picture him telling the other boys from class about it when he sees them. It'll probably make a great story.

At least I made myself a bracelet out of liquorice and Polo mints, for emergencies. This is an emergency, so as soon as I'm back I dismantle the bracelet and eat a Polo. It helps, but not as much as I'd like.

'Is everything all right?' the Senior Fashion Buyer asks me, when I hand over the latte.

'Fine,' I lie.

She clearly doesn't believe me, but she's too busy to do anything about it, which is good.

The next day, Starbucks announces a new chocolate and banana skinny milkshake combo that becomes an instant sensation in the office. Several times a day, interns are despatched for supplies. At least once a day, that intern is me.

Most times, Liam is there. He always gives me his

half-amused smile and stares at my outfit. I wish, I really wish, that I could be a normal, sexy teenager, in a mini and layered vest tops, dripping with attitude. But I can't. It's not me and it's too tiring to try and pretend every day.

Seeing him there, knowing he thinks I'm freakish and noticing the softness of his hair, the flecks of green in his blue eyes, and the way his mouth moves when he smiles, makes me realise how much I *really* like him. He is totally my most favourite unattainable boy right now.

I try and take my mind off him by thinking about Crow's ideas for the new label. It doesn't work. Edie manages to distract me a bit. Unfortunately, she does it by making me seriously worried about Jenny's mum.

Chapter 23

'It's the way she seems to avoid everyone.'

'You know she drinks?' I say.

Edie looks at me, horrified. 'Really?'

'That's what Mum thinks.'

'Gloria didn't *seem* drunk. But . . .'

Edie plays with the straw of her smoothie. We're in the V&A, because it's my second home and Edie needs to get out of the library at least once in a while.

'How did she seem?'

Edie pauses to consider. 'Like she was sleepwalking. Like she wasn't really there.'

'What was she doing?'

'She was in her bedroom, with the curtains closed. I asked her if she was OK and she said, "Yes, thank you," but her voice was cracked, like she hardly used it.'

'Do you think she was hungover?'

Edie shrugs and does her 'creeped-out' look again. 'I don't know what to think.'

There's only one thing for it. We have to ask Jenny. We stay up really late so we can call her after she gets back from some trip to Brooklyn with Charlotte.

'Why don't you just Skype me?' she says, airily. 'Jackson's got Skype. See you in a mo.'

So after five minutes of playing about with the camera on Mum's computer (my semi-broken laptop doesn't have one), we manage to get a grainy, slow-moving image of Jenny in some room with a grand piano in the background, and she gets one of us with our heads squashed together, looking worried.

'It's Gloria,' Edie says.

'Still creepy, is she?'

This isn't getting us anywhere.

'Does she have a medical problem?' I ask. How do you ask someone if their mum's an alcoholic? 'Is there someone we should call?'

There's a pause, while Jenny's face flickers and we wait for an answer.

'You can call her doctor, if you like. His number's in the phone book. But he'll just tell her to take her medication and she won't take it. We've been there before.'

'Medication for what?'

Jenny pauses a moment. 'Depression.'

'Oh!' Edie and I say it together. Depression doesn't seem so bad, somehow. Not as bad as drinking, anyway.

'What – manic depression?' Edie asks, sounding technical. 'Is she bipolar?'

'No!' Jenny says. And it could be the grainy image, but I'd swear she looks almost wistful. 'Not manic. Just depressed. Chronically depressed. But she'll get through it. She always does. Look, I've got to go now. Just remind Mum to feed the kittens, will you? Bye.'

And that's it. She reaches forward to switch off the camera. The picture goes fuzzy. She's gone.

Edie gets up.

'I'm going over,' she says.

'What? To New York?'

'No, idiot. To Jenny's flat. I've got the key. If I get the doctor's number now, I can call him first thing tomorrow and get that medication Gloria needs. Hopefully we can get her better before Jenny gets home.'

Yeah. Edie would love to be able to tell Jenny she fixed her mum while she was away. Like she's a broken clock or something.

'I really don't think you should . . .' I stop myself before I finish the sentence. Trying to tell Edie not to get involved when she has world-saving to do is like trying to tell Stella's kittens not to be cute. She can't help it.

'Tell me how it goes,' I sigh.

'Of course,' she says, with an optimistic smile.

It doesn't go well.

Edie's waiting for me when I get home from work next day.

'It was a nightmare!' she says.

'Tell me about it,' I mutter. I'm thinking about unattainable boys and unapproachable mothers, but I know Edie isn't. She tells me about it.

'I went to the doctor's and they said they couldn't talk to me, because Gloria had to be there, but in the state she's in now, she won't go. That was bad enough, but then I had this idea. I went back to the flat and checked in the bathroom to see if she already had some medication – Prozac or something – that she was meant to be taking.'

'And?'

'I opened the bathroom cabinet and the stuff practically fell out. There were enough pills in there to knock out half of London. So I took some into Gloria and asked her which ones she was supposed to take and she wouldn't touch them.'

'Why?'

'She said they make her brain go numb and she's never, ever taking them again and if I go round and try and make her, she's calling the police.'

'Oh, great. Apart from that, it went really well, I'm guessing.'

'Don't make fun of this, Nonie. It was horrible.'

I apologise. I know I shouldn't be teasing her at such a difficult time. And in fact, I really admire her for at least trying to do something. It's just a shame it didn't work.

'So what can we do?' I ask. I'm worried about Gloria, and also about the cats. If they don't get fed, we will have dead, musical-themed kittens on our hands and that doesn't bear thinking about.

Edie smiles slightly. 'It's sweet of you to offer to help, but you're busy at Miss Teen. I'll be fine. Gloria wouldn't call the police on me. I think I'll just keep popping round until I can work out what to do.'

'That's not your job, you know,' I point out. I'm thinking of Mum. Mum doesn't like interfering in other people's lives if it can be avoided. It usually ends in trouble, she says. Plus Edie's looking more stressed out than ever by this. It can't be doing her any good.

'I know,' Edie says. 'But it doesn't seem to be anybody's job.'

'Tell you what,' I offer. 'You check on Gloria, and I'll check on you.'

She grins. 'Deal.'

Even so, she leaves with the air of a girl who has the weight of the world on her shoulders. A part of me badly wants to tell her to go on holiday, have fun with Hot Phil and chill out for a while in California, like she obviously needs to. But the rest of me is in awe of how she seems to absorb other people's problems and make them her own, until she can fix them. She's not the most fun person to be with right now, but she's still amazing.

I know what Crow would do. She would make Edie a pom-pom necklace or something to show she was thinking of her. I haven't got time for pom-poms, so I make do with another bag made out of Harry's old CDs (which he has officially discarded, or I would be officially dead). It's not exactly Edie's style, but she's always liked Harry and it might make her smile. At least, I hope so.

Chapter 24

Edie has Project Gloria to worry about. I, meanwhile, have Project Flying Pig. It's my plan for finding my perfect job in fashion . . . and for proving to my mother that she is totally wrong about me.

Every time I bump into someone at Miss Teen who looks vaguely busy and important, I quiz them on what they do. They look annoyed to start with, but eventually they tell me. I am the only person who really understands the coffee machine, so it pays to be nice to me.

It feels like no two people do the same thing. There are brand managers, merchandisers, forecasters and buyers. They don't even make the clothes. Then there are pattern cutters, sample makers, garment technologists and production managers. Plus whole departments of PR, HR, and a bunch of other stuff that's starting to make my head spin. I obviously couldn't possibly do what they *all* do, so I try and work out who I most want to copy. And the awful thing is, so far Mum's right. They're all great, but I really don't want to do *any* of their jobs. Not exactly. I want to be a part of their world, but I can't find my niche. It has to be here. I just haven't looked hard enough.

Andy Elat stops me in a corridor one day.

'You're getting a bit of a name for yourself, kid,' he says.

'As something good?' I ask nervously.

'As something persistent. What's with all the interrogations?'

I explain about my need to find my perfect job in fashion. He nods wisely.

'I've never known a kid so immersed in the world as you, Nonie. It's not just what you do, it's what you *know*. Plus how you dress.' At this point he laughs. Not very politely. But at least he doesn't tell me to go home and change.

'So?' I prompt.

'You'll find a job, or it'll find you.'

Hah! I wish Mum had been here to hear this.

'A job running a label?' I ask.

He narrows his eyes. 'I'm trying to picture it. You in a suit? I mean, maybe, but . . . You good at spreadsheets?'

I nod. I hate spreadsheets. I really loathe them. They always go wrong on me. I think they're just traps waiting to spring on me and add up to the wrong number, but if I need to be good at them to get a job in fashion then . . . OK.

Andy frowns. He doesn't look convinced.

I realise I'm frowning back. Was Vivienne Westwood

good at spreadsheets? Was John Galliano? I bet not, but then, they were good at designing and making fabric into an art form. I can't do that either. There must be *something* I can do. I just wish Andy had said, 'Hey, you've already organised a catwalk show, haven't you? And look at all that chutzpah you've got. You'll be fine.' But he didn't. I'm back where I started.

Ever since the night at the Tate Modern, I've sort of assumed that my career in fashion was sorted. Apparently it's not. That would be OK – I'm only seventeen and I don't have to decide everything yet – except I've wanted to be a part of this world since I was tiny and nothing's changed. In fact it's worse. Since I met Crow, I've wanted it even more badly. I am both desperate and incompetent. This is not a great combination.

Andy wanders off down the corridor, wishing me luck over his shoulder. I don't think I need luck. I think I need another life, another brain and a whole new personality. Project Flying Pig was perfectly named. Maybe I should get a job as a project namer. I'm so qualified. Yaaay.

When I get home, to my amazement, there's an email from Crow waiting for me on my laptop.

Hi Nonie! Isn't it cool? I know! I can email! There's this great computer class and we all go every weekend. Joseph runs it he is realy cool. How is London? Victoria started seling school bags, Im helping the girls make them. Shes doing realy well. Ill give you one when I get home. Or you can buy one. Bye! Crow xxx

What? Victoria? *Victoria*! Who is seven, maybe eight, max. VICTORIA is already an entrepreneur, selling school bags, and I can't even find a decent job at Miss Teen. This does not make me feel good. Although I'm pleased for her, obviously. I wonder why Crow wants me to buy a bag, though. Normally she just gives us stuff. Are we slightly less friends now that she's at home with her family? Has she got a new set of friends, maybe?

I don't want to think about it. I don't want to tell her about what Andy Elat said, either. Instead, I email her back a few paragraphs about Jenny's kittens. And about how there's this boy from French class at the local Starbucks, and isn't that a funny coincidence?

I'm interrupted by a knock on my bedroom door. A very tall man with a notebook pokes his head in and asks if he can have a look around. This is bizarre, but I say yes anyway. I assume Mum's let him into the house. I hope so.

He has a good look at all my furniture, peers through my window and admires my view, then whips out a tape measure and does some quick measurements.

'Impressive property,' he says, pocketing the tape measure.

'Yup,' I agree.

And he, presumably, is the man Mum has called to try

136

and help her sell it, which is why she stood over me for an hour while I tidied my room recently. Yaaay.

Things are going to be different, Crow said. This is what different feels like. It doesn't feel good.

Chapter 25

'How would you describe me?' Edie asks.

'Hmmm?'

'I've got to describe myself for this essay question for Harvard. What am I like?'

'Grumpy? Stressed? Unnaturally intelligent?'

I'm lying on the floor of her bedroom, stroking the youngest of the kittens, who has finally been christened Starlight, after *Starlight Express*. Edie throws a scrumpled-up piece of paper at me, and misses. I roll it over towards Starlight.

'Bad at ball sports?'

'Look, Nonie! This is serious.'

'Somewhat lacking in a sense of humour? What? *What?*'

I dodge the next flying ball of paper. How she ever made the netball team is a mystery to me. Persistence and sheer height, I assume.

'Tall?'

She groans and turns to face me.

'OK, I give up. I'll do it later. What did you want to talk to me about?'

I sit up. This is more like it. I tell her all about Project Flying Pig and my disastrous discoveries. I'm not exactly expecting sympathy. Edie is Miss-I've-always-known-my-perfect-job. But at least she's someone to talk to. Someone who isn't Mum, or in New York, or Uganda.

'Oh, poor you!' she says, surprising me. 'You're like a fashion encyclopaedia, Nonie. There must be something you can do.'

'Something that doesn't involve spreadsheets?' I ask hopefully.

'Loads of people can't use spreadsheets.' As a girl who can, and regularly has to help people out who can't, Edie would know this. 'I always thought of you as a stylist or something.'

Hmm. Cool job. Working out what models should wear on shoots, or celebrities should wear on the red carpet. I could so do that. After I get my degree in fashion marketing or something – which is never going to happen, as Mum has so kindly pointed out. Stylist jobs are fought over like prize pieces in a sample sale, so you need a decent college degree to get a good one. This is one of the many things I know about the fashion industry. Unlike where I fit, of course.

Still, it's a job I could almost see myself doing. Something I hadn't really considered before.

'Helpful,' I say to Edie. 'Insightful.'

'What?'

'Two other things you are. When you're not being grumpy and stressed.'

'Oh. Thanks.'

She turns back to her desk and pretends to doodle something in a margin, but I think she's scribbling down 'insightful' before she forgets.

There's a scrabbling noise in front of me and I look down to see Starlight pouncing like a tiger on one of the poor unsuspecting balls of paper. He gets it in a death grip and bites a piece out of it, before batting it in my direction. I bat it back. Starlight is adorable and I can quite see why Edie asked Jenny if she could adopt him. Jenny was thrilled. Now she knows she's going to be out of the country for months, she's been anxious to find different homes for all the kittens. Which would be easier if she hadn't called the others Sondheim and Fosse. I mean, *Fosse*? It's pronounced 'Foss-ee'. I thought she said 'Flossie' at first, but no. Bob Fosse was a top choreographer, apparently. Beyoncé has used some of his moves for her videos. Even Bob would have been a better name.

Edie's mother, who's allergic to cats, is being very understanding about the whole thing and is dosed up to the eyeballs on antihistamines.

'How's Gloria, by the way?' I ask, thinking of mothers and pills.

'It's hard to tell,' she says. 'She's worried about climate

change at the moment. She's concerned that London will flood and the carpets in the flat will be ruined.'

'But they're on the fourth floor!'

'I know.'

'At least she's talking to you, I guess,' I add.

Edie nods. 'It's a good sign, isn't it? That's what Mum says. She says I shouldn't be going round there so much, 'cause I'm so busy with all my other stuff. But Gloria won't let anyone else into the flat, even Mum. So I just *have* to go.'

She shrugs and turns back to her essay.

'How's the writing going?' I ask.

'This? Ugh.' She groans.

'Is it really bad? How much do you have to do?'

She frowns at the thought of it. 'Only a page or so. But it's got to stand out. They get so many applications. People describing how amazing they are. They'll be going through millions of these.'

'Millions?'

'Well, thousands, anyway. From all around the world. How can one English girl who plays the clarinet stand out? I mean, what have I been doing with my life?'

She holds her head in her hands. Anyone would think she'd spent the last seven years watching TV, or hibernating. I try to reassure her, but she's beyond listening.

Even when you're sure what you want to do and you're a super-genius, it's not that easy. Me? I haven't got a chance.

Chapter 26

However, a part of my brain can't help hoping. As my internship comes to an end, I've started visiting a new fashion Mecca. Every day at about five-thirty, when all Miss Teen's fashionistas have drunk their fair share of tea, coffee and milkshakes, I head down Oxford Street and round the corner. There's a nondescript concrete building along a dead-end road. I stand on the other side of the street and stare up at the windows, above the sign that says 'London College of Fashion', and imagine the lives of the students that get to go there.

In my head I'm a successful, Edie type with lots of A levels and professors who hang on my every word. I'm studying fashion Public Relations or whatever (something spreadsheet-free, anyway) and getting qualified for my mega-job as a . . . still haven't thought of it yet. I excel in class, and at night I go out with my gorgeous, studenty boyfriend and we meet up with all our fabulous fashion-student friends and check out each other's outfits and go to cool parties, where people like Harry DJ till dawn.

One day I'm standing there as usual and I've just got to the gorgeous, studenty boyfriend bit when I notice someone standing beside me. He's very close and I have a feeling he's been there for a while, but I've been so busy daydreaming I haven't noticed. I turn to look at him properly and nearly jump out of my skin.

Liam. Not in Starbucks uniform now, but simple jeans and a tee-shirt. A nicely cut tee-shirt, actually, that shows what good shoulders he's got . . .

'Hi Nonie,' he says. He gives me his smile. I melt. 'Come here often?' he asks.

I look up the windy, dead-end street and across at the nondescript concrete building.

'Well, recently, a bit,' I admit. I might as well.

'Me too,' he says.

'WHAT?'

He grins. 'Me too. Boys think about careers in fashion too, you know.'

'I know,' I stutter. 'It wasn't that. It was . . .'

It was that boys *I like* don't think about careers in fashion. But I can't say that. I just look at the pavement and feel stupid.

'So, are you thinking of applying?' he asks.

'I wish.'

'Why, you wish?'

I sigh. 'Because I won't get the grades.'

'But you're quite good in French.'

That's it. Quite good. And it's my best subject. And my dad's French. If that's the best I can do, what hope have I got?

'Yeah,' I say out loud.

He smiles at me again. 'Not very talkative, are you?'

At this, I can't help smiling. I am totally talkative. I can talk for England. I get told off for talking all the time. I've talked myself into and out of some of the trickiest situations in my life. But Liam is the one person I know who's only ever seen me when I'm deliberately keeping my head down – in French – and when I just can't think of anything to say, like now. This is typical. He's looking at me in quite an interested sort of way, I've just noticed. This will almost certainly be because he likes quiet women. So if he ever did get to really know me, he'd be horrified.

'I am usually,' I say. 'Talkative, I mean.' Then I lapse into silence again.

'Anyway,' he says, filling it. 'I want to come here to study fashion journalism. Then I'm going to get an editing job at a major magazine and become a style guru. Everyone's going to turn to me to find out what's going to be big next season.'

I look at him in his jeans and tee-shirt. He looks at me in my frilly dress, worn as a top and wrapped round with Harry's bicycle chain belt, over neon-pink cycling shorts and clogs.

We know what he thinks about my freaky style-free

zone. But now that I look more closely, I realise that as well as his beautiful tee-shirt, he's wearing really interesting sneakers. Interesting because, even though they're old and scuffed and well-used – perhaps *because* of all these things, they are perfect. They are exactly how a sneaker should be. Not showy, just . . . natural. Like his tee-shirt. Like his jeans. He looks as if he doesn't think about his wardrobe at all, but to get it looking that relaxed, but right, you often have to think about it really hard, or just be naturally talented at styling.

'I didn't know you were interested in fashion,' I say.

'Huh! Thanks!'

I realise that didn't come out quite as complimentary as I meant it to.

'I mean . . . Wow. Good. Sorry. I mean . . . I like your sneakers.'

Liam's lips curl up and he gives a sexy laugh. 'I like your belt,' he says.

'Thanks.'

'And your dress-top thing.'

I'm blushing, I can feel it.

'Er, thanks.'

'And your shorts.'

My cheeks get hotter. He's teasing me, of course. His teasing makes me tingle. I can't believe I just said I liked his sneakers. I mean, of all the stupid, childish things to say.

'Well, they are an interesting colour . . . the shorts, I

mean.' Like my face. 'Anyway, I'd better go. See you on Keep your head d— I mean, see you in French.'

'Keep your what?' Liam seems intrigued. He's the sort of boy who's intrigued by a lot of things. A bit like I'm intrigued by him, I suppose. Or maybe not. I'm more than intrigued. Intrigued isn't the right word at all. Embarrassed is close, though.

For a moment, I'm tempted to tell him about Keep your head down Friday. For a moment, I really, really want to have a conversation with him and tell him what's going on in my head, and find out what's going on in his. But that would be crazy. It would get out, and that would give the Belles something else to tease us about. Anyway, I'm 'the girl who's not very talkative'.

'Doesn't matter,' I say.

He gives me his perplexed look again. Yup – that's me. Destined to perplex the boys I like. We talk about nothing for a minute or two and he heads off home.

I stay where I am for a while. Now, in my dream, the gorgeous studenty boyfriend has black hair, get-lost-in blue eyes and a half-amused smile. I desperately try to make him blond and serious. Or frizzy and spotty. Anything. But the image won't shift. And it hurts. My heart actually hurts.

So do my hips. Harry's bicycle chain is a lot heavier than it looks. I go home to change and make at least one ache go away.

Chapter 27

Harry, for once, is home, sitting in the kitchen with a men's magazine (the sort Liam wants to edit one day) and a Coke.

'Are you OK, little sis?' he asks when he sees me.

I explain about the bike chain hurting.

He smiles. 'I was wondering where that had got to.'

I feel guilty. 'I thought you weren't using your bike any more.'

'I'm not. I need to sell it. It's taking up too much space, Mum says. She needs the place tidy. For . . .'

He doesn't say it. For when people come round to look at the house, so they can buy it and Mum and I can go to our converted warehouse somewhere trendy. Yaaay.

'How's your flat-hunting coming on, by the way?' I ask. I sort of don't want to know the answer, but I sort of do.

He shrugs. 'Isabelle's in charge. I'll just go where I'm told.'

I give him a sharp look. Harry is passionate about his surroundings. If I touch anything in his room – any tiny thing – I hear about it for weeks. Not in a good way. I'm surprised to hear him sounding so uninterested.

'Don't worry, sis!' he says, catching my eye. 'It'll be fantastic. Isabelle's dreamed about this for years. She wants to find the absolutely perfect place. And you'll have to come and visit. Often. Promise?'

I promise. Something wasn't quite right about that conversation and I'm not sure what, but Harry's gone back to his magazine and it's too late to find out. And I'm already picturing Liam writing an editorial piece about men's fashion trends and working out which photos to use . . .

Harry's bike is in the basement, in the corridor outside Crow's workroom. I go downstairs to put the chain there, so Harry can re-attach it before he sells the bike. Afterwards, I stand in the workroom for ages. It's so empty and dark without Crow.

She'll probably be making school bags with Victoria at the moment. I bet that's fun. Maybe it's such fun she won't even want to come home. When I first met Crow, I couldn't understand how she could want to live in London when her family were in Uganda. I didn't know how dangerous their life was back then. But it's much safer for them now. The war that caused so much killing and kidnapping is mostly over. Her mum and dad have returned to their village. They have a great school (the one Edie helped raise the money to build). Soon Henry will be teaching there, along with Crow's dad. I wouldn't blame her for deciding to stay, if she wanted to.

Suddenly I feel lonely and frightened. I decide to go up the steps into the garden for some warmth and sunshine. It's not good to stand here like this, shivering. I need some air.

Outside, Mum is talking to a man I don't recognise about lawn sizes and property values in our street. She turns round, sees me and looks startled.

'Oh. Darling. Hi.' She doesn't seem desperately thrilled to see me. 'Er, this is Peter Anderson. From next door.'

The man steps forward and I realise I do recognise him. He looks like a thinner, taller version of Colin Firth. The last time I saw him properly, he was standing in the middle of our living room and swearing loudly about Harry's music. He smiles at me and I smile back, although I don't really feel like smiling right now.

'Great house,' he says. 'I've always liked it.'

He looks almost proprietorial. Mum looks totally guilty. And I realise why. Mr Anderson must be a potential buyer for the house. Perhaps he's going to knock the two together and make a mega-home. The people a few doors down did that and built a swimming pool *under the lawn*. 'More money than sense,' Mum muttered at the time, but it sounded pretty cool to me.

'I've always liked it here too,' I whisper. Mum gives me a half-smile, but doesn't say anything. Things have been even more difficult since my exam results arrived last week. If anything, my school was over-optimistic. My chances of going to college are virtually nil. In fact, I'd be lucky to get a job in Starbucks at this rate. I head back indoors. Mum calls after me, but I don't hear what she says. I don't think I really want to know.

Chapter 28

I see Mr Anderson a couple more times before the holidays end. He's not quite holding a tape measure and paint samples yet, but you can just tell he's mentally redecorating. It's a relief when I go and spend a few days with my dad in Paris, before school starts again.

I tell Dad all about Crow, and he's reassuring. He says she's made her home in London now and he's sure she'll want to come back, however great the holidays were. I also tell him about us moving and he tries to be understanding, but it's clear he doesn't want to be mean about Mum behind her back. That's the funny thing about my parents. They're hopeless when they're together, but they're generally quite nice about each other when they're apart.

Dad's right about Crow though. When I get back to London there's an email waiting for me from her, saying which flight she's on and how she can't wait to see us all again. I'm so relieved I feel like a cork bobbing up from the bottom of the ocean. I spend the evening making a huge, glitter 'Welcome home' sign, so I can take it to the airport when I meet her off the plane.

It must be something about the African sun: she's grown about ten centimetres. And she's got extra poise and confidence too. She's wearing a tribal print maxi-dress with a contrasting turban and bead sandals. She comes running over, sending passengers and trolleys flying. We hug as hard as we can. I have weeks of hugging to catch up on.

'How was it? How was your dad? Did he make you work all summer? How was Victoria? What did you do? I love your dress! Is your mum OK?'

'Hey! Stop!' she says. She laughs. I realise this is normal me. Talkative me. Possibly too talkative. But it's so good to see her.

'It was good,' she says. 'Henry! Over here!'

Poor Henry is trying to steer an overloaded baggage trolley. He looks relieved when he spots Crow and comes to join us. We lug the heavy bags down to the Tube and Crow and I talk non-stop the entire way home. If only Liam could see me now.

If only I could see *him* now . . .

But anyway, Crow is full of news about her family, her village, the school and all the new facilities they've got thanks to the support of people like Edie, and the textiles project.

'What's that?' I ask.

'All the girls and some of the women meet after

school,' Crow says. They design fabrics, and there's this factory that prints them, and they make things to sell. Dresses, shawls, blankets . . . Victoria had the idea of making the school bags. Look! Here's mine.'

Instead of her normal satchel, she is wearing a rectangular cotton bag, lined on the inside to make it stronger, and big enough to hold a few school books and files. Hers contains her sketchbooks and pens, as always.

'For every bag they sell, they raise a dollar for the school. I brought some to sell in London. D'you think anyone will like them?'

'Well, I do,' I say. And I realise I don't feel quite so bad now that she wanted me to buy one. I hadn't realised they raised money for the school. Golly. Victoria's not only an entrepreneur, she's a fundraiser too.

'Your little sister's amazing,' I add.

Crow smiles happily and takes my arm in hers.

'Yes she is, isn't she? It was so good to see her. I want to spend much more time with her. I didn't know she missed me so badly. And I missed her too.'

She turns to put the bag away, so I can't see her face. It's quite good that she can't see my face now, either. I'm wondering how soon it will be before she goes to Uganda again. And whether she'll come back next time.

Henry, who's sitting opposite us, catches my expression and gives me a kind smile.

'How was your summer, Nonie?' he asks. Henry is very thoughtful that way.

'Great,' I lie. 'Busy. You know . . . working . . . and stuff.'

He smiles again, polite but confused. I haven't made it sound particularly incredible.

'Ready for your final year at school?'

Henry, like his dad, can't think of anything nicer than a whole year of lovely school to look forward to.

I nod and grin. If there was an A level in lying, I would ace it.

Chapter 29

I'm not ready at all. I'm terrified. I always thought being in the top year at school would be amazing. We'd be the oldest, tallest, coolest girls and everyone would look up to us. I've been looking forward to it since Year Seven. But I hadn't realised that this is it: our exams are about five minutes away and then we have to start on the rest of our lives. In my case, a full-length career of hot beverage manufacture and boy-perplexing.

I let Crow settle back into London life for a week or so before I catch her in the workroom and explain to her about my summer of rubbish discoveries.

'You know that label?' I start.

'Which one?'

'Yours. Well, you'll have to count me out, I'm afraid. You need people with experience to run it for you. And qualifications. Which it would take me years to get, if I even could, which I can't, because my grades will be so pathetic. Plus I don't know what I'd do anyway.'

'Nonie!' She looks shocked. Disapproving too. 'Don't be silly.'

'I'm not. I'm just being realistic.'

She shrugs. 'We'll talk about it later.'

'We haven't *got* a later,' I say. 'This is your moment. Andy Elat said so. You'll have to do it on your own.'

Her eyes widen with hurt. But it's for her own good. She doesn't need me dragging her down.

'At this *"moment"*,' she says, almost mocking me – which she's never done before – 'I'm thinking about school. A label is too much work right now.'

'Did your dad say that?'

'He did,' she admits. 'But it's what I think too.'

'OK, no label,' I sigh. But I haven't given up yet. If I can't actually help Crow, I can at least advise her. She was on the brink of something truly amazing in the spring. Just because I can't do it, doesn't mean that she can't. I don't say anything more, because I can tell she wants to change the subject, but my brain is ticking away. Project Flying Pig isn't dead yet.

Meanwhile at school, I notice for the first time how my teachers sigh when they hand me my first assignment. As if they know they're going to get the answer back in bullet points and it's going to look as if I spent ten minutes on it, which I probably did. For the first time, it makes me sad. For the first time, I realise, I actually care.

I try asking Edie for advice, but she just tells me about

'splitting the workload into rational, weekly sections'. This is not helpful to me in any way. Nor is the rest of Edie's behaviour, which is to bury herself so hard in her books and personal statements that I hardly ever see her, even at school.

I'd talk to Jenny about it – by Skype if necessary – but of course she's not even doing A levels this year and she's so into her musical she probably can't remember what they are.

Of all the lessons, the one I've had the most sleepless nights about is French. This year, Keep your head down Friday has shifted to Keep your head down Wednesday. However, the same rules apply. The news is out that Jenny will be performing in *Elizabeth and Margaret* and if one more person sets their ringtone to 'There's no business like showbusiness', I am liable to thump them.

I'm determined to concentrate properly for once, so I keep my head down even more than usual, but it's no good. Liam is four rows in front of me. His hair has grown slightly since the summer, so it rests on his collar. He's been away on some sort of outdoor holiday in Ireland and has a light brown tan. When he shifts his arm out to the right, I can just see the hairs on his skin . . .

When I walk into the room each Wednesday, I hold my breath and wait to see if I'll get a flash of his half-amused smile as I head to my seat. But the first week he looks slightly disappointed, and by the third week, his smile has faded completely. What have I done wrong? I'm supposed to be thinking about the French film industry in the *Nouvelle Vague*, but all I can think about is that smile, and the way it vanished.

Halfway through class, my school bag starts vibrating against my foot. My phone. I carefully manoeuvre it out of the bag without the teacher noticing and slide it under the desk. A text from a number I don't recognise.

'Where's the belt?'

I don't understand. Is this some sort of bullying by total confusion? I ignore the text and go back to thinking about the smile.

My phone vibrates again.

'Why are you dressed like a ruler?'

This is unfair. I look down. I'm in a perfectly acceptable Keep your head down Wednesday outfit. Sand-coloured jumper. Maxi camel skirt. Desert boots. OK, it has a certain sameness to it. True, if you squared off the edges I might look like a wooden ruler, possibly. But it is unobjectionable.

More vibrations.

'???????????'

Somebody is objecting.

I look around. Of course, I can't help looking at Liam first and I catch the swish of his curls. I'm sure he was just staring at me. I decide to try something out and text back: 'Which belt?'

'The bike chain.'

Aha! It *is* Liam. He's the only person here who ever

saw the bike chain. My heart is suddenly pounding like a road drill. I am SO not thinking about the French film industry.

I type rapidly. 'It was heavy. And my brother needed it back.'

More vibrations. He's a super-fast typist. 'And the ruler look?'

I'm in the middle of a long and complicated reply, which I'm about to delete anyway, when somebody jogs my chair – quite a common occurrence – and my phone clatters to the ground. Madame Stanley looks up with a sigh and tells me to add it to her collection of confiscated phones on the front desk. Liam looks very guilty when he catches my eye on the way back to my seat. After the lesson, I find him waiting for me outside the classroom door.

'Sorry about that,' he says.

'No problem.'

'But I wish . . .' He pauses. He looks embarrassed. I look embarrassed. We look embarrassed together.

'What?'

'I liked you in the summer. I thought you looked cool.'

'*Really?*'

'Yeah. Amazing, actually. Like back when you wore that kimono.'

'You liked the *kimono*?'

'Well, not liked, exactly. But it was interesting.'

'Believe me, looking interesting isn't always a good thing.'

I glance across at the Belles, who are a few metres away, chatting to the most popular boys while adjusting their miniskirts over their long, smooth legs.

'Well, I think it is,' Liam says.

My name is being called, loudly and repeatedly, by the girls from my school who want to get back.

'Better go,' I say.

He smiles. The corners of his mouth turn up very slightly and I badly want to kiss them.

'Sure,' he says. 'You've got my number.'

He disappears off with his mates and I go and join my school friends. I am *so* confused. Certainly, I have his number, but WHAT AM I SUPPOSED TO DO WITH IT? I'm the girl he 'liked in the summer', apparently. It's now autumn. I am therefore quite obviously the girl he doesn't like any more. This is hopeless, and typical.

I try and ignore the part of my brain that's already planning an interesting outfit for next Wednesday. But I can't help it. The only thing I'm sure of, in a large world of confusion, is that if I have to choose between being interesting to Liam and invisible to the Belles, the bike chain look wins every time.

Chapter 30

hen I get home, I can see a light on in the basement window. This means that Crow's in her workroom again. She hasn't been there much since our discussion about labels. When I do see her, she goes on about Joseph and his amazing internet classes in the summer, or GCSEs and other school-related things. Her dad has definitely had an effect on her. She's stopped making her dresses to sell in the Portobello Road and she's told Andy Elat she won't be designing another collection for Miss Teen in the foreseeable future. The only thing she's working on, as far as I know, is a new design for Isabelle's wedding dress.

I let myself in and Crow smiles when she sees me. I curl up in the velvet armchair while she fiddles with the dress on the mannequin.

'Does my outfit remind you of anything?' I ask her.

'Stand up,' she commands. I do. 'Hmmm.' She thinks for a while. 'A tower block in Kampala. A beige one.'

'Someone at school said a ruler.'

She raises one eyebrow and nods in agreement. 'He was right. You should wear your usual stuff.'

'Who said he was a he?'

She looks at me and laughs. 'I've known you a long time, Nonie. It's the coffee shop guy, isn't it? The one you told me about. Anyway, he's right. What do you think about this, by the way?'

She's fiddling crossly with a seam on the latest wedding dress. 'I don't know what it is,' she adds. 'Usually I have such a clear idea from the start and all I have to do is make it look the way I imagine. But this dress . . . it keeps going wrong.'

I shift my attention from Liam to the dress. This version will be a white chiffon shift with a slight 1920s feel. It will hang from satin ribbon shoulder straps and fall to Isabelle's ankles. Crow is working on the cotton toile that will make the pattern. The final dress will be weighted by thousands of tiny white mother-of-pearl beads and silver sequins, which will be applied by a workshop in India. Isabelle's really excited and emails Crow about it almost every day, apparently.

'It's beautiful,' I tell her. 'But you've got ages to get it right. And, I've been thinking. Remember the MIMOs?' She looks confused. 'The men in matching overcoats who were setting up that fashion house? They're still looking for someone. If you don't want to do your own label, you could do theirs. I really think you should get back to them about your creative directions.'

'But I don't have any. I have school. I have exams. So do you. We need to revise.'

'I know . . . but they might not wait. '

Crow shrugs. I thought I'd got used to her shrug and it didn't annoy me any more, but right now I am super-annoyed. I have to make her snap out of her laid-back attitude.

'They sounded really excited about you. And they've got so much money, they could make any design you could think of. You just need to tell them what you want to do.'

Crow shrugs AGAIN and doesn't speak.

'Christopher Kane's doing a line for Versace,' I point out.

Nothing. Even though Christopher Kane is one of Crow's favourite designers.

'Stella McCartney went to Chloé. Alexander McQueen went to Givenchy. It's how most of the big names got famous and this is your chance. You've got to talk to them, at least. Show them some ideas.'

I look across at her pleadingly. Her lovely, large mouth is set in a thin line and for once, it's not because it's full of pins. She doesn't look impressed, but she should be. Not only by the big chance, but by how noble I'm being in suggesting it to her. Even though we both know there wouldn't be a job for me.

'I promised Dad I'd study really hard this year.' She looks up. 'At home,' – and I realise by 'home' she means Uganda, not her flat down the road from here, and suddenly that hurts – 'lots of girls have to leave school to help their families. They can't do exams or training. In London, people take school too much for granted.'

She's not looking at me when she says this. She's deliberately avoiding me, in fact. But I think when she says 'people' she means 'you, Nonie'. And I could do without having a best friend who sounds like a Ugandan version of my mother.

We end up sitting in silence for the next half hour, while she unpicks a side seam on the dress and pins it into a new position. She does it very carefully, but at first the change seems so tiny that I can't see why she bothered. Then suddenly the dress hangs differently and seems to come to life on the mannequin. She's so good at this! I can't bear it that she's not grabbing this amazing opportunity with both hands.

I stomp upstairs in frustration, muttering something about assignments. She doesn't say goodbye.

Chapter 31

I'm in the middle of English homework when Mum puts her head round the door, sees that I'm working, and smiles. She's dressed to go out. Little black dress, Jimmy Choos and freshly waved hair.

'I'm off to a private view. Won't be late. What is it tonight?'

'*The Great Gatsby.*'

'Going OK?'

I nod. Actually, Crow isn't the only person who's decided to turn over a new leaf. I'm fed up with dreading every result I get. When I'm not with my friends I've been secretly experimenting with putting in some real effort into my assignments and, so far, it's working. My English teacher has stopped picking them up by her fingertips like she used to do – as if they were toxic. This time, I'm hoping for a B.

Mum comes over and kisses the top of my head. I smell the familiar mixture of Rive Gauche, Jo Malone shampoo and Elnett hairspray. She takes my face in her hands and smiles at me again.

'You're really trying this term, aren't you, darling?'

There's a happy gleam in her eyes and a new lustre to her hair. I've been noticing it a lot recently. Just like I've noticed the single white rose that gets delivered anonymously every Monday morning and is instantly put in a little crystal vase on the desk in her cubbyhole at the top of the house. And the way she leaps several centimetres whenever her BlackBerry goes off. And the secret glow on her face if it's the message she was hoping for. Well, I know that feeling now. It's the feeling I got when Liam texted me about the bike chain. It's love, or something close to it. Extreme like, anyway.

It's useful, because it's put her in a permanent good mood and it means that when I asked her if I could possibly go and see Jenny perform in Chicago after half-term as part of my eighteenth birthday treat she said yes almost straight away. She's trying to be nice to me and hasn't mentioned flying pigs since the summer. She hasn't really talked to me about it, but it's totally obvious what's happened. The white roses were the biggest giveaway.

Vicente.

They got the spark back when he visited in February. You could see it when they danced together. I guess it was always waiting to happen. I wish she'd just come out and tell me, but she won't. She's embarrassed. Maybe she realises it looks a bit bad for me – falling in love again with the man she was with before I came along and ruined it. And things haven't really changed, because it's thanks to me and my 'important academic year' that she can't go off to Brazil and spend some proper time with him.

'D'you think she would?' Jenny asks. 'Brazil? Really?'

I'm Skyping her about the trip to Chicago. But we've got distracted by men. As you do.

'I don't see why not,' I say.

'It's such a fairytale,' Jenny sighs.

'What d'you mean?'

'Well, you know, pining for someone for so long, then finally getting it together with them. I mean – eighteen years. It's a lifetime.'

I have a feeling that in her head she's turning Mum's life into a musical and she's imagining the number where Mum falls into Vicente's arms and he whisks her round the stage singing 'Finally!' Or words to that effect.

'Anyway,' I say, keen to change the subject, 'how about you? You must be surrounded by gorgeous men.'

'I am!' she giggles. 'Totally gorgeous and adorable. And so *talented*. But the ones I like are mostly dating each other, or girls from the chorus. I spend most of my time rehearsing with Gary Lee, who plays Prince Philip, and he's hooked up with one of the ladies in waiting. You should see her do the splits. She's *amazing.*'

'What about you? Are you ready? You start previews in three weeks.'

'I *know!* We've got our first full rehearsal with the orchestra soon. It's going to be awesome. And the sets are so cool. The ballroom at Buckingham Palace. The Royal Yacht Britannia. A massive tent in Africa. Wait till you see them!'

I hope she's not avoiding telling me something awful. Usually, at this point, she's incredibly nervous about her performance.

'Yes,' I say, 'but what about *you*? Are you OK?'

'I'm fine,' she assures me. 'Just tired from all the dance classes. I have to do extra ones because I'm so rubbish. It's kind of weird having a starring role. I have to buy presents for everyone for opening night. I've got no idea what to get them.'

I'm about to offer some ideas, but she carries on without listening.

'Luckily, Carmen's going to take me shopping. It'll be cool. Carmen keeps being stopped for autographs, but she says you get used to it. It's bizarre but you just have to be really natural about it . . .'

She goes on for five minutes about the difficulties of being a STAR in a MUSICAL, and I realise that I even miss her babbling away about herself. She's not always the easiest friend to have around. Her life is usually some sort of drama, but I've got used to that. Or I had. I suppose I'll have to un-get used to it for a while, until the show is over.

At least I can visit her. Although how I'm supposed to pack enough stuff for three days into one 'standard checked-baggage size' suitcase is a mystery to me.

Just before half-term, I'm busy trying to fit my under-wear into one of the teeny-weeny pockets of my case, when Crow comes round with a package for me to take.

I look at her. We haven't spoken much since the whole discussion about 'people' not taking school seriously enough. I look at the package. It is the size of a folded-up dress. A folded-up Jenny dress, with voluminous skirts and a nipped-in waist. The sort of thing Crow always does when Jenny has a big moment coming up.

'Something for her to wear on her opening night?' I ask.

Crow nods.

'Something you just ran up between homework assignments?

Crow nods again, looking guilty.

'I don't suppose you've managed to . . .'

She shakes her head. She looks towards my suitcase. It is full. Totally full. I've only packed about three sweaters and some leggings. A girl needs a little variety to choose from. But it's bursting at the seams. She looks more guilty. We both wonder where the package can go.

I sigh. 'I'll fit it in somehow.'

She gives me a grin. And I realise she's right. It wouldn't be the same if Jenny went to a big event without wearing something of Crow's.

'I promise I'll look after it.'

She grins some more. So far she hasn't said a word. Unlike me, she is *seriously* not a talker.

'Got some stuff to do at home,' she mutters, and leaves.

I look down at the parcel. It says all I need to know about how she feels about Jenny, and misses her, like me, and wants everything to go well for her. Then I set about unpacking my suitcase and working out how to squeeze it in.

Chapter 32

'Oh my God, I LOVE IT!' Jenny gasps, the moment she opens the parcel.

She twirls round my hotel room in Chicago, holding the dress in front of her and admiring herself in the full-length mirror on the wardrobe.

'Crow emailed me about my measurements. I did wonder why. I assumed it might be a dress or something, but not THIS.'

I smile encouragingly. Crow doing all her own email-ing now, with no need for me to be involved. Yaaay.

'And of course, I was a totally different shape, so thank goodness she did,' Jenny rattles on. 'All that dance prac-tice. Look. Feel.'

She shoves an arm in my face. Gingerly, I feel her shoulder. It's rock solid with muscle. She does the same with a leg. Same story. Her figure has changed, but not too much. She looks thinner, but healthy. And she's bouncing round the room as if she's high on energy pills.

I'm thinking about the power shower she dragged me out of so she could open the parcel. I could do with another few hours just standing under it. It was wonderful. However, I'm not allowed to. She whisks me round the corner to Starbucks for breakfast, then off to the shops so we can talk about all the relationships we're not having, while window-shopping for stilettos (Jenny) and anything unusual that might impress Liam in French (me).

After what feels like twenty minutes, Jenny looks at her watch and gasps. It's lunchtime already, and she has a matinée to perform at 2.30. There's just time for a quick – but massive – sandwich, before we head off to the theatre for the show.

Backstage is full of shouting, banging, creaking and little snatches of piano music and singing, as people finish limbering up their voices. Jenny lets me sit with her while she puts on her hidden microphone, dark wig and makeup, transforming herself from a modern-day redhead teen into a demure royal from the 1940s. It's fascinating to see her face change. She shows me photos of Princess Elizabeth from those days, and I watch as Jenny's features become the beautiful, reserved face of that girl.

There's an announcement, to say they have 15 minutes to go. Through a speaker in the corridor, I can hear the sound of the audience filling the auditorium. Jenny's busy perfecting her eye makeup in a mirror that's surrounded by light bulbs, just like you'd expect. I decide I might as well take my seat. I give her a good luck hug and leave her to it.

In the lobby, there's less shouting and banging, but still just as much of a buzz. Chicago audiences love to check out new musicals during the previews. They arrive in their heavy coats and thick jackets, talking and laughing. I could swear I just saw Oprah Winfrey handing her coat to someone. This is SO EXCITING! Then I feel a tap on my shoulder, turn round, and there, in front of me, is Isabelle Carruthers, grinning at me. Behind her, about ten men and a couple of women are pretending not to stare in awe.

'Nonie!' she says. 'I didn't know you'd be here. But I should have guessed. Where are you sitting?'

'In the third row,' I say. 'But how come *you're* here?'

'Oh, I had to see Jenny. I promised I'd come. And you must sit with me. I'm sure I can persuade someone to move.'

'Where are you?' I ask.

'In the front row.'

Yeah, right. Like someone who has tickets for the FRONT ROW of a new show is going to move, just so two girls can sit together. But it's typical of Isabelle to try, at least. When you're with her, it's impossible to dislike her. She seems to have inherited the niceness gene as well as the beauty one.

I head for the stalls behind my future sister-in-law. Heads turn at every step. Isabelle has her ringlets tucked into an oversize beret and is wearing a sequinned slip dress over a polo-neck jumper, skinny jeans and boots. She has no makeup on at all and looks heartbreakingly gorgeous. She completely ignores the stares. When we get to the front row she bends down and says something to a couple of men sitting near the middle. There's a brief conversation, and next thing I know, one of the men is offering me his seat and the other is shifting along so Isabelle and I can sit next to each other.

This is a woman who can make any man in the world do whatever she wants, and she's marrying my brother. Why?

'Crow's been doing a beautiful job with your dress,' I say, thinking back to the beaded shift.

Isabelle smiles, but her lips quickly wobble into a nervous pout.

'I hope Harry likes it. I was describing it to him, but he said he just hoped it didn't make me look like a human waterfall.'

'Oh! That's mean.'

'He's always teasing me. It's one of the things that's so sweet about him. Most of the men I know don't dare tease me. It makes a refreshing change. But even so . . .'

She bites her lip. I sense that 'human waterfall' is not the image she wants in her head as she walks up the aisle. However, I don't have any time to reassure her, because at this moment the orchestra strikes up and the audience falls silent, waiting to see if Jackson Ward has another hit on his hands or not.

For the next two and a half hours, we sit back and enjoy ourselves. The sets are as grand as Jenny promised, the costumes are stunning and the songs are great. Princess Margaret has the best ones, and also the best dances. Which is lucky, because Jenny is not a natural dancer and she's explained that she practically has to be carried around the stage by Prince Philip when they have their waltz scene. He's still recovering from the bruises she accidentally gave him during rehearsals. She's still recovering from the ones she gave herself.

By the time Jenny has been crowned Queen, with her husband by her side, and they've announced that Sir Edmund Hillary has conquered Everest (note my new grasp of history! Yay!), and the stage is filled with singing, dancing Londoners doing the hokey-cokey, it's perfectly clear that Jackson Ward doesn't need to worry. This is another hit, definitely.

Isabelle and I stand up, along with the rest of the audience, for several curtain calls. There's lots of cheering and demands for an encore. A few extra-keen people are even attempting a hokey-cokey in the aisles. It's a thrilling moment. I only wish Edie could have been here to share it and, for Jenny's sake, Gloria too.

Chapter 33

Twenty-four hours later, I'm back in London. So's Isabelle. Thanks to her and a bit of eyelash batting, I got a seat in First Class and frankly, I could have moved in. My seat turned into a bed and I really should have slept all the way home (as Isabelle did – she has a shoot today and needs to look dewy-eyed), but that would have been a total waste. I ate yummy meals. I tried on the special pyjamas. I popped into the loo and used all the gorgeous little creams in my special First Class washbag. I watched the latest movies on my own, special, tiltable screen. I checked out all the celebrities in the seats around me. I read all the latest magazines.

It was fabulous, but as a result I'm now completely shattered and not entirely ready for school. Mum is 'disappointed, Nonie. I thought you were more mature.' Worth it, though.

A few days later the previews are over, and it's the official opening night in Chicago. The next morning, I Google the show to see what the critics have to say.

The first one I read is a bit hesitant: 'Lots of royal heart, but needs more soul'. However, all the others call it: 'A right royal entertainment', 'A royal night out', 'A royal success for the King of Broadway, Jackson Ward'. Et cetera. They love Carmen Candy as Margaret. They love Gary Lee as Prince Philip. And they love 'the new British singing sensation, Jenny Merritt' as Elizabeth.

Various theatre blogs show pictures of the opening night party. Jenny, in her burnt-orange crop, looks fabulous in the dress Crow made for her – a shorter version of the Met Ball dress, in green and peacock blue, beautifully fitted to show off her new dancer's body. She's standing between Jackson Ward and Elton John. Looking perfectly relaxed, as if she does this every evening.

As soon as I can, I Skype her.

'ELTON JOHN?'

'I know! He said he loved it.'

'Yes, but . . . ELTON JOHN?'

'He's an old friend of Jackson's. He's invited me to his house in the south of France in the summer. D'you want to come? You didn't get much of a holiday this year.'

I'm still struggling. 'ELTON JOHN?'

'Yes, Nonie,' she says patiently. 'Elton John. He's really nice. He's a fantastic piano player, by the way. He played at the party. So did Alicia Keys.'

'ALICIA KEYS?'

'Yes.'

'*She* was there?'

'Uh huh. She was in town.'

'And she played piano?'

'Yup. I sang with her. It was great.'

Oh. My. God.

It's not that Jenny's met these people. It's not even that they've invited her on holiday and PLAYED THE PIANO FOR HER. It's that she thinks this is perfectly normal. She's not boasting. She's not freaked out. She's just . . . comfortable. This is Jenny's world now, and I'm finally starting to convince myself that she'll be OK.

I have to tell someone about this. I call Edie.

'It's going to be a total smash,' I tell her. 'And Elton John was there! And Alicia Keys!'

'Greeaaat,' she says. She makes it sound like one of my yaaays. Now that I think about it, I could swear she's been crying.

'Are you all right?' I check.

'Uh huh,' she says.

There's a pause. 'You're not, are you?' I say.

There's another pause. Then a sniffle.

'What is it?'

'It's my parents,' she says. 'They've stopped everything. They say I've overstretched myself and that's why I'm so tired and miserable the whole time. They've stopped orchestra. They've stopped volunteering. They've banned me from even doing the website. '

'Oh, Edie! All your favourite stuff!'

She blows her nose. 'It's OK. They're right, I suppose. I need to concentrate on my interviews. Mum even offered to visit Gloria for me, but that's something I have to do myself. It's just . . . you know . . . It's . . .'

She tails off. She's so tired she can't even think of the words any more. Her parents may have a point.

'Oh no. This is my fault!' I say. 'I was supposed to look after you. But I've hardly seen you.'

'It's not your fault,' she sighs. 'It's not anyone's fault.'

I'm shocked. Edie's one of my best friends and I should have seen this coming. She's been super-stressed for more than a year now and I can't remember the last time she didn't look tired or pale. But we just got used to it. Plus we've all had other things on our minds, I suppose.

'Just think,' I say, desperate to cheer her up, 'this time next year you'll be at Harvard, exploring Boston, making new friends.' I SO picture her as Reese Witherspoon in *Legally Blonde* that in my mind she has a pink laptop and a chihuahua, although I know that in real life she wouldn't be seen dead with either.

She mumbles something about how greeaat that will be, but right now, I think all she wants to be is asleep.

That was totally not the conversation I needed to have about Jenny. I go down to the workroom, hoping and praying that Crow will be there, so I can tell her how cool Jenny looked in the dress, and namedrop like crazy.

But my hopes and prayers don't work. The workroom's empty. It's been empty a lot, recently. The lights are off. The mannequin is bare. In fact, it's so depressing that I turn the lights on, just to cheer myself up a bit. Then, as usual, I can't help wandering around the room, picking up bits of fabric and flicking through Crow's old sketches to admire them.

It turns out that not all of the sketches are old, though. Some of them are things I haven't seen before. Lots, in fact. Crow has covered pages and pages of notebooks and loose paper with ideas for a new collection. Not just pictures, but notes in her scrawly handwriting and even little scraps of fabric attached to the pages. She's been working on an idea Edie gave her ages ago: dresses made out of Fair Trade cotton from Uganda. Crow's taken it a stage further and designed lots of new prints. The dresses themselves have lots of clever draping, so they come in all sorts of curvy and boxy shapes. There are several designs I want to wear right this minute. And the fabrics look amazing.

So much work has gone into them. I had no idea Crow had even been thinking about them since she got back. She told me she was too busy for designing. She must be keeping me in the dark for some reason.

It doesn't take me long to work out what that reason might be. She needs someone to help her get her designs off the ground. She always did. And it's obvious that person can't be me. Perhaps she's waiting until she finds a new 'me' to help her out. Perhaps she's got someone in mind, but she hasn't asked them yet. Or worse. I suddenly remember her new talent for email. Maybe she's already asked someone and she's waiting for a reply.

Well, I refuse to be counted out quite so early. I may not be able to run a label, but I'm sure there's something I can do. I flick through a few more sketches. They're so lovely and they show her creative direction really clearly. Aha! Which gives me an idea – my one last chance of doing something useful.

Looking around like some sort of comedy burglar, I grab a selection of the best sketches and sneak them up to the top of the house, where Mum has a colour scanner-printer thing. I carefully scan in each one and use Mum's email account (which I set up for her and regularly have to update for her) to send myself the files. Then I replace the sketches in the workroom, as messily as I can, so they'll look the way Crow left them.

I feel a bit guilty going behind her back, but then, she's sort of been going behind mine by not telling me about her new ideas. And I've helped her out secretly before, when I signed her up to do her first catwalk show. That worked out OK. This will work out OK too. She will see that I was doing this for her own good and forgive me. Everything will be fine.

Then she can move on without me, if that's what she really wants to do.

I go to my room and look up the email address for the MIMOs' headquarters in New York. I include the scans of the pictures, and also an explanation of what Crow had in mind for the fabrics. She tends to use three words (badly spelled) where most people need twenty to get the gist of what she means. I can just feel what she was after. She wants to mix sexy, modern, urban shapes with tribal fabrics with an African vibe. She wants to be on the pulse with her designs, and to use ethically-sourced, Fair Trade cotton, which is on the pulse too. My fingers are shaking as I type, but it's exciting. It flows out of me. It makes me feel sure I'm doing the right thing.

Chapter 34

In the days that follow, I wait for a reply from the MIMOs, but nothing comes. I see Crow in the workroom a couple of times and carefully don't mention the new sketches. Neither does she. She hardly talks. When she does, it's about how much she enjoyed browsing the markets 'at home'. Or how much Henry's looking forward to his new teaching job there next year. Or how impressed she was by little Victoria's sewing techniques. If she talks about London at all, it's mostly about homework and looming mocks next term, and how stressful A levels must be. In fact, talking to Crow right now is a bit like talking to Edie, which is something I could never have imagined.

Talking to Edie herself is, if anything, worse.

'I can't remember a thing,' she tells me, looking shaky during registration one day near the end of term. 'I've got my Harvard interview tomorrow and I just feel sick at the thought of it. Even with questions like, "Why do you want to go to Harvard?" – I can't remember what I'm supposed to say.'

'You've wanted to go there all your life, practically,' I remind her. 'Just say whatever you think. You don't need to practise.'

After all, her schooldays have been one long preparation for this moment.

'Huh,' she says. 'That's what Phil said. He told me to lighten up.'

'He's right,' I point out.

'That's what you always say. Maybe he's right about getting a new girlfriend, too.'

'WHAT?'

'Yeah. They hooked up a few weeks ago. He said he was fed up with me never coming over. He said I've changed and he can't wait forever for me to have a life.'

'And he told you all of this just now? Before your interviews? When you're super-uptight?'

I've always liked Hot Phil, but suddenly I hate him. How could anyone be so cruel? No wonder Edie looks like a shadow of her normal self.

'He didn't mean to tell me,' she says in his defence. She can't help being kind, even now. 'It just sort of came out. He was really sorry about it.'

'I bet he was.'

'She's called Ramona, apparently.'

I also hate Ramona. She may only be a name to me, but I hate her anyway.

I wait for Edie to cry, but she doesn't. She's too tired even to cry any more. This is hopeless.

'When's your interview?' I ask.

'Tomorrow afternoon. At this posh old club near Piccadilly where you can't wear trousers. If you're a girl, anyway. I think if you're a boy, you have to.'

'I'll come with you. You need someone to hold your hand.'

I'm half expecting her to tell me not to be so silly, but she doesn't.

'Thanks,' she says. 'Mum's working so she can't make it. It would be nice to have someone there.'

However, it doesn't help as much as I'd like. She comes out of the interview in tears, convinced that she's totally messed it up. I offer to go to a movie with her in Leicester Square, or go out for burgers somewhere, but all she wants to do is go to bed. It's the same after her Oxford visits.

Like her, I find myself counting the days until Jenny comes home. Edie wants her for Gloria's sake, but I want her for my sake. I need her cheerfulness and energy again. I need less discussion about revision timetables and frankly a lot more conversation about talented artists and potential holidays with international pop stars.

Chapter 35

At Heathrow airport, Jenny arrives looking like a curvy, redheaded Victoria Beckham, with a new set of matching luggage and a record-breaking pair of sunglasses that cover most of her face. I wave my glitter sign so she can spot me through the shades.

'Sorry,' she says, lifting them up to kiss me hello. 'They don't call those flights the red-eye for nothing. See?'

She shows me her eyes. They are indeed red and puffy. She should try flying First Class. It is so much more comfortable and relaxing.

'Nice glasses, though,' I say. I notice that they're by Tom Ford. This is probably as close to Tom Ford as I'm ever going to get. I try them on.

'Why are you wearing them?' I ask, peering around at the arrivals lounge, which has suddenly gone dark. 'Afraid of getting papped by a paparazzo?'

Jenny immediately goes pink. She goes pinker, faster, than anyone I know, including Edie. She's so pink I can even spot it through the new super-shades. She looks at the floor.

'Oh my God! You are!' I say. 'You really are!'

'Well,' she admits, 'it was sort of happening in Chicago. I even had someone try and sit in the seat next to me so she could interview me on the plane.'

'Seriously?'

She nods.

'What did you say?'

'I said no!' she giggles. 'My publicist has to approve all my interviews or I get in big trouble.'

'You have a publicist?'

She goes pink again. 'Actually two. One in London and one in America. Jackson says I need them. Basically, they work for him, but they help me too.'

'Wow.' I hand Jenny back her shades, which she obviously needs more than I thought, and pick up my 'Welcome home Jenny' sign. I feel a bit embarrassed about it now. The last thing she wants is a big sparkly arrow pointed at her head.

I start to head for the Tube, but Jenny holds me back.

'Don't worry. My publicist said I should just get a cab. Those flights are so tiring.'

We make our way slowly to the taxi queue while I work out how much the cab is going to cost (probably as much as I earned at Miss Teen last summer, I should think) and Jenny talks non-stop about how well the show went, and how the cast party at the end of the run was

THE BEST NIGHT OF HER LIFE and how she cried the whole of the next day at the thought of not working with them all again.

She's moved on to describing their knitting obsession, and the hot pair of legwarmers she made for the Queen Mother, when she suddenly realises she's lost my attention.

'What is it?' she asks, looking in the same direction as me, towards the front of the queue. She even puts her Tom Fords on her head, so she can see properly.

'It must be my imagination,' I whisper. 'It's just – I could have sworn I saw—'

'Vicente!'

Jenny has a loud voice, honed by many hours on the stage, and she's just spotted him too. A head whips round, to reveal a silhouette with a chiselled jaw and straight nose. He's peering in our direction. Jenny calls the name again. She may be small, but she is redheaded and was recently in *Vogue*. When she wants to, she stands out.

He sees us and looks amazed. It's definitely him. Jenny runs up to him and kisses him on both cheeks. I'm not sure what to do: keep our place in the increasingly long taxi queue, or go over and say hi. However, with Jenny beckoning like a mad thing, I don't have much of a choice. I struggle with her bags and deposit them around Vicente's feet, looking as embarrassed as I feel. 'Nonie! What a charming surprise,' he says. 'And Jenny too. It is Jenny, isn't it? Have you been somewhere exciting?'

By the time Jenny's finished telling him about the

musical, he's at the front of the queue and the other people in it are staring at Jenny and me with such intense hatred that he really has to offer us a place in his cab, to save us from the mob. We gratefully accept.

Jenny looks around the spacious, black interior of the cab with its tip-up seats and sighs happily, settling into one of them so she's facing Vicente and me.

'A London taxi,' she says. 'What a treat. This is strange, though, Vicente. Shouldn't you be in a limo or something?'

Vicente laughs. 'Why? When one can find such attractive company on a taxi ride.'

'Are you going to be in London long?' I ask.

'A couple of weeks,' he says. He's still looking surprised and uncomfortable, despite all his charm. As if he hasn't recovered from seeing us yet. Then his phone goes off and he discreetly checks a text. Instantly, he gets that warm glow that I know so well from Mum. He looks up, catches my eye and looks as self-conscious as Jenny did when I asked her about the paparazzi.

Jenny coughs quietly. Then she coughs again. I realise she's trying to get my attention. She gives me the Look. I pretend to ignore it, but she won't let me. Luckily Vicente is busy texting back, so he doesn't notice. I do my 'Shut Up' Look to Jenny, but her eyes are almost completely round with staring by now. She flicks her glance to Vicente and back to me, and nods knowingly, before smiling a sickly smile.

I've known Jenny a long time. Most people might

assume she had a piece of grit in her eye and was trying to get rid of it, but I know what she's trying to say is: 'D'you think that was your mum texting Vicente? Is he here on a secret romantic visit, maybe? Ahh, look, he's texting her back! Isn't that cute?'

I shrug. I'm desperately trying to tell myself I'm wrong about this, but the trouble is, I agree with Jenny. That's exactly how it looks to me too. And I realise why Vicente's so uncomfortable. Mum's been trying to keep her new relationship quiet from me for months now. I can't say it's the greatest feeling, from my point of view, but the fact is, she's in love. And the man she loves has flown all the way from Brazil to spend Christmas with her. She might as well come out with it.

I decide to spare her the trouble.

'You should come to dinner again,' I tell him, when he's finished pressing send. 'I'm sure Mum would love it. Harry's over for the holidays – for some of the time, anyway. He'd love to see you.'

Vicente looks flattered, but mortified. 'Oh. That's very kind of you, Nonie. Of course, I was going to get in touch and invite you out somewhere. Harry and I have already fixed something up . . .'

Oh, God. This is awful. Here's me trying to be all generous and helpful, and I'm just making myself look stupid. He obviously had the whole holiday arranged so that he could see Mum and Harry and spare me from knowing. And now I've ruined it. But it's too late.

I look across at Jenny, hoping the conversation didn't seem as awkward as it felt. But as soon as Vicente looks out of the window she rolls her eyes at me and mouths 'Ouch'.

Great.

Chapter 36

Christmas is a succession of awkward meetings. I'm used to them in the fashion industry, but these are happening in the kitchen at home. Mum looks shocked when I tell her about meeting Vicente in the taxi queue, but she graciously makes the best of it and invites him round to supper. Granny's staying in town and comes round too, thrilled to see him and eager to talk about weddings. Again. Vicente has offered to help pay for Harry and Isabelle's, and Granny wants his opinion on every detail. I can tell Mum and Vicente would rather be alone together, but there's not much they can do about it now.

For a few days Harry and Isabelle are there in person, and these are the most awkward times. Isabelle, as always, is delighted to discuss tiara size, veil length, place settings and flowers. Harry isn't. Watching him, I realise that big weddings aren't his thing. He and Vicente have the same ill-at-ease posture, as if they'd rather be anywhere but here, but they're both too polite to say so and try to be as helpful as they can. They look comically similar, and I can't help feeling sorry for them both.

I catch Harry on the landing one day and say, 'You know, you don't need to do this big affair if you don't want to. I'm sure Isabelle would get married on a beach if you asked her.'

He looks at me as if I'm totally crazy. He often does that. Then he laughs.

'I couldn't do that to her. She's been planning this day for years. And Granny would kill me. Slowly. Besides, all I have to do is show up in a top hat and tails, not get too drunk and tell Issy I love her. I can manage that.'

I nod, because I sort of agree, as far as it goes. But it must be very different for boys, because my idea of my wedding day SO does not boil down to looking smart, not getting drunk and telling someone I love them. Although all of these are a good start, obviously.

I wonder if Isabelle realises how uncomfortable all the wedding talk makes Harry, but she doesn't seem to notice. Nor do Mum and Granny. It's as if Harry is just a necessary piece of a very large and lovely jigsaw puzzle. I feel more and more sorry for him. I mean, if I loved a boy and he asked me to marry him (let's say, a few years after fashion college, when we were living in Paris and I was managing the career of a super-top designer) and he wanted to do it in – oh, I don't know – jeans, a beautiful tee-shirt and perfect sneakers, somewhere quiet in

Ireland, I'd go along with it, to make him happy. As long as our day was romantic and special and meant something to us. But Isabelle is so used to everybody doing exactly what she wants that she's probably forgotten to check that it's what Harry wants too.

I'm tempted to say something to her, but I made such a big mistake with Vicente that I decide to keep out of it. I limit myself to encouraging smiles to Harry every now and again, and trying to change the subject when Granny gets on to her third hour of Successful Friends' Weddings In Gorgeous Country Houses, and precisely which brand of champagne to use for the toasts.

Jenny doesn't help. Her jet lag turns into a major cold and she's in bed for a week, then moping around the flat feeling sorry for herself for a week after that. However, a few days after New Year, she calls me, sounding much better. Positively chirpy, in fact.

'Can you meet me at the V&A in an hour? I'm trying to get hold of Edie and Crow too. It's time we all got together. Oh, and I've got some news.'

I leave the house and skip down the steps to the street. This is more like it. The V&A, my friends, and a bit of intrigue. Perfect! Exactly what I need to cheer me up with term starting soon. I just hope the news isn't that Stella is pregnant again. I'm not sure I could go through all that kitten naming a second time.

I'm the first to arrive. Or at least I think I am.

Then I spot Jenny by the information desk, signing autographs.

She grins when she sees me and comes over.

'Tourists from Chicago. Said they saw the show three times.'

Crow joins us. She's wearing a cream dress that seems vaguely familiar, and about seven fake pearl necklaces, accessorised with silk flowers. The overall effect is graceful, unusual and cool. I look at the dress and realise it's the toile for Isabelle's wedding dress, hoisted up with a belt and worn over a jumper. Crow is still a few centimetres shorter than Isabelle, so it looks totally different on her. I give Crow my quizzical look. Toiles are for mannequins and, occasionally, models to wear in the studio. They aren't worn in public. This one is all half-finished seams and chalk marks.

Crow shrugs. 'I liked its unmade-ness. It was like a sketch of a dress. What do you think?'

Now that I look at it properly, I think it looks absolutely great. Strange, but great. The way it drapes reminds me of the new designs she's not telling me about.

'Is the proper dress finished now?' I ask. 'Isabelle's, I mean.'

'Nearly,' Crow says. 'She's going to use it at this model award ceremony she's got in a couple of weeks.'

'WHAT?'

Crow shrugs again. 'She changed her mind about

getting married in it. She was worried in case it made her look like a human waterfall. She wants me to do something with antique lace now.'

Oh well. At least Isabelle listens to Harry on some things. But Crow must be on her tenth design for this dress by now. Meanwhile, Jenny is dragging us through to the café at the back of the museum without waiting for Edie, who'll know where to find us anyway.

Heads turn. Not on an Isabelle level, but nevertheless, they turn. Jenny has an aura about her now. Even though she's in jeans and the mismatched knitted cardigan, she's still got the chic, burnt-orange hair, the Tom Ford glasses (on top of her head) and a sort of a glow. But even more heads turn to look at Crow. I *wish* I'd thought to wear a toile before. It's such a good idea. My own zebra-print leggings and orange mohair shrug look positively tame by comparison.

We settle at a table and Jenny updates us on the kittens.

'I've found a home for Fosse and Stella! Our downstairs neighbour's taking them. Oh, and Fosse's called Eliza now. After Eliza Doolittle in *My Fair Lady*. The lady refused to call a girl kitten Fosse. Or Bob.'

'Or Flossie?'

'I *told* you, Nonie. Flossie's such a stupid name.'

'Unlike Sondheim.'

'Stephen Sondheim is, like, *the* composer! Apart from Jackson, of course. He's totally famous!' Jenny seems shocked that I don't get this. I guess it's her equivalent of me and the Met Ball. I notice no-one's adopting Sondheim the kitten yet, though.

'Wait a minute,' Crow interrupts. 'Did you say your neighbour's taking Stella *and* Eliza. Stella too? Why?'

'Ah,' says Jenny. 'Yes. Well. That's part of my news, you see, so it'll have to wait till Edie gets here.'

We fall into one of those awkward silences. Crow gets out a sketchbook and starts filling in a sort of doodle she did earlier. Hard to tell exactly what it is. It looks like an animal print from far away, but when I peer more closely, I realise it's made up of lots of silhouettes of girls holding hands. Pretty.

While we wait, I tell Jenny about the Harry and Isabelle situation at home, and Granny going on about weddings.

'Mm hmm. Sounds good.'

She's not listening. Talking about someone else's wedding doesn't really compare to having your dressing room filled to the brim with flowers on opening night, or jamming with pop stars into the early hours.

'Any news on Starbucks boy?' she asks.

I shake my head. I think I've caught him looking at me a few more times since the ruler conversation, but that hardly counts as news. Luckily, Edie arrives to rescue the conversation.

'I was reading. Sorry,' she says breathlessly. 'Missed the bus stop. Had to run back . . . Anyway, hi guys. What's it all about, Jen?'

'Well,' Jenny says, taking a deep breath and grinning from ear to ear. 'Get this. We've got a new theatre. The owners are really excited about the show. They confirmed yesterday. It's all incredibly fast and scary. We open on Broadway in the summer. I. Am. Going. To. New. York.'

There's a stunned silence. Jenny grins some more.

'Wow!' says Crow, who's the first to speak.

'Really?' I ask.

Oh my God. In six months' time, it's just possible that all my friends will be in America, and I'll be in London, working at a hot drinks counter somewhere. What's going on here? I feel shaky and slightly sick.

'Yeah,' Jenny says, bouncing on her seat. 'Not Off-Broadway. The actual Broadway. Well, not Broadway exactly, it's 43rd Street, but that's practically 42nd Street, so it's even better for a musical, really, because of the tradition, you know? It's practically unheard of nowadays for a new musical to get such a prestigious theatre straight away. But they love us. And we're going to get bigger sets and better costumes . . .'

'Better costumes?' Crow interrupts. 'That's interesting. I've always loved theatre design . . .'

But Jenny and I aren't listening. By now, we're both looking at Edie, who hasn't said anything yet.

'Well?' Jenny asks.

'I can't believe it,' Edie whispers. 'You've only just come back.'

'I know!' Jenny says happily. 'Oh, and there's a few

more tweaks we need to make to the show, but that always happens . . .'

She's sounding like an old pro now and relishing every minute.

Edie, on the other hand, isn't. Judging by her expression, when she said 'I can't believe it', she didn't mean it was unbelievably great. She meant something else entirely.

'Are you OK?' I ask.

She sits there, stock-still, staring at Jenny.

'And you're going to go? To New York? In the summer? For months, presumably?'

'No,' Jenny says, crossing her arms and getting those two bright spots on her cheeks that always make me nervous. 'Not in the summer. In two weeks. I can stay with Jackson. I need to take more dance classes and he knows some great people I can work with.'

'Presumably they're talented artists,' I suggest. Everyone ignores me.

'I could be gone for a year,' Jenny sums up.

She stares defiantly at Edie. Edie stares angrily back.

'So *that's* why your neighbour's taking Stella,' Crow says.

Edie looks grim. 'This isn't about Stella, Crow. This is about Gloria. This is about the fact that Jenny's mum has been living on her own since last summer, and she is positively ill. And her only daughter is going to live in New York for a year. For a whole *year*. So she can be in a *show*.'

All the time, her eyes are boring into Jenny's. If I were Jenny, I'd be pulling down those Tom Fords any time now, but Jenny's braver. She continues to stare right back.

'There's something you don't understand, Edie,' she says quietly. 'You've been visiting Mum since the summer and looking after her. And that's fantastic. But I've been doing it since I was three.'

I gasp. 'Three?'

'That's when she had her first episode. She blames Dad for walking out on her. I'm not so sure. Maybe it would have happened anyway. But all my life, I've never known if my mum was going to be the bright, fun one, baking shortbread and making up skits for us to do, or the silent one in the corner, who couldn't even take me to school.'

'Jen!' I say. 'That's terrible. I never knew. All this time I've known you – you never said.'

For the first time, Jenny looks away from Edie, and towards me. She shrugs.

'I don't know . . . I thought about it. But at school I just wanted to be normal. I was glad you didn't know.'

She might have been, but I'm not.

'I could have helped!' I point out.

'You did. You were always nice to me. You just didn't know that you were helping.'

There's a silence, while we take it all in.

'And now?' Edie says. 'Now that she needs you more than ever? I suppose I'm expected to step in?'

Jenny shakes her head. 'Not at all. It's great if you do,

but if you don't want to . . . The thing is, guys, this is my biggest chance. Starring in a Broadway show? At eighteen? That doesn't happen to you twice. You have to take it and go. Mum will understand.'

'Huh!' says Edie, affronted. 'You *would* say that.'

'No, I mean it. She'll understand, because it's what she's always wanted for me. It's what she wanted to do herself, before she met Dad. She'd be devastated if I didn't go. She was her happiest ever when I was in *Annie*. And she loved it when I did the play last year. She even liked me being in that movie. But this is on another level.'

'I agree,' Edie says, folding her arms.

Crow and I sigh with relief.

'It's certainly on another level,' Edie continues. 'Because this time, she's *really* ill. If you go, I dread to think what might happen.'

'You can't blackmail me,' Jenny says. And now she does pull the Tom Fords down, before grabbing her bag and standing up to go. 'I thought you were all going to be so happy for me. I had no idea you were going to . . . hate me.'

There's a catch in her voice as she turns to leave the café. I'm desperate to call her back and say she's got it all wrong. That I *am* really happy for her. But Edie is shuddering and white-faced with shock. She seems to need our help even more.

Crow and I do what we can to reassure Edie that everything will be OK, but we don't make much progress. It doesn't help that we have no idea *how* to make things

OK. We can't ask Jenny not to go to New York, but it's awful to think of Gloria all alone in her flat. Besides, Edie isn't listening to us anyway.

We lapse back into silence. I'm thinking about something Jenny said. About how some chances don't come along twice. When they do come, you have to grab them and go. It's as if she was telling me I did the right thing to send Crow's sketches to the MIMOs. Just think, in a year Jenny'll be starring in a Broadway production and Crow could be going into the MIMOs' headquarters to design her latest collection. Maybe they could share a flat together. Maybe Harry and Isabelle could stop by for tea . . .

Edie rootles in her bag for a tissue and wipes her eyes. I realise I need to try a bit harder to make things better.

'Don't be too hard on Jenny,' I say. 'You're the one who thought of going to America first. You know – Harvard. Remember?'

'Funnily enough, I've been thinking about that a lot recently,' Edie says. 'I've thought about it all holidays. And I'm not going.'

'HELLO?'

'You heard me. I'm not going to Harvard. Well, obviously I'm not going because I did a rubbish personal statement and I failed the interview. But I'm not going to study law. I'm not going to join the United Nations. You were right, Nonie. I'd hate being away from home. I'm thinking of not applying to university at all.'

'Oh. My. God. Not seriously?'

She shrugs. 'I'm just being realistic, Nonie.'

'No you're not! You're being totally mad. You're the cleverest girl in the school. You've just been working too hard. Honestly, Edie, you need a rest.'

She looks at me with her hollow eyes. 'Sure. Whatever. Anyway, at least it means I'll be around to look in on Gloria, so that's nice for Jenny, isn't it?'

I stare at her. I hardly recognise her. And I'm not even sure I particularly like her right now. If she didn't look so miserable, I'd say something about using Gloria to make Jenny feel guilty. But the thing is, she looks *completely* miserable. I know she'll change her mind about Harvard when she's had some sleep, but right now, she seems serious. I hesitate, not sure what I can do to help.

'Please, Nonie,' she says, 'just go away.'

This doesn't seem like the best idea, but right now I can't think of a better one. Reluctantly, I do as I'm told. Crow stays behind, still doodling in her sketchbook. I leave them both to it and wish I'd never come.

Back at home, Granny is putting on her coat.

'That was such fun, darlings! I can't *wait* for June.'

Mum is putting away a stack of wedding magazines about a mile high. Harry looks like he's been hit by a bomb.

'Nonie!' Granny says, giving me a quick peck on the cheek. 'We were talking bridesmaids. How do you feel about ecru lace? It's beige, really, but when you say ecru it sounds so much nicer, don't you think? What is it, darling? Don't you like ecru?'

'Ecru's fine,' I lie, to avoid getting into a longer conversation.

Oh great. I'm going to be a beige bridesmaid. Yaaay.

Chapter 37

or the next week, Edie's out of contact visiting her grandparents, and Crow isn't answering her phone. Which could mean she's avoiding me, or she's lost it, or simply that it's run out of battery. It's impossible to tell with Crow. Meanwhile, Jenny's in contact all the time. Her main topics of conversation are how mean Edie was at the V&A, what she should pack for New York, and knitting. I'm trying to remember why I missed her so much.

However, things aren't all bad. Vicente has gone back to Brazil and Granny's gone back to her house in the country, which helps a lot. Oh, I get a text from Liam, asking if I had a good Christmas and saying he'll see me in class next week. Which is kind of obvious, so why is my heart beating so fast, and why do I have to get my phone out and check the message every three minutes?

I decide to be totally cool about the whole thing, and wait until we go back to school before I reply.

Two seconds later, I text him back, saying I had a fab Christmas (one of my many not-so-truthful statements, but this is not the time for the whole Crow/Vicente/Jenny/Edie story) and agreeing that we will, indeed, see each other next week. And I add a kiss at the end of the text, because it just seems wrong without one. True, he will now think I'm freakish *and* desperate, but I can't help myself.

Two days before school's due to start again, I finally get an email from the MIMOs, about the sketches I sent them. They don't explain why they waited so long to get back to me. That's the way things seem to work in fashion. You either have to wait half a lifetime or you have to do something in the next ten seconds. It's one bit of the industry I'm sort of used to by now. Anyway, they say they were very impressed by Crow's work, which they've shown to 'various key stakeholders and other interested parties' and they're enthusiastic about the idea of creating a print-based teen range (with a few minor adjustments) and they'd love to 'pursue discussions with the designer directly'. I promise that the designer will get back to them just as soon as she can.

Then I spend an hour trying to work out how to admit to Crow what I did. I suppose I should try and call her, but I doubt she'd answer. I write a long email, explaining all about finding the sketches in the workroom and how fabulous it is that the MIMOs are so excited. I include my original email, so she can see how much I worked on it.

Maybe it's useful that Crow's on email after all. Right now, it's easier than talking to her face to face.

I wait a few minutes for a reply, but I guess she's not online. Nothing comes. The next day, nothing either. I think about calling her, but I'm sure if she wanted to talk about it, she'd call me. Which doesn't happen. I wait for her to show up in the workroom, but she doesn't come. I'm starting to wonder if I've made a huge mistake. However, there's nothing I can do and anyway, I'll be seeing Liam in less than twelve hours. Which means I have a whole bunch of other stuff to think about.

The first day of school is Wednesday. Which means French. Which means I wake up at 4.45 in the morning and can't go back to sleep. This is useful, as it takes me at least two hours to find an outfit that is quirky but not too way out, and gives me a vague hint of a figure without looking like I tried too hard. By seven AM my bed is covered in almost every piece of clothing I possess. In the end, I settle on a jumper Crow gave me for Christmas, knitted out of soft, merino wool with silver and raspberry tiger stripes, plus denim hotpants, leopard-print leggings and Doc Martens. It is comfortable, warm and colourful. It also has a sort of jungle theme going on, which I like.

At breakfast, I can only face half a slice of toast. By the time we get to the French labs at Wetherby, the sound of my heart beating can probably be heard on the other side of London, where the converted warehouses are.

Liam is in his usual seat in the front row. He's had a haircut and lost some of the curls, but he's as cute and kissable as ever. He's not dressed for the freezing London weather. He's wearing a shirt with an open collar, a shoelace for a tie and a very old, battered blazer that is several times too small for him.

He looks sexy. But he's absorbed with chatting to Ashley about something. His eyes don't flicker in my direction as I pass. I'm sure he must be able to hear my heart pounding, but he doesn't show it. As soon as I sit down, he casually gets his phone out and starts tapping away under the desk. Seconds later, my phone goes. I have it in my lap, just in case. I'm so thrilled – and scared – that I reach for it too fast and drop it. Luckily Madame Stanley has, yet again, forgotten something and isn't there to confiscate it.

I retrieve the phone and read the message. It is one line. 'Grrrrrr.'

Does this mean what I think it means? Does this mean that, with his head down and never looking in my direction, he noticed the jungle theme? Is he being a leopard, or a tiger?

I can't help laughing. He hears me, looks round and gives me a grin. Yes! The boy I have texted a kiss to is pretending to be a jungle animal to make me smile. I am so happy I can hardly breathe. I grin back. Even when our teacher finally arrives and hands out our A-level mocks schedule, I'm still grinning. A little voice in my head tells me I should be cool and laid-back and mysterious, but it's too late. I am MUCH too happy to be cool right now.

After class, he reaches out to catch my hand as I go by. I stop dead, incapable of further movement, feeling the warmth of his skin.

'I was wondering,' he says.

'Mmmm?'

'Some of us are getting together to check our uni applications. Make sure we've got them right before the deadline. Want to join us?'

'Uh, me?'

'Yes, you. We're meeting in the ICT room on Friday, then going to a caff down the road.'

'Uh, really?' I say.

'Really,' he assures me.

Behind him, I notice the Belles hovering in the doorway, looking too shocked to think of any fashion-related put-downs for the time being. Then I turn my attention back to Liam.

'Right. Great. Sure. Sounds good,' I say.

'You're really not that talkative, are you?' he laughs. Then he looks concerned and wipes his lips with a finger. I realise I've been staring at them a bit too intently.

'Have I got something here?' he asks.

'Not yet,' I whisper. But not loud enough for him to hear. However, after we've applied to university and had a cappuccino or two, he's welcome to try my lips against them if he likes.

*

'NONIE? OH MY GOD!'

Jenny's in my bedroom. She came over to update me on her packing arrangements. Now, thank goodness, we have something else to talk about.

'Do you think he really means it about the application thing? Are you really doing that? Wow! And do you mean *Liam*? The one who thinks you're freakish? He didn't sound that into you.'

'I know.' I grin.

'Oh, and have you told Edie?' she asks, with a sad note in her voice.

'Not yet.'

I don't want to make Edie even more depressed, after the whole Hot Phil and Ramona thing. However, I'm going to have to tell her soon. If I don't, I'll pop.

'You'll have to introduce me to him properly,' Jenny says, flipping her attention back to Liam. 'Before I go. Otherwise, who knows when I'll get to check him over? Can I come along to the café thing?'

Oh great. That's *really* going to help. However, she's off to New York any minute and once she goes, I don't know when I'll see her again. If she's going to meet my possibly-if-things-go-well-maybe-future-boyfriend properly, this might be her only chance. So far, she's only seen him from the back of French class, so she doesn't get how cute he is at all.

'OK,' I say, after a bit of hesitation.

'Great!' she grins. 'And I'll be very quiet. Promise. You'll hardly notice me.'

We go to the Wetherby ICT room on Friday afternoon and the cool people from French are all sitting at computers, along with a few other boys from Wetherby that I don't recognise. No sign of the Belles. Everyone says hi and they seem friendly enough, but I'm only watching one pair of lips.

The half-amused smile goes into overdrive when Liam spots Jenny, but he makes space for me to sit next him, which is all I care about. We fiddle about with application forms. Mine are for every fashion college I've heard of, to do PR. I'm still not quite sure what I'd do with the degree if I got it, but as the chances of me even getting into college are so slim, I'm not worrying about that too much right now. I'm worrying about whether Liam has noticed my new leggings, and likes them, and what you're supposed to say to a boy to totally impress him.

Eventually, we head off to a café that serves English breakfasts and strong tea (and cappuccinos, luckily), and has a relaxed, friendly vibe. I'm sitting next to Liam again. We talk about stuff for a while, but my brain is entirely occupied with trying not to notice the curls on Liam's neck, and how close his hand is, resting next to mine on the table.

'Concentrate,' the brain keeps saying. 'Focus on what people are saying. Look intelligent. Say something interesting.'

As a result of which, I entirely lose track of the conversation and say almost nothing. I'm the quiet one again. It's the Liam effect. Luckily, once the uni stuff is out of the way, Jenny does the talking. Mostly about herself, but nobody seems to mind.

'They're changing the name of the show,' she says. 'From *Elizabeth and Margaret* to *The Princesses*. It sounds catchier.'

'*The Princesses?*' Ashley checks. 'By Jackson Ward? I've been reading about that. And there was something on an entertainment channel over Christmas. They were saying Catherine Zeta Jones was interested in a part, but they've already got someone for it.'

Jenny nods. 'I'm not too sure she wanted a part, exactly, but she was talking to Jackson about it. Mind you, he's known her for years. They often catch up.'

And so it goes on. Things I think about as private chat between me and Jenny are suddenly news items. And things I think of as news are suddenly private chats that Jenny has with her musical mates. The other guys are really curious about the show, not because my best friend is in it, but because they've read about it online, or seen it mentioned on TV. It is not possible to 'hardly notice' Jenny any more. It's not that I'm jealous of her. Jenny's just Jenny and she's doing what she wants to do. But I feel as if she's not 'mine' any more. She's becoming public property.

I continue to maintain my witty and impressive silence, but nobody seems to mind that either.

Liam describes how he and I are going to go to the London College of Fashion together, and how we're going to totally wow everybody there with his literary ability (apparently – so far the best thing I've seen him write is 'Grrrrr') and my stylishness.

'Stylishness? Nonie?' Jenny says.

'Oh yes. She's very stylish. Just in her own special way.'

He does the half-amused smile. Even with Jenny there, I have to physically hold on to my seat to stop myself throwing myself at him. However, I practise being demure and not getting too much cappuccino froth on my lips, for once. I want them to be clean and foam-free later, just in case.

Chapter 38

It was just a simple kiss goodbye. A very brief one. But a kiss, nevertheless. On the lips. While his lips were in the process of doing the half-amused smile.

It was perfect. The sort of kiss that you suddenly think about at odd moments, like when you're brushing your teeth, or making toast, or in class, or breathing.

I think about it all week. Including while saying goodbye to Jenny as she heads for New York, and sitting through French, tingling, and meeting up again for 'revision' the following Friday afternoon, when he does it again.

I'm still thinking about it first thing on Saturday morning, when I wake up to the sound of the alarm. Except it isn't the alarm. My alarm doesn't go off on a Saturday morning. It takes me a moment to realise what the noise is. My phone, going off in my bag. And I think this must be the third or fourth time it's rung, because I'm pretty sure I've been dreaming through the ringing for a while.

Usually he texts. Why is he calling this time? Does he need to make another kiss-rendezvous? And why is he so desperate? I mean, it was good, but this is a bit extreme.

I check the screen, but it isn't Liam calling after all. It's Edie. Outside, it's still dark.

'Hello?' I say groggily.

'Oh, Nonie,' she says. 'Thank God. You've got to come over. Please. I need someone to help me. My parents are at this Scout thing with my brother. Can you come?'

'Sure,' I say. 'What's the problem?'

'It's Gloria.'

'Gloria?'

'Yes. I'm at Jenny's flat. The ambulance is on the way. Please come soon.'

Oh my God.

I leap into my clothes as fast as I possibly can, pausing only when I realise that my jumper's on back to front and I have boob-mounds sticking out of my back. I don't waste time on the laces for my Doc Martens, which is why I end up falling, very loudly, down the stairs outside Harry's room.

As I'm picking myself up, his door opens. He looks at me, bleary-eyed.

'Hi!' I say, surprised. 'I didn't know you were home.'

'Got in last night,' he mutters. 'Late.' He looks at his watch. 'Four hours ago, in fact. What's going on?'

'It's Edie,' I explain. I tell him about Gloria and the ambulance. His face clouds over.

'I'm coming with you,' he says. 'I can drive you in Mum's car. Give me a moment.'

Two minutes later, he's back, dressed in jeans and a slouchy cardigan over the tee-shirt he slept in. We race to the car together and are at Jenny's flat in record time. Seeing the ambulance outside, with its lights flashing, makes the whole thing seem suddenly more real, and frightening.

The door to the flat is half open. Harry and I step cautiously inside. At first, the place seems eerily quiet, but then we hear shuffling noises coming from Gloria's room. I'm about to go in, when Harry puts an arm on my shoulder and stops me. Instead, he pops his head round the door, to see if everything's OK.

Instantly, Edie comes rushing out and into my arms. She doesn't say anything. Just hugs me. Moments later, a paramedic in green overalls comes out and motions us out of the way. They bring Gloria out on a stretcher. At least, I assume it's Gloria. The face, eyes closed, looks like it belongs to a woman thirty years older than the Gloria I knew, and half her weight. Straggly hair lies limp against her cheek.

'Is she . . . ?' I whisper.

Edie shakes her head. 'I thought so. That's why I called you. But they found a pulse. Look, I'd better go with them.'

She's anxious and distracted. She heads off after the paramedics, but they tell her to go home and get some rest. Everything's under control. She tries to insist on going in the ambulance, but they won't let her.

'Look, love, there's nothing more you can do. We'll look after her. Best if you leave us to it.'

They carefully manoevre the stretcher down the stairs. Edie looks so panic-stricken that Harry says, 'Why don't Nonie and I drive you to the hospital? Then you can check she's OK. And we can drive you home.'

Slowly the panic starts to fade from Edie's face.

'Are you sure? Don't you have loads to do?'

'Nothing more important than this,' Harry assures her.

We head quickly for the car and make it to the hospital not long after the ambulance. Then comes the long wait, in various different queues, until we find out where they've taken Gloria and how she is. Slumped in a chair in a badly lit waiting room with a hot cup of tea, Edie explains what happened.

'The phone rang last night. It was this weird call. Nobody said anything. Just breathing. And I messed up finding the number. Then I woke up in the night and I realised – it must have been Gloria. I dashed over to the flat, but it was too late. There were pills and bottles everywhere. She was lying in the bed and she'd been sick. I don't know when she took them, but by the time I got there she wasn't moving. I tried to wake her but I couldn't. I thought . . . I thought . . .'

I put my arm around her. Harry gently takes her tea

off her and holds her little hand in his big one. She cries quietly, but for a long time, her body shaking with the sobs. We sit with her until she feels a bit better, and then some more, until a male nurse eventually comes over and asks us to follow him. By this time, I have flicked through more celebrity magazines than I've previously read in a lifetime and know about every diet and every broken marriage in the history of Hollywood. I also know it will be a while before I drink hot tea from a vending machine again.

'She's over there,' the nurse says. He points us in the direction of a large ward with several beds in it. Gloria is in the furthest one, screened by some inappropriately cheerful yellow curtains. Her eyes are still closed but her face looks slightly less grey. There's a drip in her arm and wires attaching her to a monitor that's busy flashing meaningless numbers.

The nurse has already gone. After staring at Gloria for a while, we find some female nurses sitting round a table at the entrance to the ward, chatting. Harry goes over to them. Instantly, they all look up, stop talking and flash broad smiles. The Harry effect. Even when he's wearing last night's tee-shirt and hasn't brushed his teeth. I don't know how he does it, but I wish he'd give some of it to me.

After a couple of minutes of questions from Harry and adoring gazes from the nurses, he comes back over to Edie and me.

'She's stable. The fact that she was sick saved her. That and you getting there, Edie. She'll be OK, but it'll take time.'

He hesitates. There's something else, but it's clear he doesn't want to tell us.

'Please,' I say. 'Whatever it is – I think we should know.'

At first he shakes his head, but Edie and I as combined forces are hard to resist. Eventually he gives in.

'They said that in this sort of case she's likely to try again. We need to keep an eye on her.'

'Oh!'

There's a gasp from Edie. I wonder if she's going to cry again, but she doesn't. Instead, she bites her lip and goes very still. I put my arm around her and help her back to the car. I'm so glad we've got Harry with us to worry about all the practical stuff like paying for parking and negotiating a way through the busy London traffic.

We take Edie back to her house. We're expecting it to be empty, but to our surprise, her whole family is there. In the hall, her mum folds Edie into her arms and starts crying.

'Thank God you're safe, darling,' she says. 'We've been so worried. I tried calling you the minute I got your message. We came back straight away, but we didn't know where you were or how to find you.'

She looks up at Harry and me.

'I can't thank you both enough. You must be exhausted. Come and have a cup of tea.'

We all troop into Edie's kitchen, where her mum bustles around making drinks for everyone. I don't think I can face another cup of tea right now, until one's put in front of me with a big spoonful of sugar in it. I don't normally have sugar in tea, but the sweetness turns out to be just what I need. And Edie's mum's right. I do suddenly feel exhausted. Even though I've spent most of the last few hours just sitting around waiting for things to happen in the hospital, it's been more tiring than I realised.

'What happened?' Edie's brother Jake asks. His eyes are wide. 'Did she die, that lady?'

Harry smiles gently. 'No, she didn't. She's going to be fine, actually. Your sister's a real hero.'

I don't even need to look at Edie. I know how pink her cheeks will be. She's got her head down anyway, hiding her face with her fringe while she checks her phone for all the texts and messages she's missed from home while we were at the hospital.

'Sorry about the Scout thing,' I say to Jake. 'Did you miss much of it?'

'Most of it,' he shrugs. 'But we wanted to check Edie was OK. Mum said Edie sounded really upset in her message. And then Mum started crying. And Dad looked really upset too. And I didn't really feel like doing scouts anyway after that.'

'Oh, *Jake*,' his mum says, looking mortified.

Harry and I catch each other's eye. He has the ghost of

a smile, but he's trying to hide it. I guess he's touched, like I am, by the way Edie's family sticks together in a crisis. How kind they all are. How easily her mum gets embarrassed. They're not like our family at all, but they're great.

'Well, I'd better be going,' Harry says eventually. 'There's this thing I was supposed to be at . . .'

Edie glances up from under her fringe and puts her phone on the table.

'Er, thanks,' she says. 'For everything, Harry. Thanks very much.'

She stands up. Harry goes round to say goodbye. She sticks her hand out to shake his, but he's already leaning in for a quick hug, so she gets him in the stomach with her pointy fingers. Harry laughs and gives her a very formal handshake and a bow. She looks just as mortified as her mum did earlier.

On the sofa later, watching old episodes of *Glee* with Edie and Jake, I can't help wondering about our families. I can't possibly imagine Mum dropping everything to come and rescue me from some emergency. But on the other hand, we're natural huggers.

And thinking about hugging reminds me of kissing. Which naturally leads me to thoughts about Liam. I get my phone out and stare at it. Do I dare text him? Lately, we've only texted about practical stuff like meeting arrangements. Is it a bit too much for a girl to text a boy when she wants to talk about something terrible that's just happened? Will he think I'm getting serious, and go off me instantly?

I decide I'll have to risk it, but keep it as light and vague as possible. I think about what to say for a full episode of *Glee*, going through the various options until I finally come up with: 'Are you around?'

I wait. And wait. And no text comes back. Greeaat.

Then, just as I'm about to leave Edie's and go back home, something comes through.

'Sorry babe. Working for my dad today. Hope you're ok. Miss you x'

I keep staring. It's hardly Shakespeare. But it uses the words 'babe', and 'miss you' and 'x'. As far as I'm concerned, it's a Jane Austen novel – with a happy ending. Despite the day, and the memory of Gloria's grey face on the stretcher, it fills me with a warm glow that starts in my tummy and spreads out to my earlobes.

'Are you sure you're OK to go home now?' Edie's mum asks, checking me for signs of stress. But suddenly, they've gone.

'I'm fine,' I assure her, truthfully. 'Absolutely fine.'

Chapter 39

They keep Gloria in hospital for a week, to start her on some medication and to keep an eye on her. Edie visits her every day, and Harry pops in too. I manage to go a couple of times, but the rest of my time is taken up with revising or thinking about Liam, texting Liam, receiving texts from Liam, seeing him in class or generally wondering when the next kissing goodbye opportunity will arise.

I know Edie's called Jenny to tell her the news. I don't know what Jenny said, but it obviously wasn't what Edie wanted to hear. Her face clouds over whenever Jenny's name is mentioned.

I call Crow to let her know what's happened. I haven't seen her since before term began and I'm really missing the sight of her light in the basement workroom. More than anything, I just want to talk to her.

'It's sort of good news, in a way,' I explain. I don't want to alarm Crow too much. 'Gloria's agreed to see a therapist and talk things through. Plus she's going to let social services visit, so Edie won't have to go round so often.'

'Good,' Crow says.

There's a bit of silence, while we both work out what to say next. Crow and telephones don't mix brilliantly.

'Er, did you get my email?' I ask, eventually.

I've been meaning to ask this for a while. I sent the email ages ago. Since then I've been a bit busy with Liam and kisses and Gloria and stuff, but at the back of my mind I've still been worrying about Crow's total lack of contact. I thought she liked emailing these days.

'What email?' she asks.

FOR GOODNESS' SAKE!

'The one about the MIMOs. The one about your sketches for cotton print dresses,' I say, crossly. The one about her whole new career as an international designer! Honestly! What email does she think it would be?

'Mee-mos? Oh, *that*,' she says. 'I remember. Those sketches were just stuff I did when I was supposed to be revising for maths. I didn't expect anyone to see them.' She sounds guilty again, which is how I feel.

'I'm sorry I sent them without asking you. But it seemed such a shame to waste them. I was so sure the MIMOs would be really excited about them.'

'I'm glad you liked them.'

'The MIMOs? I thought they were a bit weird, but—'

'No, the sketches,' she says. 'I liked the way you

described them.'

'Thanks,' I say. 'I thought they were amazing. But what I think doesn't matter any more. You need to talk to the MIMOs direct. I sent you their details. Promise me you'll talk to them, Crow? Promise?'

'OK.' She sounds unconvinced. Maybe she has something totally different in mind. But I so want to be able to help her. I want it to be *my* thing she does. Not whatever else she's thinking of.

'How's your family?' I ask, as an afterthought. I'd hate her to think I'm just obsessed with her sketches. Although I suppose I am.

She sighs down the phone.

'It's difficult. Now Edie's stopped doing her website, there's not so much money for the school back home. Please don't tell her, I know it will make her sad, but she was so good at raising money. Now it's harder for my dad to buy books. And maybe they won't be able to pay Henry to be a new teacher after all. So I'm designing some fabrics for the school bags because they say if the bags have my name on, they're easier to sell. But you mustn't worry, Nonie. I wasn't going to tell you . . .'

I'm so shocked I don't know what to say. She wasn't going to tell me? Why? Has she given up talking to me altogether? I have no idea how to end the conversation. I can hear a sort of judder in my voice as I say goodbye. I've obviously done something terribly wrong. Was it sending off the sketches, after all? I'm not sure. I'm not really sure about anything Crow-related any more.

Even Mum notices something's up. She's spotted that Crow's hardly around at the moment, at least.

'That girl's working too hard,' she says one day. 'She needs some fun.'

WHAT? This, from the woman who would physically chain me to my laptop if she knew how. I say nothing.

'It's her birthday soon, isn't it? Her sixteenth?'

I nod.

'Sixteen's a big deal,' Mum goes on. 'I'm sure if she was at home, her family would do something to mark the occasion. And Crow's never really celebrated, has she?'

This is true. Up to now, we've normally been busy doing a collection or something and she hasn't had much time to think about it. It only highlights what a fashion desert this year has become.

'I'm happy to organise something for her,' Mum offers. 'If she wants. Can you find out what she'd like?'

I try and think of an excuse not to call her, but I can't come up with anything, and besides, just because she doesn't want to talk to me, that doesn't mean she should miss out on a birthday party. So I call, and it's as if nothing ever happened. She's thrilled by the party idea and very grateful to Mum. I'm more confused than ever, but glad that Crow still gets on with at least one member of my family.

They decide on a grown-up dinner party, with close

friends and family members. Mum suggests going to a posh restaurant in Mayfair. I'm not sure why. Our kitchen is perfectly good enough. But Crow loves the idea. And I suddenly realise that I really, really need somebody else to be there too.

'Would you come?' I ask Liam after French. 'It will be truly awful. I mean, lovely for Crow, but full of my family. And they'll probably ask you the most embarrassing questions. But . . . well, I don't want to be there on my own.'

I know this is putting pressure on him, which I feel bad about, but at the moment I always feel I'm on my own unless he's there.

He's very brave about it. Positively cheerful, in fact.

'I'd love to meet your family,' he says. 'I've been waiting for you to ask. They all sound totally mad from the way you talk about them. Particularly your granny. Bring it on!'

The restaurant is grown-up and sophisticated. Panelled walls and big, round tables with white tablecloths and a spotlight on each one. Photographs by one of Mum's artists on the walls, which is spooky, but hopefully a lucky sign. And waiters who couldn't be more attentive if we were Elton John and Alicia Keys.

Crow arrives in a special party outfit that consists of silver dungarees, a red and black ladybird cape and two little bobbing antennae in her enormous hair.

'Ladybirds are lucky,' she explains. 'I want this to be a

lucky year for me.'

Hopefully, having a giant silver ladybird at the table will be lucky for us all. However, once she sits down she blends so easily into the conversation that you sort of forget about the antennae and the cape. She spends ages chatting to Harry about Victoria's bag-making empire in Uganda. Well, not exactly empire. Just this female co-operative making stuff, but it feels like an empire to me. And to Harry too, by the sound of it. He's seriously impressed and offers to buy a bunch of bags to give to his friends at fashion shows. Maybe they will pay for part of a new computer for the school.

I'm sitting opposite them both. Harry gives me a puzzled frown and asks me what I'm thinking. I'm actually wondering whether Crow has talked to the MIMOs yet, but I lie and say I'm admiring Edie's new haircut. She has finally, after many years, got it cut into a short bob and she looks beautiful. Crow suggested it, apparently. She's sort of taken Edie under her wing since the Gloria thing. We all look across to where Edie's sitting at the other end of the table. She's brightened up a lot since Gloria came out of hospital. And the new haircut was a seriously good decision.

'Better,' Harry says, with a grin and a raised eyebrow. 'Definitely better. She's quite fit, in fact. Don't tell her, though.' This – from a boy who is constantly surrounded by models and engaged to a super-version – is about as good as it gets.

Liam, meanwhile, is being monopolised by Mum. After she's asked him all the boring questions about A-level subjects and college applications they get onto favourite photographers, and it turns out that Liam knows nearly as much about Henri Cartier-Bresson as Mum does. In fact, it's all going so bizarrely well that I start to wonder if the evening will be all right after all.

Then it's Granny's turn. I wince as she starts asking him about his family, and where they're from, and where-abouts in Kensington they live exactly, and all sorts of 'subtle' questions designed to work out if he is from good stock and whether there might be some relative in the background with a yacht, or a trust fund, or something else useful. I can't bear to listen. Because I know that Granny's about to find out that Liam's dad is a chef. Not a Michelin-starred one, but a chef at the local caff where we do our revision. And his mum's a receptionist at the hospital where we took Gloria. As it happens, they do have a dinghy, which they keep at his uncle's place on the west coast of Ireland, but if I tried to show off my graceful calves by jumping off that, I'd probably sink it.

I tune out, although I can't help noticing Granny's lips turning down a bit more with every new piece of infor-mation, and Liam's turning up – because I've warned him about this and hopefully he's finding the whole thing quite funny. Instead, I focus on my food, which is a yummy steak, and Mum, who's now talking to Crow about wedding-dress designs.

'The Galliano dress sounds amazing,' Crow says. 'Isabelle was telling me about it. He's doing the one for the reception. It's a narrow column dress at the front, but there's a panel that balloons out at the back to make a sort of hidden train.' Her fingers flutter as she describes it with her hands.

'Beautiful,' Mum says wistfully. 'I like that Seventies vibe. It sounds just like what I've been imagining for myself.'

And then she gasps, shuts her mouth, stares at me for a moment, grabs her glass to hide her embarrassment and chokes on her wine.

It would have been fine if she'd just carried on talking. I wouldn't have noticed. Or I'd have assumed she was being theoretical, or picturing some future party. But the gasping and the staring and the choking have given the game away. And my shocked expression must mean she knows it.

'I'm sorry,' she says to Crow. 'I was thinking about . . . something else. So, tell me about . . . the other dress. The one for the evening do. Who's doing that one?'

The trouble is, it's too late. Mum's got as far as picturing her wedding dress, and she still hasn't talked to me. If she's actually marrying Vicente, it must mean she's thinking of moving to Brazil, because there's no way he could live in London. He's got all his eco-projects to look after.

No wonder she hasn't wanted to talk about it.

Liam touches my arm.

'You OK?'

I nod. This is Crow's evening and I can't spoil it for her. The conversation goes on for a bit, but I can't concentrate on it and nor, I can tell, can Mum. Then the restaurant lights go low and a man comes out of the kitchen with a big chocolate birthday cake, lit with sixteen tall white candles. It's beautiful. Liam touches my arm again. I realise that everyone else is clapping, so I clap too.

The evening goes from uncomfortable to weird. The man carrying the cake isn't one of the normal waiters. It's the man from next door. The one who's going to buy our house when Mum goes to Brazil.

'This is Peter Anderson,' Mum says, for the benefit of the people who don't know. 'He owns this restaurant. He kindly gave us the best table.'

Oh. So that explains the whole restaurant-in-Mayfair thing.

Harry and Edie shove up so that Peter can sit at our table. We all sing happy birthday to Crow. We eat cake. We drink coffee. Mum offers to pay the bill and Mr Anderson says no, he wouldn't dream of it. We get our coats. We go outside. It isn't until Liam's face is about two centimetres from mine that I realise he's about to kiss me goodbye. Normally I spend the previous half-hour building up to this moment. Now I hardly get the chance to savour it at all.

He looks into my eyes, worried.

'Tell me tomorrow,' he says.

'What?'

'Whatever it is.'

I watch him go, and I wonder. There are things I haven't told Crow, or Edie, or even Jenny. There are things I thought I'd never tell anyone. But this time I think, perhaps, I will.

Chapter 40

We meet at the caff. Liam's dad offers to make me a special sausage and egg combo, because he says I need feeding up, despite the steak last night. I suppose I don't look my best at the moment.

'So?' Liam says, while we're waiting.

I've already told him about Crow and the MIMOs and how worried I am that she's avoiding me, but he can tell there's something else.

'It's Mum,' I say. I've decided to tell him everything. 'She's getting married. She let it slip last night.'

'And? She's been single for ages, hasn't she? This could be good.'

'It *is* good,' I say carefully. 'She's been single all my life, really, apart from the odd boyfriend. It's great.' I pause.

'So?'

'So . . . it's just that she's marrying the man she should have married in the first place,' I explain. 'Before I came along and messed things up. And he lives in Brazil.'

Liam looks at me, puzzled. 'Whoa!' he says. 'Back up a minute. *You* messed things up? How?'

I explain about Vicente and Harry, the affair with Dad. Me being an accident. Mum wanting to go back to Vicente but not being able to. It's super-embarrassing and personal, the whole thing, but actually, it's great to be sharing it at last. At least it's not just my secret any more.

Liam shakes his head. 'I don't get it. This is all stuff that happened before you were born. Or just after. How do you know?'

I think back. It's trickier than I thought. 'I'm not sure, really. Things Mum's let slip. Things I've heard her saying to friends. Stuff Granny told me. Granny confirmed it, really.'

'And he lives in Brazil?'

I nod.

'So your mum will go there, you think?'

I nod again.

'What about you?'

I shrug. 'No idea. I mean, I'll stay here, obviously. But I don't know where I'll live. Somewhere.'

For a brief second, Liam gives me his smile. He looks relieved. I realise that he was worried I'd be going to Rio and he's glad I'm not. It's lovely to feel wanted. Fabulous, in fact. Worth telling him for.

'We'll find you somewhere, don't worry,' he says. 'Assuming we have to. But you really need to talk about this with your mum. I mean, *really*.'

'I know,' I shrug. 'It's just, we never get round to it.'

'Well, you've got to.' He sounds very firm. Like me telling Edie or Jenny what to do. Or Crow, for that matter. I realise that we're more alike than I imagined. 'I had no idea you were going through all of this.'

I smile. 'I'm not "going through" anything. It's just stuff that happened, that's all.'

He takes my hand in his and starts playing with the rings on my fingers.

'You are, Nonie,' he says. 'More than you know. You can't carry this around with you for ever. Talk to her. Promise me.'

I promise, to keep him happy. But I know that there's no point. What is there to say? It's life. It's over. Lots of children are accidents. What's the big deal?

'No, I mean *really* promise me,' he insists.

I laugh. 'I *really* promise,' I say.

It's the first time I've lied to my boyfriend and I hope he can't tell. Luckily, his dad chooses this moment to put my fry-up in front of me. I dig into it with a big, innocent grin and change the subject as fast as I can.

I half expect Edie to collar me at school and ask about what happened at the birthday party to make me go all quiet, but luckily it seems she didn't even notice. Even though she's looking a lot better now, she's still in a world of her own. She says she's busy with her own uni applications, which her parents have persuaded her to do after all, but I know she's thinking about something else. Something other than our Shakespeare mock A-level paper, which is coming up any minute. She's working something out and she'll tell me when she's ready. I just have to wait.

Eventually, she comes up to me just as we're about to go into the exam. Now is not the best time to give me new information. I'm struggling to remember the finer points of King Lear's decision to take early retirement (on which I thought I was an expert at about three o'clock this morning) and wishing I'd retired a bit earlier myself.

'About Gloria – I've realised I've got to see Jenny face to face,' Edie says.

'Uh huh,' I mutter. I try to look like I'm listening harder than I really am.

'It's the only way to make her see sense.'

'Yeah, sure.'

'Because now it's really serious.'

'Uh huh. Absolutely,' I add, not concentrating.

'So I've persuaded Mum and Dad. I found some cheap flights and I'm going to New York at half-term.'

'Uh huh. I mean, WHAT?'

'New York. At half-term,' she repeats. 'To tell Jenny properly about Gloria. And explain how she really has to come home now.'

'Close your mouth, Nonie,' our teacher says, rounding the corner. 'And you can go on in, girls. We're ready for you now.'

They might be ready, but I totally am not. I worked hard for this paper, and now I sit, staring at it, unable to make sense of the questions. Edie? Alone in New York? And having a showdown with Jenny? This can't possibly be good. Edie is a rubbish traveller. And I know Jenny doesn't show it, but she must feel guilty enough about leaving Gloria as it is. She really doesn't need Edie to make it worse.

I do the best I can with the exam, but all the while my brain is churning. I have to do something to stop Edie, or Jenny, or both, saying something they'll regret for ever. But how can I do it if I'm stuck here and they're both on the other side of the Atlantic?

'You're not going,' Mum says. 'Don't even think about it, Nonie. You've only just come back from Chicago.'

Harry gives me a sympathetic look and helps himself to what's left of our Chinese takeaway. 'But Nonie's been working really hard,' he says. 'And you should have seen her that day at the hospital. She was brilliant. And Issy'll look after her. She'll be in New York for Fashion Week.'

'Absolutely not,' Mum says, lips in a thin line. 'She has mocks. This is an important academic year. She can't just flit about like a . . .'

There's a pause while she thinks of something that flits.

'Model?' Harry suggests.

He seems innocent enough, but Mum flashes him a

look. When she was my age, she was successfully modelling in several cities and knew New York like the back of her hand.

'It would be a cultural visit,' I point out, after I've given Harry a grateful grin. 'Think of all the galleries I could go to. And museums. You know. The Met. And the, er . . .'

I kick Harry under the table. I need help here.

'And the Guggenheim, of course,' he says, kicking me back. 'Just think. Nonie's lived eighteen years and she's never seen it. And the Frick.'

'The Frick, obviously,' I say.

'Do you know what the Frick is, Nonie?' Mum asks.

Damn.

'Yes. It's—'

'—your favourite, Mum,' Harry butts in. 'You know how much you love that place.'

Mum smiles fondly. Whatever the Frick is, she's obviously got some happy memories of it.

'Well . . .'

'And it would only be for three days,' I add. 'And Isabelle could look after me. Not that I'd need it. And if I don't go, Edie will do something . . . Edie-ish, and it will be a disaster. Honestly. *Please?*'

I can see Mum hesitating.

'What did you get for your last three assignments?' she asks in her strictest voice.

'Two Bs and a C.'

Of course, if I was Edie, this would be a horrible

admission of defeat, but for me it's actually quite amazing. Mum seems to think so too.

'Honestly?'

I nod. 'You can check.'

She sighs. I can tell she's thinking about changing her mind.

'And I'll help pay for it,' Harry chips in. 'The gigs are going pretty well at the moment. And I seem to remember that I gave you a rather small birthday present, Nonie.'

'It was a book,' I remind him. 'A nice one, about Alexander McQueen.'

'A book. Exactly,' he says. 'An airline ticket would be so much better, wouldn't it?'

Well, of course it would. (Even though Alexander McQueen was a fashion god and that book is gorgeous.)

Mum laughs. 'I know when I'm beaten. I'll call the head in the morning, Nonie. If she says you've earned it, you can go. Oh Harry, you are incorrigible, you know.'

She gives my brother a tender smile. He drives her crazy sometimes, but she can't help giving into him. She's like most females in that respect. And he makes it easy for her. He knows all about art, because he studied it at college. He has a great career. He dates supermodels. If he tidied his room a bit more, he'd be almost perfect.

'Thanks,' I tell him later, when we're watching TV and Mum's back upstairs, working.

'No problem,' he says with a friendly shrug. 'I just

called Issy, by the way, and she says you'll just catch her at the end of Fashion Week. She can't wait to see you. She'll even take you both to the Frick, if you ask her nicely.'

He looks across at me, challenging me to ask him what it is. But I refuse to rise to the bait. I'll look it up later. Right now, I'm thinking about Isabelle. I feel really mean for taking advantage of her, when I'm starting to wonder if she's actually the one for my brother. Maybe I can use the time in New York to work it out once and for all: is she marrying Harry for love, or is she just using him so she can go down her petal-strewn aisle in the perfect tiara, with her ecru lace bridesmaids following on behind? She's always struck me as unnecessarily nice for someone so beautiful. It makes sense, somehow, to spot a fatal flaw in her character. But if there is one, won't it make Harry miserable for ever? I sort of want to find it – just to prove she's human after all – and I sort of don't.

Chapter 41

Next day, the head admits that I've worked harder this year than in the previous six years put together, and Mum says yes, I can go. I tell Edie the news about my trip.

'Really?' she says. 'Are you sure? I think I can manage on my own.'

'Don't worry, it's sorted,' I tell her. As opposed to 'No you can't – you'd be a walking disaster area,' which is what I'm thinking.

Liam is thrilled for me, and really jealous. He's always wanted to go. We spend long evenings on Instant Messenger, saying how much we're going to miss each other, which in my case is totally true, but there's something else that I'm not admitting to.

I'm quite relieved that there will be a few days at least when he can't pester me about talking to Mum. I know he thinks it's a great idea for us to have a heart to heart about Vicente, but frankly, I'd rather do that Shakespeare mock ten times over. And it wasn't fun the first time, believe me.

'If you tell me ONE MORE TIME how much nicer it is in First Class, I will personally attack you with this plastic spoon,' Edie says about halfway through the flight. I realise I might have mentioned the big seats a few times, and the legroom, the clothes, the magazines and movies, and the celebrities . . .

Edie is deep in one of her four guidebooks, and making notes.

'I've got it down to twelve major sights that we can't afford to miss,' she says. 'If we start with Ground Zero at the south end of Manhattan Island and work our way systematically north towards Central Park, we should be OK.'

'This is a trip to see Jenny,' I point out. 'Not an expedition to the North Pole.'

'Yes, I know,' Edie says irritably. 'But while we're there . . . I mean, imagine not seeing the Guggenheim, or the Met, or the Public Library. Oh, goodness. I've left out the Statue of Liberty.'

She goes back to her notes and starts scribbling again.

Frankly, the Public Library, lovely though I'm sure it is, would not make my top twelve sights. Not since I'd have to fit in Saks Fifth Avenue, Barneys, Bergdorf Goodman, Bloomingdales, Tiffany and all the little shops in the back streets of SoHo. And the Frick, whatever that is. But I don't have a list. I'm more a 'take it as it comes' sort of a girl.

Also, I have better things to do with the rest of this flight than make lists. Liam gave me a longer than usual goodbye kiss yesterday, to last me until I get back to England. I close my eyes and try to remember it. Turns out, this is even more fun than sitting in First Class.

We land in the evening. A bright yellow taxi whisks us down freeways and through tunnels until suddenly we're in the high-rise corridors of Manhattan by night. To start off with, Edie tries to chat to the taxi driver and ask for his advice on places to see, but we eventually realise that he's not talking to us, he's talking into a headpiece attached to his phone, and he's speaking a language we don't even recognise. Edie gives up on the tourist advice and makes do with staring out of the window at the lights.

We reach a wide, low-rise road, where the trees are hung with fairy lights. West Broadway, in the heart of SoHo. I'm thinking it can't get any more magical, when the driver pulls up.

'Here,' he says gruffly. He points at the meter and I start scrabbling around for dollars. I'm the one in charge of money on this trip. While I'm counting, he extracts our bags from his boot and the second I've paid him, he's gone.

'Huh! Not exactly an advert for his city,' Edie says to his departing tail-lights.

But I don't care. I can't help grinning. I'm in New York. It's freezing cold and so far we've only heard one word in English, but this street is beautiful. The lights all around us are twinkling their welcome. We're about to hang out with a supermodel during Fashion Week. So far, so extremely good.

Isabelle has spent the whole day doing shows and interviews. She's been up for sixteen hours. She opens the door wearing no makeup and looking like a Botticelli angel.

'I'm sorry I'm not going to be here much,' she says, showing us around. The apartment has two small bedrooms and an open-plan kitchen and living room overlooking the street. It's furnished with a mixture of antique textiles and junk shop finds and I love every centimetre of it.

'I'd show you the city, but I'm only here until tomorrow night, then I'm off to London,' she says. 'I'll have to leave you to it, but I'll tell you where to go, if you like.'

'That would be great!' Edie says. She may have several pages of notes on exactly what to do in New York, but she's gradually returning to her old self, and her old self can never have too much information.

'First, though, you must be starving,' Isabelle says. 'I always am when I get in. What would you like? I recommend the Thai curry. Or the dim sum.'

She rummages through the drawer of a mirrored

console table and throws us a menu. It's several pages long, covering every world cuisine I can think of. And several others that I suspect have been made up by New York chefs, just to be different.

She's right about us being starving, but wrong about us feeling adventurous. We settle for burgers and chips. Later, while we're making a small dent in the largest portions of food I've ever encountered – apart from in Chicago – she tucks her long legs under her and asks us about London.

'How's your mum, Nonie? And your granny?'

I try not to wince and tell her they're fine.

'And Harry? He had a cold the last time I saw him. That was eleven days ago. Did he manage to get rid of it? He looked so tired and grizzled, poor thing. I gave him every vitamin I could think of, but I'm not sure he took them.'

'He's fine too,' I assure her. 'He sends you lots of love.'

Actually, I'm making this bit up. It's just occurred to me that he probably should have sent her lots of love, but he was so busy telling me about his favourite old record stores in the area that he forgot.

Nevertheless, I'm a good white liar, and Isabelle glows with pleasure.

'Well, I'm seeing him in three days anyway, so I can check up on him then. And make sure he takes those vitamins.'

I look around her living room. Harry is everywhere, in

subtle ways. There are framed album covers by his favourite old bands. A road bike that surely must be his, hung on the wall just inside the door. A photo of Isabelle in the shirt she wore to their engagement party that I'm certain he took. I recognise his style. She's even wearing one of his old tee-shirts now, I realise.

As she sits back and chats to us, occasionally running her fingers through her world-famous ringlets, I'm surprised that Harry doesn't talk about her more often. Perhaps you just get used to it after a while – living with that much beauty. But hard as I try, I really can't persuade myself that she's using him just so she can have a big wedding. She seems so genuinely in love. It's a relief, I suppose. Good to think that Harry will be happy. Except something's still wrong. But I am far too tired and full of chips and burger to work out what it is.

Chapter 42

Next morning, we're woken by the phone ringing. At least, Edie and I are. Isabelle is already out of the apartment and preparing for her first show.

'Wow!' Jenny shouts when I pick up. 'I can't believe you're really here! You're SO AMAZING to come and see me. And you've come at the craziest time. I'll tell you all about it. But it means I'm a bit manic at the moment. Anyway, I'll meet you at the Soho Grand in half an hour, OK? It's down the road from you. I've only got an hour this morning, but I can't wait to see you!'

And while I'm still breathing in to reply, she rings off.

We quickly go through one of Edie's guidebooks, trying to work out what and where the Soho Grand is, but luckily it turns out to be a rather nice-looking hotel, just a few doors down from the apartment. Half an hour later, we're all dressed and ready, standing in the hotel's designer lobby and waiting for Jenny to appear.

She's late. While we wait, we watch various famous

faces go by. As far as I can tell, half the fashion world must stay here during New York Fashion Week. I'm secretly hoping to see Joan Burstein again, but have to make do with several models, two movie stars, three fashion editors and Paris Hilton. Not bad for a fifteen-minute wait, I consider.

When Jenny arrives, she's very apologetic.

'Traffic! Ugh!' she says, hugging us tightly, each in turn. 'But oh my God! You're in New York! I still can't believe it! Now come with me.'

We go up the designer stairs to another designer area where a bunch of incredibly well-dressed, important people are having coffee with other well-dressed, important people. I can't see any spare seats, but Jenny has a word with an even better-dressed hotel manager and somehow, three seats around a little table are miraculously found.

'Jackson comes here all the time,' Jenny explains. 'So does Charlotte. They know me now. It's very useful.'

I still think I'd be more comfortable in a café across the road. My Doc Martens and fake fur bomber jacket are clashing badly with the designer atmosphere. Jenny looks pretty scruffy in jeans and a multi-coloured, hand-knitted sweater. Her hair, however, is still *Vogue* perfect, which helps. So does Edie's new dress, as made for her last week by Crow, which is covered in exposed seams and chalk marks but shows off her legs and looks really cool. Even under the multi-pocketed parka she insists on wearing to hold all the guidebooks. At least I have a new school bag that Crow gave me, using her girls-holding-hands print. It's the chicest thing about me.

'Anyway,' Jenny says, talking fast and waving her hands with enthusiasm. 'I told you it was a crazy time. There's so much going on with the show. There's a whole new ball scene that's just incredible. It'll take me till the summer to learn the dances, but the costumes will be A-MA-ZING. I bet even the Queen didn't get to wear such good ones. And they're changing my part.'

'Oh, no!' I gasp, before I can help myself.

'Oh, Nonie. Will you stop worrying?' she says crossly. 'They're making it better, not cutting it. The producers have been arguing with the director for weeks, but they've finally agreed that the problem with the show was that Elizabeth wasn't interesting enough, compared to Margaret. And they needed a better ten o'clock number.'

'A what?' we ask.

'A ten o'clock number,' she sighs, as if we're supposed to know what that means. 'The song that really gets the audience involved in the second half. Before you build up to the finale. You know.'

Well, we don't, really, but we nod anyway.

'And they're giving it to me,' Jenny continues, eyes shining. 'It's the bit where Princess Elizabeth hears that her father has died. She's on tour in Africa, away from home and her young children. She realises that by the

249

time she sees them again, she won't just be their mummy, she'll be Queen.'

'Wow!' I say. It's not so much the story, but the gleam in Jenny's eyes as she tells it. You can tell she's excited by this bit.

She looks thrilled at my reaction. 'Anyway, she has this moment she's missing her dad and she's scared. She never really wanted to be Queen – not in our story, anyway – but she has to abandon her private feelings and throw herself into her new life ruling the country, and never let anyone know how hard it was, ever. That's the ten o'clock number.'

'That's a *song*?' Edie asks. 'They're putting all of that into a *song*?'

Jenny looks affronted. 'A *Broadway* song. They can put a whole lot more in, I can tell you. But this one's great. The lyrics are amazing. And Jackson's written such a sad melody for it. Makes me cry every time. Which is lucky, because I have to. Cry, I mean. We started rehearsing it last week and I have another session with Jackson and Marty, the musical director, tomorrow. You can come, if you've got time. And if the TV people will let you.'

'The TV people?' I ask.

'Yes. Jackson's doing this reality TV show. About the making of a musical. Bringing it to Broadway. It's mostly him at home, working on the songs and talking to Marty and the producers and people, but they like to show him out and about with the cast. They're filming my bit at the theatre. Oh, God. Got to go. Jackson wants to know if you can come round for supper tonight. See you then? I'll text you his address.'

And that's it. She's gone. We both feel as if we've been hit by a tornado. I had put Edie under strict instructions not to bring up Gloria until we've had a bit more time with Jenny, but that wasn't a problem after all. She hardly had a chance to get a word in edgeways.

She looks at me, stunned.

'Was that real?' she asks.

I nod.

'She didn't even ask us how the flight was. Or how we are. Or how Isabelle is. Or anything. It's all about Jenny.'

'To be fair,' I point out, 'she didn't have much time.'

Edie snorts. 'She had enough for the ten o'clock number.'

It's true. She had a lot of time for that.

Chapter 43

The next eight hours are some of the busiest of my life. Edie is like a woman possessed. She has studied her guidebook until she could walk around New York blindfold, and she whisks me from one 'Oh my God' moment to the next. One minute we're peering at the Statue of Liberty through the rain-spattered window of a sightseeing boat, and the next we're standing at the Ground Zero building site, watching the rain fall on the hole where the Twin Towers used to be. Then we're in the subway, getting only slightly lost, before finally arriving in Fifth Avenue, where all the shops are – or, as I like to call it, home.

Edie doesn't enjoy this bit as much as me. Edie complains, in fact, that it is not necessary to see Saks *and* Bergdorf Goodman, Tiffany *and* Abercrombie & Fitch. Edie seems to think that we are wasting valuable museum-visiting time. I disagree. I am picturing the best locations for Crow's future collections for the MIMOs. I am deciding that Bergdorf Goodman is probably my favourite, but I might have to go to Barney's on Madison Avenue to make sure. It's not until Edie sits down on the floor of Abercrombie, and refuses to move, that I realise that now *I* am the woman possessed. Besides, we're due at Jackson Ward's for dinner soon, and we need to change out of our sightseeing clothes.

As I struggle into an old silver-knit mini-dress of Crow's, hoping it's suitable for meeting a musical legend, I'm wondering how I can ever repay Harry for my ticket. New York is even taller, louder and more inspiring than I imagined. It has so much energy – it even makes London look laid-back, which takes some doing. Only one thing scares me slightly. You would have to be totally and utterly amazing to stand out here. Just being 'great' isn't good enough. Jackson Ward has managed it somehow, with his Tonys and Oscars. So has Isabelle. But I wonder if Jenny has realised how much she's taking on by performing in this city. And I wonder what I've let Crow in for by trying to get her that job here, too.

With Edie map-reading, we get the subway to Jackson Ward's apartment on East 73rd Street, not far from Central Park. However, the first surprise is that his apartment isn't an apartment at all. It's a house. An actual old house, with a front door and stairs and, by the look of it, a lot of history. I'd been hoping for a skyscraper. Possibly even the Trump Tower, but this is cool anyway.

'I *told* you it was a house,' Jenny says in the hall.

She probably did. I probably wasn't listening. She gushes so much about Jackson Ward and his fabulous life that I tend to tune out.

Jenny leads us through to a grand reception room. Mum would love the place. It's full of sculpture. Stone ones, bronze ones, wood ones, even weird, twisted ones that are made out of no material I recognise. Edie sighs appreciatively. We are in a world of culture. She is happy.

'Come and meet everyone,' Jenny says.

At the far end of the room, a short, balding man in a silk shirt is sipping cocktails and chatting with a remarkably tall, white-haired woman and a short, pretty girl with a pale face, geek-chic glasses and almost waist-length dark hair. They all come over to shake our hands.

'How do you do? Awfully nice to meet you. This is my wife, Jane, and my lovely daughter, Charlotte.'

He does the whole speech in the fakest English accent I've ever heard. I can sense Edie wincing beside me, so I smile extra politely to make up for her.

'Ignore him,' Charlotte says with a friendly smile. 'He's always like this with strangers. Shut UP, Dad. He'll get better, though. Now, come over and make yourselves comfortable.'

I can't help noticing, as we pass various side tables crammed with expensive knick-knacks, that there are at least two photos of Charlotte and her mother posing on a yacht. If only Granny were here. She'd be SO impressed.

'So, girls,' Jackson asks, 'how was your first day in New York? What did you do with yourselves?'

Edie is less distracted by the Oscars and Tonys. She answers first.

'Ground Zero was so poignant,' she says sombrely.

There's a brief pause for reflection.

'And what about you, Nonie?'

For a moment, I wish we'd gone to the Met and the Guggenheim, like Edie wanted. That would be the perfect conversation to have right now. Instead, I have to admit to practically every store on Fifth Avenue. Some of them twice.

Jackson Ward grins. 'Aha! Jenny's told me all about you. A fashionista to your fingertips. I salute you!'

He takes a sip of cocktail in my honour. From then, I relax a bit and get used to being in museum-standard surroundings. Supper, which is served by a maid, manages to be super-healthy and super-yummy, which is just what we need after too many fries and emergency Starbucks milkshakes. And then Jackson sits down at the piano while coffee is served in teeny porcelain cups, and sings several of the songs from *The Princesses* for us.

He's very good. He sings and plays as if he's starring in the show himself, and it's strange to think that he hardly ever performs in public. He could probably do a stint in Las Vegas if he wanted to. As long as he never attempts anything in an English accent.

I'm so gripped that for a long time, I don't notice that

I'm sitting alone on my gold silk sofa. But when I do, I'm suddenly concerned. Edie and Jenny have disappeared. They must have gone up to Jenny's room. Which can only mean that Edie is telling Jenny about Gloria. Not just about the pills, which Jenny already knows about, but about what the nurses said. About how fragile Gloria is.

My concern is how fragile Jenny is when it comes to her mum. Oh my God. I came all this way to stop this and it's happening under my nose. As soon as I decently can, I make my excuses to Jackson and head for Jenny's room upstairs.

It takes me a few moments to find it. There are a lot of doors in this house. Then I finally open the right one and two faces whip round to look at me. Both have bright pink spots on their cheeks. The rest of Edie's face is white and drawn, while Jenny's is tear-stained and blotchy.

'You think it's my fault, don't you?' Jenny shouts. 'You think it's because of me that she's so bad. Because I don't look after her enough.'

'I think you don't look after her at all!' Edie shouts back.

Jenny's voice goes quiet, but she's shaking with anger. 'Get out! Get *out!* Go away! Leave me alone!'

There's not much else we can do, under the circumstances. Furiously, I grab Edie's arm and pull her towards me.

'We're going,' I say to Jenny. 'But look – please call me? I came all this way, Jen. Promise me you'll talk to me?'

She doesn't answer.

Edie and I go back to the sitting room. Three elegant, confused and embarrassed Wards see us politely to the door. We catch the subway home and reach the apartment in silence. I have just wasted Harry's birthday-present plane ticket after all, by spending the most important five minutes in New York listening to an old guy play the piano and it wasn't even Elton John. I could kick myself. I could kick Edie too, right now, but I don't.

Chapter 44

The next morning, over breakfast, Edie looks sheepish. She's pretending to be studious, poring over her guidebook and her super-list of things to do, but it's not working. We both keep looking at the phones: mine, the apartment phone and Edie's. Eventually, a text arrives on mine.

'Sorry for before. Not your fault. See you by the polar bears in Central Park in 1 hour? Jxxx'

This is good. This is great. Jenny's still talking to me. It's wonderful, in fact. And apparently they have polar bears in Central Park. Interesting. I thought it was just trees and swings and stuff.

'Want me to come?' Edie asks.

'No, I'll be OK,' I say. Which is code for, After everything you said to her last night? ARE YOU CRAZY?

'Oh, all right,' she agrees. I think she understood the

code. 'Tell her I send my love,' she says, 'and . . . I hope . . . she's feeling better.'

I assume this is code for a big apology and promise to pass it on.

Central Park is beautiful, even in winter with hardly any leaves on the trees and every New Yorker wrapped up in as many coats and scarves as they can find. After the towering buildings and roads roaring with yellow taxis suddenly there's peace, calm, orderliness and inviting walks along shady paths. Bizarre to think that Bergdorf Goodman is a ten-minute walk away, max. I can understand why Granny would want to come here with her mini-Isabelles and Harrys. It doesn't look like polar bear country, though.

I get to the zoo, which was on Edie's list of cultural go-sees, but pretty low down, and follow signs to the Polar Circle. Eventually, I spot a big, stone enclosure with a massive pond and there they are: two polar bears sitting on a rock, idly grooming themselves. Nearby, there's a girl with cropped, burnt-orange hair and sunglasses, clutching a hot chocolate and looking completely miserable.

Jenny gives me a slight smile when I get close.

'Hi,' she says, pushing her sunglasses up.

'Hi, how are you?'

She doesn't really answer. Instead, she watches a bear slide into the freezing water of the pond.

'I always come here when I'm thinking,' Jenny says. 'It

seems so weird. Two polar bears in the centre of New York City. Gus and Ida. They're sort of like friends now.'

'*We*'re still your friends,' I say. 'And I'm sorry about Edie, but you know what she's like . . . She sort of said sorry as well, by the way.'

Jenny leans against a railing and takes a sip from her cup.

'Did she?' she asks. 'I don't know why. She was right, as usual.'

This is exactly what I was worried about.

'Jenny, I know this is really obvious,' I say, 'but – that stuff with Edie. It's not your fault.'

'What isn't?'

'Your mum. Everything.'

'Well, that's sweet of you, Nonie, but it doesn't feel that way. Besides – suppose it happened to me one day.'

'What?'

'You know, I get like Mum.'

'Jenny! No!'

'Why not? What if it runs in the family?'

'I'm sure it doesn't. You're such an upbeat person. Trust me, Jenny, it won't happen to you.'

She gives me a watery smile. 'If it did, though, I'd want someone to be there. I'd want to know someone cared. If I was at home now I could at least do something for Mum. Help her. I've tried so hard to escape from it all, but, if she needs me . . .'

She hunches over her cup and despite the chic hair and the Tom Ford shades on top (actually Chanel, now I look closer, she's got new ones), she looks small and lost.

'Gloria's the grown-up,' I say. 'She's supposed to look after herself.'

'But she can't, can she?' Jenny whispers. 'And meanwhile, here I am. Every day I wake up in that incredible house and I go to the rehearsal studio and sing those songs . . .'

'You said that's what Gloria wanted you to do.'

'It *is* what she wanted me to do. But Edie's right about that too. It's just an excuse. I should come home with you. I know it, really. There will be other chances. Maybe not like this one, but . . . something.'

She gives me a sad smile and takes my hand in hers. I can sense she doesn't want me to talk any more. We watch the bears together for a while. They don't do much. They're pretty boring, actually. One of them is giving me a funny look and I have a nasty feeling he's mistaken my fake fur bomber jacket for a tasty seal. Luckily, he seems too lazy to do anything about it.

Jenny's more impressed than me.

'Don't you love their energy?' she says. 'Isn't it awesome?'

If she means awesome in the sense of non-existent, I totally agree. But at least the bears are cheering her up somehow. Gradually she seems a bit more positive and gets a hint of her bounce back. She checks her watch.

'God. Rehearsal in an hour. I've got to get to the theatre. Still want to come?'

'Of course!' I say. But she can see me hesitate.

'Go on. Invite Edie too, if you like. She might as well be there.'

'Thanks,' I say, and get my phone out.

Chapter 45

The theatre turns out to be two minutes from Times Square. I sit in a seat near the back, thinking 'oh my God oh my God I'm two minutes from Times Square', while around us, total chaos gradually turns into something resembling a song rehearsal, which is what it's supposed to be. You'd hardly know it, though. The place is overrun by TV people and electrical equipment. Every time the guy at the piano tries to start playing the song, he has to stop because the sound is wrong, or the lights, or something else entirely. Through it all, Jenny stands beside the piano, looking serious and focused, but holding it together a lot better than I'd have expected after the whole polar bear experience.

'Did you tell her I said hi?' Edie asks me anxiously, arriving with two bags of books and posters from the Frick. Turns out it's an art museum. I thought it probably would be.

I nod. 'She said you were right anyway,' I say. 'She

understands about Gloria. Honestly; more than you know. In fact, I don't know how much longer she'll be sticking this out.'

Edie breathes a long sigh of relief and smiles in Jenny's direction.

'Thank goodness. I really didn't think she'd listen to me.' Her smile spreads to a grin and her whole body seems to relax. She starts watching what the TV people are doing and I can tell that her Edie super-brain is already trying to work out how to make a TV programme. Just in case she ever needs to know.

After two hours of technical fiddling about, Jenny finally gets to sing her song all the way through, uninterrupted. It's called 'My Other Life' and it is a sad, haunting tune. Jenny seems to do OK, as far as I can tell. Her cheeks are glistening, so I think she managed the tears.

'OK for now,' the TV head honcho shouts. 'Take fifteen, people.'

Everyone seems happy. Various people head for the exits. Jenny heads straight for us.

'You were great!' I tell her. 'The song's amazing.'

Jenny smiles gratefully.

'Is that it?' Edie asks. 'Where's Mr Ward?'

'Oh, he's not even here yet,' Jenny says. 'That was just the warm-up. In fact, look, he's just coming in. They're going to tape him talking about the song. Then I'll have to do it again in front of him. But let's go outside while we're waiting. I need a bit of fresh air.'

We walk to the street corner. Ahead of us is a square with tall, elegant trees. It's full of tents, builders and activity.

'Look!' Jenny says. 'That's Bryant Park. They're just dismantling New York Fashion Week.'

We look, then Edie squeals. Beyond the tents and trees we can just see something else. The top of the Empire State Building. This is SO cool. I give Jenny's arm a squeeze.

'Excuse me, ladies,' says a voice behind us. 'Can I grab a word, Jenny?'

'Of course,' Jenny says.

It's the guy who played the piano for the rehearsal: Marty, the musical director. He's small, intense and more than slightly frightening. He's hardly said a word all morning, but he's been watching Jenny intently and I've noticed that he hasn't smiled once. They go off into a little huddle, and Edie and I lurk nearby, pretending we can't hear every word they're saying.

'I've just spoken to Jackson and he agrees, we're still not getting it,' Marty says, linking his arm through Jenny's and leaning in close.

Jenny looks worried. 'I'm doing my best.'

'That's the point,' Marty says. 'I don't want your best. I want something you don't even know you got. It's not the notes any more. It's not the pitch or the modulation. They're all fine but they don't matter now. It's what's inside of you.'

Jenny looks hurt and confused.

'Look, I'm only telling you this because I think you got something special, doll. Something extra. A gift. It's what Liza had. And Barbra. All the greats. But you gotta dig deep. You gotta find a part of yourself that's raw and you gotta pull it out and share it. Not everybody can do that. Most people don't even want to. I keep nearly seeing it, but then you pull back. Today I want you to show me, OK? And Jackson too. Show us you can do it. Otherwise we got just another song there, and that's a shame, 'cause it could be special and personally, I think Jackson deserves better.'

He gives her a pat on the back and strides back to the theatre. Jenny stays where she is, looking after him. Edie and I cluster round her, for support.

'I'm sure Jackson likes you just the way you are,' I say. Oops. I realise I've just given away that we heard everything. But I needn't worry. Jenny doesn't seem to have noticed.

'Who's Liza, by the way?' I ask.

'Minnelli,' she says, automatically.

'And Barbra?' Edie adds.

'Streisand,' Jenny says, striding ahead. Edie and I have to jog to keep up with her. By the time we get back, she's so completely wrapped up in what Marty said I don't think she even knows we're there any more.

We take our seats at the back of the theatre, and she goes down to the stage, where she looks lost in thought while the TV people check all their equipment again.

This time, Jackson Ward sits at the piano. Slowly, Jenny walks over to join him. She moves as if she's treading through treacle. When she gets close to the piano, Jackson gives her an encouraging smile. A guy with a TV camera trains it on Jenny's face. Someone calls for silence. Then Jackson starts to play.

Twice, Jenny sings the first few lines of the song, and Jackson stops her. She would have had to stop anyway. Her cheeks are already glistening and her voice is cracking. I'm really not sure she's up to this amount of pressure. Perhaps it's a good thing she's coming home soon.

The third time, she gets halfway through before Jackson stops her again. He talks to her in a low voice and plays a couple of bars, as if to show her something. She nods.

The fourth time, she sings the song all the way through.

Except, I'm not even sure that it *is* the same song. Before, it was sad and haunting. But now it's not sad – it's way more than that. It's tragic. The way Jenny sings it, you feel the pain in every heartbreaking note. You're sure she's not going to make it, but gradually her voice grows and grows until at the end it's completely filling the theatre, soaring round us and through us, tingling with new determination.

I feel the tingle right the way up my spine, and the heartbreak sits in my chest. I suddenly know how I'd feel if Liam were to break up with me right now. The final note ends and the theatre rings with silence. Jackson Ward looks astonished. He glances across at Marty, who nods slightly. Then Jackson turns to Jenny and says, 'Again!'

So she does it again. Same voice. Same heartbreak. Same triumphant, soaring final note and gentle sigh.

For several seconds, which feel like several minutes, nobody moves. Then Jackson smiles at Jenny. She's looking drained and shocked, but this seems to cheer her up a bit.

Suddenly there's whooping. Various people who've been standing in the wings come forward to clap and cheer. Marty rushes over, lifts her off the ground, kisses her forehead and says 'Yes!'

I join in with the clapping, because now I understand what the gift is – the one the greats have. And Jenny's got it. She dug deep and found lots of it. It's still in the air above our heads somehow, like glitter, reminding us what we just went through with her.

Jackson gets up from his piano stool, puts an arm around her and leads her gently off the stage. As they head out, Marty checks with the TV guy.

'Did you get that?' he asks.

'Hell, yeah!' the man says.

Marty nods, satisfied.

I turn to Edie, who's still standing, transfixed, beside me.

'Did you see that?' she asks.

'Hell, yeah!' I say, grinning.

'I mean, did you see her expression? Did you realise what she was thinking?'

'Er, no,' I say. 'Wasn't she just thinking about singing?'

'I can't believe it,' Edie goes on. 'I just can't. She had exactly the same expression as she did in Mr Ward's house, when I told her about Gloria. That same pain. She just took it and used it. For a *song*.'

Edie turns on her heel and walks straight out of the theatre. I'm back in my usual position of not knowing who to let down most – her or Jenny. But I decide that Jenny needs me more right now. I watch Edie go.

When I eventually find Jenny, she's on her own, drinking a cup of green tea in one of the theatre dressing rooms and looking slightly less out of it than she did when she finished the song.

'How do you feel?' I ask. 'I mean, it was totally amazing, of course, but are you OK?'

She looks up and nods. For a moment, she looks embarrassed. Maybe she's thinking about Gloria too. But then she takes a deep breath and smiles.

'I feel good,' she says. 'I think I nailed it. Jackson seems to think so. He said that's the ten o'clock number sorted. And Marty's happy at last. So yes, I feel good.' Her smile falters slightly. 'You know I was thinking of coming home, but I guess they need me here too.'

She looks apologetic. For once, I know what to say.

'Of course they need you,' I tell her. 'And of course you're staying. You can't not do . . . that thing you did. It's a gift. I'm really pleased for you, honestly. And your mum will be so proud of you.'

Jenny bites her lip. She suddenly looks a lot older than eighteen. More like a twenty-five-year-old queen with a lot to think about. But she manages half a smile.

'Thank you, Nonie.' She shakes her head and takes a deep breath, glancing round the room for some excuse to change the subject. 'Hey, *that's* nice.'

'What?' I ask.

'Your bag,' she says. 'Cool design. I noticed it yesterday. It's cute.'

The air in the room clears a bit, as we talk about bags instead of singing.

'Crow did it,' I explain, and tell her about the Victoria thing. 'It's really useful.'

'Maybe she could send me one,' Jenny says.

I promise I'll send her a whole pile of them. Maybe someone in New York will see them and want one. You never know.

Chapter 46

Outside, I decide it's time to head for the apartment. This is where I need Edie, whose ability to read maps is fifty times better than mine. However, I do the best I can. I start off down Broadway, or at least I assume it's Broadway. It seems to be going in the right direction.

Then I notice that I'm walking on Ralph Lauren. Well, not him exactly, but a round plaque in the pavement with his name on it, and one of his sketches engraved into it. Nearby is Halston, then Diane Von Furstenberg. Each plaque explains it's the Fashion Walk of Fame. I look up. I can't be on Broadway – if I was, it would be the Theatre Walk of Fame, surely?

A nearby street sign says Seventh Avenue – not Broadway, but close. I realise I've wandered into the Garment District. That would account for the bin I just passed full of abandoned mannequin arms and legs that someone was trying to sell off for $5 each. Also the shop selling braid and trimmings, and the multiple vans unloading racks of clothes in plastic bags. There were clues. I just didn't spot them.

A thought occurs to me. I must be near the MIMOs' headquarters, on West 37th Street. Five minutes later, I'm standing opposite a red-brick building with gleaming, freshly polished windows. Busy fashion people are rushing in and out, usually armed with giant coffees. I suddenly wonder if I could get an internship here one day. After all, I'm an expert in getting coffee now. And it would mean I could stay near to Crow.

But as Mum so kindly pointed out, they wouldn't have me. Even as an intern. They have whole departments of people to do everything I do. And everyone here looks like they could make spreadsheets in their sleep. Actually, if I'm really honest, the place looks terrifying. All those people are relying on the designers to do a great job, so they can stay in business. If I was a sixteen-year-old from Uganda, I'd be pretty overwhelmed. Not for the first time, I wonder what I'm getting Crow into. But they say they want her, so they must be right, surely?

When I get back to the apartment, Edie's already there. She looks as tired and depressed as I feel.

'It's our last night,' she points out. 'Want to do anything?'

Outside, the air is cold and crisp. We have Manhattan at our feet and hours to kill.

'No,' I say. 'Not really. You?'

She shakes her head.

We must be the only unsupervised eighteen-year-olds in New York who'd rather stay in and watch movies.

We search through Isabelle's DVD collection. A lot of it is subtitled. She also has an unexpected thing for action films, particularly those involving aliens or Matt Damon. Edie, of course, wants something French from the 1960s and I want *The Bourne Identity*. We compromise on *Green Card*. Turns out, it's about a guy (Gérard Depardieu – French, to keep Edie happy) who wants to come and work in New York, but can't.

I know the feeling. He should have been a polar bear.

Chapter 47

The next morning Edie is very quiet. She's quiet while we pack – despite the sheer horror of trying to get all our stuff into two teeny-weeny little wheelie bags. And she's quiet all the way to the airport, while we say goodbye to the amazing New York skyline. She's quiet at the terminal, while I manage to sweet-talk the lady at the check-in desk to give at least one of us a window seat, and while I spend about an hour choosing between all the major fashion magazines in the world for the two that I can afford to take home.

She's building up to something again. She's biding her time and as soon as we're safely at thirty thousand feet over the Atlantic and I have nowhere else to go, she's going to let it all out, I just know it. However, after two hours, two *Vogues* (US and French) and an episode of *The Simpsons*, when she still hasn't said anything, I can't take the tension any longer.

'Er, Edie, is there something you need to tell me?'

She turns her head from the window to look at me. She's still got the clouds in her eyes. Slowly, she focuses on me.

'No. I don't think so,' she says.

I may have been dreading it for hours, but now I just need to know what it is.

'About Jenny . . . ?'

She sighs. 'Oh. About Jenny.'

Here we go. I don't actually adopt the brace position, like you do when you're about to crash, but I'm tempted. Edie on the subject of endangered rhino, or African villages without water or whatever, is a frightening experience. Edie on the subject of her own friend, who's chosen to *sing a song* instead of comfort her own mother – well, I have to admit, I duck slightly.

'I've been thinking,' she says slowly.

'Yeeees?'

'I think I was wrong.'

'Sorry?' I say, shocked. I've never heard her say this before. And I've known her since we started secondary school.

'After I'd stormed out of the theatre I came back to get you, but you weren't there,' she goes on. 'Someone said you'd gone to see Jenny. I bet you were giving her some encouragement. Being a friend for her. I'm sure it's what she needed. I didn't do that. I feel a bit ashamed of myself, really.'

'You do?'

Edie nods and looks at me sadly.

'I'm always so busy working out what people ought to do. But I can't change them. They are who they are. I love Jenny. She's doing what's right for her. I should just let her do it. Don't you think? Nonie?'

I realise I'm staring. Just staring and not talking. I mean, Edie can surprise me, sure, but this is unreal. This isn't Edie at all.

'I don't get it,' I sigh.

This makes Edie look even sadder. 'Really? God, am I so judgmental that you can't even imagine me wanting to stay friends with Jenny?'

Yes. She has hit it on the button. But of course I can't say so.

'Not at all!' I say. 'Of course not. You're amazing.'

She smiles at me.

'And you're lying. To be kind. Just like you always do, Nonie. I don't mean you always lie – although you do a lot, you know. I mean, you're always kind. You put friendship first. I should copy you more.'

Hello? Genius-girl here, the one who's on every team at school, in every band and orchestra (when she's allowed), who has personally raised enough money to OPEN A SCHOOL in Africa, wants to be more like me? What's going on here?

'Don't look so shocked,' she says. 'I mean it. And I mean it about Jenny. She was incredible, doing that song. Gloria would want her to do it. I mean, *I* couldn't let *my* mother live alone like that, but I'm not Jenny. Maybe I should just help her.'

I'm about to express more shock and disbelief, but I realise that this would be rude. Instead, I take a deep breath.

'Cool,' I say. 'Fantastic.'

'Really?'

Edie's doubtful pout suddenly turns into a nervous smile, and then a grin. She hugs me. A bit awkwardly, because we're sitting in really narrow airline seats and she's not the world's best hugger anyway, but at least she's trying and it's great. Then I realise I haven't got to listen to several hours of ranting about Jenny, and that's great too.

Five minutes later, a stewardess comes along to ask what we want to eat. I turn to ask Edie, but she's fast asleep. Her face looks more peaceful than I've seen it for months. And prettier too. I decide she needs sleep more than airline food and leave her to it.

Which leaves me with several unexpected hours of thinking time to myself. I'm not necessarily very good at thinking time. If I think too much at the moment – unless it's about Liam – I tend to think about Crow getting this job without me, or Mum and Vicente and losing our home, and I can't bear to do too much of that right now.

I try watching a romcom on the mini screen in front of me, but it doesn't work. In the end, I find myself picturing Isabelle's apartment. How gorgeous it was. How full of memories of Harry. And it gradually occurs to me. This thing that's been bothering me for ages. The thing that's not right between them. Somehow, after the whole Edie-not-blaming-Jenny revelation, I can see things in a completely different light.

It's not exactly a thrilling discovery about my brother. In fact, it's pretty tragic in its way. I find myself poring over it for hours, wondering what I should do and wishing I could just forget all about it. The trouble is, I love Harry, and I can't.

Chapter 48

uckily, Isabelle is staying at a hotel in London for the fashion shows, and not in our house. That would make what I have to say too totally difficult. Luckily, too, Liam agrees that I'm probably doing the right thing, when I explain it all to him. After my welcome home kiss. And my I-missed-you kiss. And several other kisses he can think of.

I find an appropriate moment when Harry's home, but the house is quiet. I fortify myself with a double cappuccino and a whole packet of M&Ms. Harry's in his room, packing to go to Milan for some shows, but seems pleased to see me. I feel such a traitor for what I'm about to say.

'Er, Harry,' I start, 'you know that apartment that you and Isabelle are going to get in New York?'

'Uh huh?' he says, jamming some socks into his suitcase.

'Well, how exactly do you imagine it? Exactly?'

It's not quite the speech I had in mind. Not totally as fluent and articulate.

'Well,' he says, still fiddling with socks, 'big, you know. Full of Issy's stuff, naturally. All those textiles she collects. Big enough for you . . .'

'That's not what I meant,' I say quickly. 'I mean, what about *your* stuff? . . . How do *you* picture it?'

He looks up now, annoyed. 'It's not down to me. Issy's got great taste. What d'you mean, Nonie?'

His sharp look softens when he sees how uncomfortable I am. He can tell this isn't easy for me. His brow furrows.

'Really. What *do* you mean?'

'Well,' I say, 'I saw Isabelle in New York, of course, and I know if I'd asked her the same thing, she could have told me in great detail. Because she's been picturing it and looking forward to it. She loves you so much, Harry. But whenever I ask you, or Mum does, you kind of avoid it. And I think that you *don't* think about it so much, do you? You aren't picturing your life together.'

There's silence.

'Are you, Harry?'

There's more silence. I let it fill the room. It's very unusual for Harry's room to be silent, but he needs a bit of thinking time.

He looks angry, and then frightened, and then sad. He comes over and sits beside me, but doesn't look at me. He plays with a frayed thread on the knee of his jeans.

'I try. But then I just picture myself on a beach some-where. By myself. Escaping. How did you know?'

'Because I care about you,' I say. 'Because I'm your sister. Because I know when something's not right. I think Crow knew too. She could never get the dress to work.'

Harry gives a short laugh. There's a pause. Then he says, 'When I proposed to Issy, it felt so right. It just hap-pened. She was as surprised as I was. She's so beautiful, Nonie. Inside too. She's such a perfect, perfect girl.'

I nod. Having checked Isabelle out, I agree. She is perfect. The only trouble is, perfect isn't always perfect.

'I just pictured us carrying on like we were, but, you know, for ever,' Harry says. He shakes his head, cross with himself. 'It seemed a good idea at the time. But then the wedding thing got bigger and bigger. And we started talking about kids, or at least, Issy did. Then she saw my face and backed off and suggested a puppy. At least to start with. I felt guilty enough about that.'

He looks at me helplessly. He's obviously not proud of himself, but he's lost.

'You're only twenty-four,' I say.

'She's twenty-one. But she knows exactly what she wants. And she means it. Why shouldn't I?'

I shrug. 'Not everyone's as grown-up as Isabelle inside,' I suggest. 'But you've got to tell her. You know that, don't you? Before you totally break her heart.'

He jumps up and starts shoving more stuff in his suitcase.

'That's the problem. Don't you see? I've been thinking about it for months. I can't let her down now. It really would break her heart. And I couldn't bear that. She doesn't deserve it.'

He catches my eye. It is the eye of a sister who knows him, and knows the right thing to do. I don't say anything, but he flinches anyway.

'You can see that, can't you, sis?'

I get up and head for the door. I pause there for a moment, with my hand on the handle.

'One day she'll work it out,' I say. 'The way I did. How will she feel then?'

He crumples, as if I've hit him with a cricket bat. I let myself out of his room as quietly as I can. Back in my own room, I call Liam, who reassures me, yet again, that it was the right thing to do.

It doesn't feel like it, though. Normally, when you do the right thing you feel great afterwards. A real sense of achievement. I just feel empty and miserable. If only I were doing a paper on Shakespeare's tragedies tomorrow, I'd be in the perfect mood to write it. Unfortunately, it's Business Studies. Yaaay.

'He didn't?'

Yesterday, Mum was on the phone to Granny, sobbing. Today Granny is in our kitchen. Mum is still sobbing, but face to face this time.

'He did. He told me two nights ago, from Milan.'

'*Why?*' Granny wails. 'She's the best chance he'll ever get!'

'He says he doesn't love her.'

'Doesn't love her? The boy's besotted.'

'That's the thing,' Mum says in a bit of a break between sobs. 'Besotted, not in love. Not long-term love, anyway. That's what he said.'

'Idiot,' Granny says crossly, getting a hankie out and handing it to Mum. 'He doesn't know what he's talking about. I bet she took it badly.'

This doesn't help Mum, who nods and goes back to sobbing. 'She's inconsolable, apparently. She's had to pull out of several shows. The poor girl.'

'And why now?' Granny asks angrily. 'Why suddenly now, for God's sake?'

Mum looks up helplessly and shrugs. I've been watching through the doorway and decide to make myself scarce. Unfortunately, it's hard to make a secret getaway in Doc Martens and Granny calls me back.

'Nonie! Tell me you didn't have anything to do with this.'

Lie, I tell myself. Just lie. You know you can do it. You do it all the time. Lie your little tartan socks off. But Granny is staring at me with a particular stare that only Granny can do.

'I might have mentioned I was worried about him,' I say.

Mum looks up, shocked. Granny looks absolutely

furious. The next fifteen minutes are not remotely funny. By the time it's over, I just about have the energy to creep upstairs to my room and text Liam a sad face, before curling myself up into a ball on the bed.

He calls back instantly. I uncurl myself enough to pick up the phone from where I'd dropped it on the floor. Then I curl myself up again.

'What's happened?' he asks. 'Nothing to do with your mad granny, by any chance?'

I tell him about the conversation.

'So they're saying it's your fault?' he asks.

I think back over the past quarter of an hour. And yes, that pretty much seems to sum it up.

'But you were just trying to stop Harry making a world-class mistake.'

'According to Granny, I was selfishly trying to stop Harry being happy so I could get to stay in my own precious bedroom. Mum looked extra shocked at that.'

'Hey – if he really loved Isabelle, he'd have just told you not to be so stupid. He wouldn't have called it off just so you can keep your room.'

I sigh. It's fine for Liam to be telling *me* this. I just wish he could have been there to tell Granny. I'd have liked to see him try.

'Sorry,' he says. He realises he's not being very helpful. 'They'll come round.'

'Sure.'

'Nonie?'

He can tell there's something else. Something I'm not saying. Something that's even worse.

I hesitate. Until a few weeks ago, I wouldn't have told anybody the next bit, but things have changed. Some of them for the better. Including being able to tell Liam anything and know that I can trust him.

'It was after I left. I was on my way up here, but I kind of stopped on the stairs . . . And I heard what Granny said to Mum.'

'Which was?'

I pause. I try and do Granny's voice and make a joke of it, but it comes out all cracked and wrong. '"Well, that's the second family marriage that girl's managed to ruin. What next?"'

'You're joking! Your granny said that?' he asks. He's shocked, which is comforting.

'Well, she's right,' I say. 'And I told myself I wouldn't do it. I told myself I'd be good.'

'You *are* good, Nonie,' he insists. 'God, I wish I could be there with you. You haven't talked to your mum yet, have you?'

I shake my head. He can't see that over the phone, but I'm not really thinking straight.

'Talk to her,' he says very slowly, like I'm a little child, or a tourist asking for directions. 'Talk to her soon. This is getting ridiculous.'

I promise, once again, that I will talk to Mum. Liam knows I'm lying by now, but there's not much he can do about it over the phone. Besides, now would be a really, really stupid time to bring up the whole subject of Dad and affairs and mistakes and wasted relationships. I can hear raised voices downstairs and Mum sounding distinctly upset. Even Granny can't calm her down. The last thing she needs is me going on about family history.

When I eventually go back downstairs, the house is silent. Granny has gone and Mum's out too. She's left me a note, just saying she'll be back later. I feel as if I've pushed them all away and I'm starting to wonder if I wouldn't be better off in a rented room somewhere, with Mum safely in Rio and me out of upsetting range for a change. Liam said the whole thing's ridiculous and he's probably right. It probably does look ridiculous from a distance. But from right in the middle, it feels as lonely as I can possibly imagine.

Chapter 49

*L*ater, I get an email from Crow.

'The overcoat men are in London for the shows. I'm seeing them on Saturday. What is a Senior Vice-President of Talent and Staffing Strategy? Cause I'm seeing one of those too. Oh, and Isabelle called to cancel her dress. She sounded like she has a bad cold. Is she OK? Hope New York was good.'

So she's decided to go to this meeting by herself, without asking me along. Fine. No problem. I should have expected it. As for her questions, I don't know the answers to either of them. One I can look up on the internet. The other I can only guess at. And I'm guessing a No.

At least Crow's talking to me. Which is more than I've done to her since I got back from New York, I realise. I send her back a quick message, telling her about Jenny and the song, and Harry and my big mouth. I'd forgotten she'd already started designing yet another dress and now, thanks to me, it won't be needed. I wonder what the new design was going to be? I suppose that now I'll never know.

I'm desperate to say more. To ask what happens next and find out what she'd do if she had to choose between going to New York and going back home to Uganda. After Liam, she's the person I'd most like to be here right now, sitting on my floor, even if she's not saying anything. I miss her borrowing my books. I miss her annoying shrug and laid-back attitude. I miss her ever-increasing afro and never being able to guess what she'll have decorated it with today. I miss watching her take a few scraps of fabric and turn them into a work of art.

But that's the point, really. Because she's so good at it, I have to let her go. Like Jenny, she's got a gift. I'd just be selfish if I told her how much I wanted us to stay together. Better if I pretend I'm fine with how things are. As Edie says, I'm good at lying.

When I've sent the email, I Google Jenny, to see if there are any updates about the show to take my mind off things. Usually there's a snippet or two about her, but today the internet's gone crazy. Suddenly, Jenny is headline material. There are stories about her everywhere.

'JACKSON WARD DISCOVERS BROADWAY STAR'
'WARD'S COPPER-HEAD BOMBSHELL'
'BROADWAY'S NEW BRIT BABY!'

Someone has 'leaked' the clip of her singing onto YouTube, where it's already got over ninety thousand hits. I can't bear to watch. Jenny's anguished face is not exactly designed to cheer me up right now. However, it's having the desired effect. The advance ticket sales for *The Princesses* are breaking records. Even though there are still months to go, it's the most anticipated opening on Broadway.

I print out the story to use later. Liam's suggested making a scrapbook about Jenny. It's something Mum did for Crow years ago, when she first got her design career going. It's fun to find little snippets about the show and put them in, alongside Jenny's *Vogue* pictures, the Miss Teen advert of her with the elephant and the Taj Mahal and her reviews from the play, the movie (the better ones, anyway) and *Annie*. The plan is to take it round to Gloria at the weekend. Working on it is the best way of taking my mind off . . . everything else. Except my boyfriend. He is wonderful and I don't mind thinking about him at all.

By Sunday, the scrapbook is ready. When Liam comes round to pick me up and take me to Gloria's, as agreed, he finds me at the kitchen table with my miserable brother. Harry still hasn't forgiven himself for what he's put Isabelle through. He's cut down on his own work because he's so upset.

'You going out?' he asks.

I explain about the scrapbook.

'Tell Gloria get well soon from me,' he says. 'Will Edie be there, by the way?'

'Uh huh.'

'You couldn't ask her about volunteering ideas, could you? I'd like to do something useful. See if she can suggest anything.'

I promise I will. He's obviously trying to make himself feel better. I wish I could do a scrapbook for Harry too. However, I'm not sure what a break-up scrapbook would look like. It's probably not something he wants a memento of.

When I get to the flat with Liam, Gloria is sitting in a chair in the kitchen and Edie's bustling round her, making coffee. Gloria looks slightly more like her old self, with her hair up in a loose bun and a little more flesh on her bones. It's hard to say what's happened, exactly. Maybe it's the shock of being in hospital, or the medication they gave her, or how well Jenny's doing in New York, or just her brain chemistry, but something has altered her mood. She smiles when she sees us and cries when she sees the scrapbook, poring over every page.

'Thank you for looking after my girl,' she says to me in a weak voice, and holding out a hand towards me. I take her hand, noticing the boniness of her fingers, and her shakiness as she reaches out.

'Pleasure,' I say. 'New York's amazing. You really must go.'

And then I remember that she can't. Jenny said something about travel insurance, and she looks too frail to go. I feel silly, but Liam rescues me.

'I like your flat, Gloria. Very homely.'

Gloria smiles at him gratefully. 'It's Edie who looks after it for me.' She beckons him closer and he leans in towards her. 'Edie saved my life, you know.'

'Oh, don't be silly!' Edie says, fiddling with the cafetière and going pink. The way she bustles around reminds me exactly of her mother, except a taller, geekier version, with better hair.

'She did,' Gloria says earnestly, looking deep into my boyfriend's gorgeous blue eyes. 'More than once. Many times.'

Edie laughs. 'What do you mean, many times? I only called one ambulance. And that was just . . . well . . . you know, anybody would've.' She's so embarrassed. But Gloria shakes her head.

'Not anybody. Who else would come over in the middle of the night?'

'Coffee?' Edie asks, trying to change the subject.

'And think of all those other times you came,' Gloria continues, ignoring her. 'You didn't know if you were helping me or not, but you did it anyway. And it cost you your place at Harvard. Don't tell me it didn't, because I know.'

Edie looks horrified. She probably doesn't remember telling Gloria about the stresses of last term, but she was here every day, chatting away. Some of it must have slipped out.

'Well actually,' she says, 'it didn't cost me a place, Gloria, so don't worry.'

'Yes it did,' Gloria insists. 'I know you think you were just overworking, but if you hadn't been here every morning, you'd have had more time . . .'

'It's not that,' Edie interrupts. She plonks some mugs on the table and starts pouring coffee into them. 'I got in. I found out last week.' Then she slumps into a chair beside me. 'In fact,' she admits in a stunned sort of voice, 'I got a scholarship. Look.'

She takes an extremely creased piece of paper out of her pocket and spreads it out on the table. It's obviously been folded and unfolded many times, but Edie hasn't mentioned it up to now. Sure enough, it's a letter from Harvard, congratulating her on her scholarship. We all stare at it, Edie hardest of all.

'I still can't believe it,' she says. 'The head says she gave me a great reference from school. And they took into account all the work I've been doing over the last couple of years. And my test results were good. But even so . . .'

Liam by now is looking at me.

'Nonie!' he says, sounding concerned. 'You OK?'

'Fine,' I say. 'Just thinking of Edie going off to Boston. Congratulations! Boston! Wow! America! Fantastic! Yaaay!'

I'm wittering. I know it. I just know how much I'm going to miss her. And Jenny. And Crow . . .

Oh my God. Crow's MIMO meeting was yesterday. She hasn't called or emailed to tell me about it. Does that mean they offered her a job and she doesn't want to tell me? Or they said no after all, and she doesn't want to tell me that either?

Edie coughs and looks embarrassed.

'Well, actually,' she says, 'I'm not going. I've already called them to say no.'

'WHAT?'

We all say it together, including Gloria.

Edie smiles. 'I haven't changed my mind since Christmas. Harvard isn't for me. Nor's Boston. You knew it all the time, Nonie. I'd hate living so far away from home. And I don't want to spend my life travelling. I want to work here. In London. I want to be a psychiatrist, I think.'

Gloria sighs and reaches a bony hand out to Edie, who takes it. Edie always did want to fix Gloria for Jenny. If it takes her a whole career to do it, she'll keep trying.

'I'm applying to University College London,' she goes on. 'I'll be just down the road from the two of you. If I get in. Crow'll be pleased. She always said she hated the idea of us all breaking up and going our separate ways. Even though Harvard is amazing, obviously . . .'

She chats on for a bit more, but suddenly I'm not listening. I'm thinking.

'Excuse me,' I butt in. 'I've just remembered something. Got to go. Sorry. Great to see you, Gloria.'

And I'm grabbing my bag and going, with Edie looking astonished and Liam following in my wake.

'What was that about?' he says as soon as we're outside.

'You keep telling me I need to talk to people,' I say. 'Well, I need to talk to Crow. Right now. I need to know what she's going to do. Even if it's bad news – well, good news for her, obviously – I've just got to hear it. And there was something that Edie said . . .'

'I'll come with you,' he offers.

But some things I have to do on my own. I let him kiss me good luck and promise him I'll let him know what happens. Then he finds me a taxi (he is the *perfect* boyfriend), and lends me the money so I can get there as quickly as I can.

Chapter 50

At Crow's flat, Henry answers the door.

'Is she in?' I ask.

'No. She's gone out. She said she needed time to think. She'll be back later.'

'Right. Tell her, so will I,' I say.

'Any message?'

'No. Just . . . Just tell her I really need to see her, OK?'

'OK,' he smiles. 'She'll be pleased.'

'Really?'

He nods.

I think about the wasted taxi ride and try not to feel too disappointed.

'Harry?'

I'm back in the kitchen at home, killing time. So is Harry. I don't think he's moved since Liam and I saw him earlier.

'Hello?'

'Do you mind? About what I said? About you and Isabelle . . . I mean, did I just make a mess of things?'

He looks up at me, astonished. Then he gets up slowly and wraps his arms around me in a bear hug.

'No, little sis. *I* made a mess of things. You stopped me making it worse. Why?'

I stay there for a minute, with his arms wrapped around me.

'Well, I worry sometimes. You know, that I'm not very . . . useful. There's you with your DJing, and Jenny's going to be a megastar on Broadway, and Edie being a psychiatrist. And Crow's such an incredible designer.'

'A *psychiatrist?*'

'Sorry?'

'You said Edie was going to be a psychiatrist.'

'Oh yes. And she got a scholarship to Harvard, by the way, but she's not going. She wants to study here. And there's something she said about Crow that made me think . . .'

'Bloody hell! A psychiatrist, hey? Your friends never cease to amaze me.'

Harry looks animated for the first time in days. For about two seconds. Then he sits down again and lets his hair flop back over his eyes.

'So?' I ask, sitting opposite him. 'What about me?'

He gives me a smile. Weak, but real. 'Hmm. What about you?' He pauses, pondering, for ages. It's not looking good. 'Well, you're constantly obsessed by your boyfriend, your exams, your latest argument with whoever and what you're going to wear.' He sees my face fall. My chin is practically on the floor. 'But hold up, sis! You notice things about people. You're there for them when they need you – like helping Crow when you first met her, or going to New York for Jenny. You care, and it shows. It makes you interesting. That, and the fact that only you can wear those leggings with that particular shade of mohair. One of the reasons I come home so much is because you're here. Hey! Where are you going?'

I've just realised something. Where Crow might be. I blow him a kiss and head out of the door.

It's a beautiful, sunny day. Groups of visitors are taking pictures of themselves on the museum steps. Inside, little children are leaning back to admire the massive glass chandelier in the lobby. So are their parents. I rush past them.

I've nearly walked through the costume section when I spot her. She's hard to miss, in a gold lurex dress with matching cloak and Mickey Mouse ears. She's sketching an elaborate pair of Manolo Blahnik evening shoes.

'Oh, hi,' she says, looking surprised. 'This is a coincidence.'

'No it's not,' I tell her. 'I come to the V&A all the time. So do you. Listen, I need to know what happened yesterday with the MIMOs. Let's go to the café. You can tell me all about it.'

Crow puts her sketchbook away in her school bag and follows me through the sculpture hall and down the corridor to the café, where we sit at a table under one of the huge, space-hopper lights. I wait for her to say something. She waits for me.

'Well?'

'What?'

'What did they *say*?' I ask. 'Do they want you to design for them? Do they want you to go to New York?'

Crow cocks her head to one side, considering. I could shake her.

'Yes, I suppose they do,' she says eventually. 'That's what the Senior Vice-President of Talent and Thingy emailed me afterwards, anyway.'

'Right. Great,' I say. 'Well, you can't say I wasn't useful!'

I give a light laugh. It sounds like water gurgling down a drain.

'Useful?' she asks.

'By finding you the job. Sending in the sketches. You know. All that stuff.'

Crow's looking at me like I'm slightly crazy. She seems puzzled. Grumpy, possibly. Certainly not grateful.

'But they didn't want me to do my ideas.'

'Mmmmm? Which ideas?'

'The Fair Trade cotton. The prints. They liked my sketches, but they just wanted me to use fabrics from their normal suppliers. They told me not to worry where they came from.'

'You could do that, couldn't you?' I ask.

'But I don't want to,' Crow says. 'Working with the people from home was the whole point. And the prints were what gave me my inspiration.'

I imagine Crow sitting, arms folded, facing the MIMOs and them trying to get her to change her mind. I bet it was difficult. I can't help smiling a bit at the thought.

'You can always compromise though, can't you?'

Crow shakes her head. 'Why should I? *We* never compromised.'

'So what did you say?' I whisper.

She shrugs. 'I said no, of course. I never wanted to work for them anyway. I was only at the meeting 'cause you told me to go. And I hated it. I don't want to go to New York by myself. I don't want to work for a big company. They weren't even interested in my designs. Just all that stuff about me in the papers. And I only got that because of you.' She looks grumpier than ever.

I don't, though. I look happy, I just know I do. I can feel a little cloud of happiness floating up from me and towards the space-hopper light.

'Edie said you didn't like the idea of us all breaking up,' I say. 'I hadn't realised.'

'Nonie,' she says, 'you can be so stupid, sometimes.'

'Yes,' I grin, 'I know. Sorry. But I wanted you to follow your dreams. It's your moment.'

'I *am* following my dreams,' she huffs. 'I want to study

art for a bit, while you go to college. That's why I haven't been bothering you recently. So you could revise. I did tell you. I want to learn about Picasso. He really liked African art. He's cool. Then I want to do my own label, like we said. Just a small one, to start with, doing my own stuff. You can help me with the ideas for it. You're brilliant at it, Nonie. Better than men in matching overcoats. And anyway . . .' She pauses for a moment while her eyes glisten. 'I only want to do it if it's with you.'

My eyes glisten too. She did tell me, all of it, at one time or another. I just wasn't listening. Her face lights up and even the Mickey Mouse ears seem to jiggle with the force of her smile. At this point, for the first time in my life, I realise just how much Crow needs me. As much as I need her, in fact. And I can see just how much she's been missing me while she stayed away so I could study. I make the ears jiggle even more when I go to hug her. She hugs me back, hard. I like that we're big huggers in my family.

Chapter 51

*L*iam doesn't seem particularly surprised when I tell him.

'But I thought she'd completely grown out of me!' I protest.

'Just shows how rubbish you are at sussing people out,' he says, with a reassuring kiss for the tip of my nose. 'You used to think I hated your dress sense, remember? I just thought you were too cool to talk to. Until you completely messed up in Starbucks that day. That was funny.'

'But I used to be so good at it!'

'What? Ordering coffee?'

'No. Sussing people out.'

'You think?'

He doesn't sound very convinced. I try and think back. I'm sure there was a time when I could instantly sense what people were thinking. But actually, when I try and remember particular moments, I was usually totally wrong.

'Have you talked to your mum yet?' he asks, changing the subject.

'Yes. Yesterday. About my revision timetable for the Easter holidays.'

'I didn't mean that.'

'Oh.'

I know what Liam means. I may be wrong about almost everything, but there is one thing I'm sure of, and that's that it would be pointless talking to Mum about why she didn't marry Vicente all those years ago. Pointless, and painful – like sticking pins in myself. Why put myself through it?

Anyway, soon it won't be relevant any more. She's got the same loved-up glow that I have. She's constantly on her BlackBerry, writing love notes. Or she's out on mysterious 'gallery openings' that she won't discuss. I'm pretty convinced Vicente is over in London on a regular basis so he can see her. I'm guessing she's waiting until my A levels are over before she announces the wedding. She doesn't want to stress me out completely in my 'important academic year'. But there's only an important academic term of it left. In a few weeks, she'll sit me down in the kitchen for a little discussion. Yaaay.

'I'll talk to her soon. When there's a good moment,' I tell Liam. He sighs with frustration and gives up.

Besides, I'm too busy to talk to Mum. I have enough A-level revision to last me a year, and it's all got to be done in the next six weeks. Edie pretends to be stressed too, to keep me company, but basically she's back to her old self now and we both know she's going to fly through the exams without really trying. In fact, she's got so much spare time that her parents have let her start doing her web campaigning again.

'I love the school bag idea,' she tells me over lunch in the cafeteria a few weeks later, after the Shakespeare paper. (I aced *King Lear*. I totally aced him. Ask me anything about his motivations – anything. First exam I've enjoyed in my life.) 'I've been emailing the people in Uganda about it. Crow could license other co-operatives to use her designs, and then they'd make even more money. What?'

'You look different,' I say. 'Not that I wasn't listening or anything, but there's something about you.'

She looks down. Then grins.

'Crow got fed up with all my old clothes and she's been making me some summer dresses. Do you like this one?'

I check it out. It's got the clever folds and drapes that Crow was experimenting with in her sketches. It looks simple, but it somehow makes Edie's figure look even better than it is already. I tell her so and she blushes gently, before launching into a big speech about all the other things she's going to do to raise money and awareness about the importance of education for girls. Including tee-shirts. There are always tee-shirts where Edie's campaigns are involved.

Chapter 52

Turns out she doesn't need the tee-shirts, though.

I get a call from Amanda Elat at Miss Teen.

'What's all this about Crow's bags? I didn't know Crow was doing bags.'

'She isn't,' I say. 'She's designed some fabric for this project in Uganda . . .'

'Oh!' Amanda says. 'That explains it. Sort of.'

'Explains what?'

'Why I've had fifteen calls this morning. And why my inbox is overloaded. People assume this is all to do with Miss Teen. I wish it was.'

'What was?'

'Queen Fadilah, of course,' she says. 'You must have seen the coverage?'

Well, I haven't. I know who Queen Fadilah is, because I read fashion magazines and celebrity magazines, and she's always in both — either for being the most stylish royal in the world, or for being the most brilliant at supporting good causes. Even Edie knows who she is because of her latest campaign for millions more children to be educated. In fact, she reminds me of Edie, except in Dior and Louboutins.

Last week she made a speech about education at the United Nations in New York, apparently (Queen Fadilah, that is, not Edie – Edie's chances of going to the UN are still pretty much nil). She also went to the White House to talk to the President. At both events she was photographed by practically every paparazzo in existence, and ever since, the fashion press have been analysing every inch of her gorgeous outfits. Normally I would know this, but I've been busy with exams. I never thought I'd be too busy to catch a major fashion moment, but that's how good I've been recently.

Anyway, Queen Fadilah dressed casually for both events, which in her case meant Dior palazzo pants and Louboutin flats. What got everyone really talking, though, was the bag she had over her shoulder. It was surprisingly simple for the Queen – a cotton school bag, in fact – but they LOVED the print. It looks like an animal print from far away, but when you get close you realise it's . . . girls holding hands. People asked her about it and she said it was to raise money for a girls' school in Uganda, and wasn't it cute?

They want to know more about it. And by 'they' I mean half the fashion bloggers on the internet. It's become a major quest, to find out all the details about the bag, and the print, and the designer, and the school. *I* want to know how on earth Queen Fadilah got her hands on it.

'Jenny's in New York,' Edie points out when I tell her. 'This can't be a coincidence.'

We call Crow to come and join us, and we track Jenny down before her next performance.

'That's right,' she says over the phone, as if it's the most natural thing in the world. 'She came to one of our previews with her daughter, before the UN thing. Princess Alima wanted to meet me backstage. I guess she's a princess too, so we sort of have a lot in common.'

Edie sniggers.

'Uh-huh,' I say. Should I remind Jenny she isn't a real princess? Probably no point.

'Anyway,' she goes on. 'We had loads of mementoes of the show to give her. And she saw those bags you sent me lying around and liked them, and we put all the mementoes in one for her to take away. And of course I told her about Crow and Victoria and the school-bag project and everything, and she said her mum might be interested and could she have a spare? So I said yes.'

I call Amanda Elat back and explain it all to her. She doesn't sound as thrilled as I'd hoped.

'That's fine,' she says, 'but I wish you could tell the million people who keep asking me about them. I'm still getting called several times a day, you know.'

Edie's blogging again. I suggest she puts the story up on her website. By now, Liam has joined us too.

'You should write it up, Nonie,' he says. 'For one of the big fashion websites. I bet they'd love to know the story. I can find out the address of an editor if you like.'

'Why me?'

Everyone turns to look at me. Edie, Liam and Crow. They're all staring at me.

'Because you know the people involved,' Edie says. 'You were the one who gave the bags to Jenny.'

'Because you write so well,' says Crow. 'That email you wrote to the overcoat men – it was perfect. Even I didn't know what my ideas were until you described what I meant.'

'Because you'd love it,' says Liam. 'You can't stop talking about fashion. If you write like you talk – well, I'd read it.'

He's noticed I'm a talker! And he still likes me! This is one of the best days of my life.

I don't believe them, of course, but I do what I'm told. When three of your best friends, including your boyfriend, are telling you to do something, it's at least worth a try.

So I write an article explaining about Crow designing the bags, and Victoria and her friends raising money for the school, and Jenny meeting Princess Alima backstage. It's like putting an outfit together, except with words. Not like writing about Shakespeare at all (although I'm not so bad at that now, either). And when it's done, I offer it to the online version of one of my favourite fashion magazines, and they commission me to write another, longer piece for their printed magazine. And two blogs want pieces about Crow as well, and about the production of the 'Holding Hands' print bags by women's co-operatives around the world to meet the sudden, massive demand. Now, if I Google myself, the internet seems to be full of stuff I've written, or people quoting stuff I've written, and it's amazing. My English isn't toxic at all. If it's about bags, fundraising and famous royals, it's actually quite good.

Chapter 53

'How's production going?' Mum asks one summer day, as I'm grabbing a piece of toast in the kitchen.

'Of the bags? They can't make them fast enough. Thank goodness Andy Elat's offered to help with distribution and stuff. I saw ten people on Oxford Street with them yesterday. It's crazy. There were orders for half a million bags, the last I heard, and loads of co-operatives are making them. Edie says they're going to be able to buy whole new libraries with the money. And pay for more girls to go to school. Queen Fadilah keeps going on about it in the press. She's offered to give me an interview next month. I'm just working out my questions for her.'

'I'm glad,' Mum says, in a 'That wasn't what I really wanted to talk about' sort of way. 'I've made coffee for us both. Why don't you sit down?'

'Sure,' I say. Then I stop dead. All the blood runs out of my head, into my feet. I have hot legs (not in a good way) and I feel dizzy. It's just occurred to me: I took my last A-level paper two days ago. We're in the kitchen. It's time for Mum's 'little discussion'. No escaping it now.

Somehow, I make it to the nearest chair. It's not so much sitting as letting my legs buckle under me. Mum pushes a mug of coffee towards me.

'I should have told you this ages ago,' she says.

I start nodding then shaking my head. 'You didn't need to,' I whisper. It comes out as a sort of a squeak. She gives me a funny look.

'I've been seeing someone for a while,' she goes on. 'I wanted to talk to you about it, but I know it's hard for you. I wanted to wait till all your exams were over. Silly, I know . . .'

For a moment, I'm not really listening. I'm having an imaginary conversation with Liam. He's going, 'Oh my God, you were totally right. You CAN suss people out. I am SO sorry, Nonie. Will you forgive me for ever doubting you?' And I'm going, 'YES! See? Told you.' The conversation we'll be having later today, in fact, when he's finished working at his dad's caff and I've finished here, with Mum, and crawled over to him.

'. . . nearly a year now,' Mum's saying. I've obviously missed a bit. Hope it wasn't crucial. 'But actually, it started in February last year, after Harry's engagement party, so—'

'Yes, Mum, I know. Honestly,' I interrupt. Can we just speed this up?

She looks surprised, then smiles.

'I suppose I can't really keep things from you, can I?' she says. 'I mean, sharing a house with my only daughter. Of course you're going to work it out for yourself. It's just that you didn't say anything. I tried to tell you at Crow's birthday party, but then everything went wrong . . .'

'Look, Mum,' I say, 'I'm thrilled for you. I really am. He's a lovely man. But can we keep the house? Please? I mean, Harry's not getting married any more, so he'll be here a bit. He can keep an eye on me. And you'll have your own place in Brazil, so . . .'

'Brazil?' Mum says. She looks surprised.

'Yeah. Won't you be going there? Or is he coming here? But how will he run his projects?'

'Just like he always has done,' Mum says. 'From his office in the garden. Except it will be our garden. Wait a minute . . . *Brazil?*'

'Well, he lives there,' I point out.

'Peter? No he doesn't. He lives next door.'

'*Peter?*'

'Peter Anderson. Who did you think I meant? Wait – not Vicente?'

I nod. Of course, Vicente. Who else?

'But, you've always loved him,' I say shakily. This Peter Anderson thing is very confusing. 'And he sent you all those white roses.'

'Roses? Oh – no, that wasn't him,' Mum says. 'Well, he sent that big lot last year. Very over the top, I thought. But Peter's been sending them since then. They're my favourite flower. Hang on a minute – *Vicente*? What made you think it was Vicente?'

So I explain, in a very wobbly voice, about everything I know. The time she and Vicente were 'on a break'. Her meeting Dad and accidentally getting pregnant with me. Wanting to go back to Vicente and not being able to. The wedding that never happened. The whole lot.

I've no idea what Mum's reaction is, because I'm staring at a particular pattern in the marble tabletop as I talk, but I can feel the blood heading back up from my legs and settling in my face, which is now hot enough to reheat my untouched coffee.

I get to the end and there's silence. I look up at Mum at last and she's just staring at me. She can't speak for a moment. She looks anguished. Eventually, her voice comes back.

'You thought that?' she says. 'All this time? Why? I mean, how did you put together all that stuff?'

'Phonecalls,' I explain. 'You talking to your friends. Granny. You know . . .'

'That woman!' Mum looks exasperated now. Then she takes both my hands in hers and looks into my eyes. 'I'm so, so sorry, darling,' she says. 'Do you know – of all people, it was Gloria who told me I should have talked to you about this, years ago. But I couldn't bring myself to do it.'

I shrug. Nothing to apologise for. Accidents happen.

Mum lets go of one of my hands and strokes the side of my face.

'Nonie! I can't bear it! Oh my God. I'm going to have to tell you the whole thing, aren't I?'

I shrug again. She might as well, if she wants to. Whatever.

'You were the most loved baby girl in the world,' she says tenderly. 'I can't believe you didn't realise. OK, it's true, after I'd started dating your dad, I knew we were never going to make it as a couple. I was pregnant, but I wondered if I'd made a mistake breaking up with Vicente. Your damned granny urged me to go back to him . . . try and make it up. After all, he and I already had Harry together. But I think it was his estate that Granny loved. She wanted me to marry his acres. Anyway, I went to see him in Brazil and he said yes, he'd love to get back together, but not with a new baby. And that's when I realised, Nonie. That's when I knew how much I loved you. Because it never occurred to me, not even for a second, to think I'd missed out on Vicente when I could have you. Even though you were still about the size of a jelly bean inside me, I loved you so much.'

She's crying by now. I'm crying. There's a lot of crying going on. I hope tears won't spoil the surface of the marble, because if so, we're in trouble. And all the time, she's stroking my face and my wonky hair.

'So I went back to Paris,' she goes on. 'I told your dad about you, and he was over the moon. He painted an exquisite series of pictures for you – the moon in a starlit sky, in fact. We were going to keep them for you but he was offered such a staggering sum of money for them, and normally he was so poor, that he couldn't say no. That money paid for his flat. All the time I was pregnant, he looked after Harry and me so beautifully. Then you were born. You were stunning. People used to stop me in the street with the pram to tell me how beautiful you were. We had a year of happy times. But I needed to work again, and I wanted to be in London. Vicente helped me buy this house because of Harry. Granny's right about him being a very generous man. And your dad helped me find contacts in the art world so I could set up my business.'

She pauses and sighs deeply.

'That's what happened, darling. And all the time you were growing up, I was so proud of how brave you were, and how beautiful you were, and your sense of style, and your loyalty to your friends. You may have been an accident, Nonie, but you were never a mistake. Never. I just can't believe you didn't know that.'

'But Granny . . .' I stutter through my tears, 'I heard her. About me stopping two family weddings. Harry's and yours.'

Mum's lips harden into a thin line.

'Your granny is not my favourite person at the moment. You were right about Harry and Isabelle. Of course I was upset, but I realised straight away that you'd saved him from a big mistake. And she was ridiculous to bring Vicente into it. I told her so at the time. I haven't spoken to her since, actually.'

Hmm. True. I thought I hadn't seen Granny around much recently. I assumed she was busy redecorating or something. But I'm not really thinking about Granny. I'm mentally having my conversation with Liam again. It's going a bit differently this time. My opportunity to say 'I told you so' isn't quite as obvious as I thought.

Mum's BlackBerry goes off to say she's got a text. She checks the screen. This time, instead of assuming I know what it's about, I check.

'Peter Anderson?' I ask. 'Wondering if we've had our little discussion?'

She looks at me and laughs.

'Absolutely! God, what shall I tell him?'

'Well, I'm still not exactly sure what's going on,' I say. 'I kind of interrupted you. Tell me about him.'

So she does. How she went round to his house to apologise after the whole 'Turn the bloody music down or I'll sue' incident and they clicked. The meals at his restaurants (he owns three), the visits to her artists' exhibitions (there are loads), and then falling headlong in love last summer. It's funny to think you can do it when you're as old as Mum, but I've checked the symptoms and it seems it's true. They were terrified that I'd hate the idea of Mum with a new man after all this time. Because, despite having a combined age of over eighty, they can be really stupid sometimes. Why would I mind? And yes, Mum is selling her share of the house to pay Vicente back, but she's selling it to Mr Anderson. He's always preferred our house to his own. He's moving in over the summer, if that's OK with me.

'So I get to keep my room?' I check. I hate this all to come down to my room after everything else, but it's important.

'Yes, Nonie. You get to keep your room.'

'Yay!'

'And I'll get that four poster you've always wanted. And your mirrored wardrobe. I kind of promised you.'

'Yay!'

'And you're OK with Peter moving in?'

'Of course. If you love him that much, he must be OK. I'll get used to him. As long as he doesn't ask me to tidy up too often . . .'

'Oh, thank God.'

After we've talked, I go back up to my room and stare out across the rooftops at the blue Kensington sky. It's the view I've known since I was tiny, but it looks new, somehow. Different. Something has changed. It takes me ages, standing there in front of the window, to work out what it is.

I've changed. A piece of me that's been missing all my life has finally clicked into place. True, I've found out that I am TOTALLY RUBBISH at sussing people out, including my own mother, and can never trust my own opinion on anyone ever again. But I feel whole, and light as air. Mum called me brave, but underneath I've always felt pretty terrified about the future. I didn't feel ready for it. I didn't feel good enough for it. Now I do.

I text Liam.

'Had the talk with mum. You were totally right. love u xxx'

I stare at it for a while. It's the first time I've told Liam in writing that I love him, although it must be pretty obvious by now. But it's sort of a big deal when you see it there on the screen. I wonder if I should really do it. Might this turn me into the sort of clingy girlfriend that every boy hates?

Then I get my light-as-air feeling again. If you love someone, you should say so. I think everything will be OK this time.

I press Send.

Chapter 54

Harry's on his decks. The room is throbbing with disco and this would normally be the point where Peter Anderson comes in and starts start swearing about the volume, except today he can't. He's too busy dancing with Mum. He has to be one of the ungrooviest dancers I've ever seen, but Mum doesn't seem to care. She's beaming at him. If Jenny were here now, she'd be 'ooh'ing and 'aah'ing about what a lovely couple they make, but that's the problem with having a friend who's a Broadway star. She isn't here. She's still performing to sell-out houses in New York, where she's 'the new Audrey Hepburn' to the fashion press and 'the new Julie Andrews' to the entertainment press. What's even weirder is that any teenage girl who can sing on *America's Got Talent* is instantly known as 'the new Jenny Merritt'. Jenny is already the old version of herself! And she's not even nineteen. She's doing a shoot for *Vanity Fair* tomorrow. They don't know what they've let themselves in for. I miss her so much.

Crow's just back from another trip to Uganda, to deliver Henry to his new teaching job and see Victoria again. She comes over, accompanied by my gorgeous, studenty boyfriend. Well, not quite a student yet. We start college together next week, and if they let me change courses I'll be doing journalism with him. I have, after all, just interviewed the world's most stylish woman. Surely they've got to let me in?

Liam's in jeans, his perfect sneakers and an asymmetrical jacket from a vintage market I bought for him with the earnings from selling my first article. It makes him look even cooler and more gorgeous than usual. I can't believe he's mine. I kiss him, just to make sure. He absent-mindedly rubs his fingers over my cocktail rings as he holds my hand. It's a thing he does. He is SO my boyfriend.

'You up for a dance?' he asks. 'I'd have asked you before, but I'm worried about your dress. Will it cope?'

I'm in a dress made of antique lace, with a sculpted bodice and a skirt in the shape of pointed flower petals, which makes me look like a fairy. Crow was going to use the lace for the latest version of Isabelle's dress, but suddenly it wasn't needed any more. We haven't told Harry where it came from, and we won't, but it seemed a shame to waste it. Crow's own maxi-dress is made out of the famous 'Holding Hands' print. She could license it to a big company and make millions. Instead, she's licensed it to a charity. She's not interested in making millions. For now, she's interested in being with her friends, learning about Picasso and doing what makes her happy. It took me a while to understand, but finally I do.

We decide to risk the lace on the dance floor. Harry's playing some 1970s funk that simply demands to be danced to. But before we join the others, I catch a look in Crow's eye.

'What? What?' I ask.

'Nothing,' she says. 'Just a feeling. Wait and see.'

I'm desperate for more information, but Liam drags me away and Crow waves me off. Mum is still boogying on down in the middle of the dance floor. She didn't go for the column dress with the billowing train in the end. Her wedding outfit is a simple white suit that Yves Saint Laurent made for her the year before I was born. It's white wool, with a short jacket and a flared skirt. It still fits her perfectly. She accessorised it with a soft cloche hat and a bouquet of white roses on the steps of the Chelsea Register Office this afternoon and she looked stunning, I thought. Even Granny approved.

'It's style, Nonie,' she said to me, as we threw rose petals over the happy couple. 'So chic. It reminds me of Bianca Jagger. Before your time, darling . . .'

Granny forgets that I'm an expert on style icons of the twentieth century. I know exactly what she means. I've seen the photos. Bianca's hat was bigger.

I'm glad Granny's enjoying the day, even though it doesn't include country houses, estate chapels, tiaras, ecru bridesmaids or any of her 'wedding essentials'. Luckily, just seeing Mum so in love seems to be enough for her. And the fact that Granny was allowed to be there at all. I had to really work at getting Mum to forgive her for what she said about me. But I hate it when we don't talk to each other in our family. I mean, it's so ridiculous. Honestly, who bottles up all that stuff?

Harry plays a slower number. Liam moves in closer. I can feel his breath in my hair. I can hardly concentrate. Mum has her arms around Peter Anderson's neck. Next to her, Vicente is dancing with his girlfriend – the one he was coming to London to visit last Christmas, but was too polite to tell me about. Beyond them, sitting at a table near the dance floor, Edie is deep in conversation with my dad. They're probably talking about the paintings he did for me before I was born. She's been fascinated by this story ever since I told her. Either that or she's trying to get him to buy some school bags.

Liam and I finish our dance and go to join them. Liam tries to practise his French on Dad, which is sweet and very sexy. Dad, out of kindness, pretends his English isn't half as good as it is and talks back in French. I could listen for hours.

And then I spot it. From behind his decks, I catch Harry staring vaguely in our direction with a look of hopeless devotion in his eyes. Even though he was devastated about Isabelle, Harry is not the sort of boy to stay downhearted for long. The room is crammed to the brim with leggy blonde model friends of the family. I wonder which one he's fallen for this time.

Crow comes to join us.

'Harry's in love again, isn't he?' I challenge her. For some strange reason, Crow is always the first to know. She'll have it totally worked out by now.

She grins, but won't say anything.

'It could be anyone here, practically. At least give me a clue.'

She shakes her head.

Edie leans across the table.

'What are you talking about?' she asks.

'Well,' I say confidentially, 'Harry's in love, but Crow won't tell me who with.'

'Oh!'

Edie gasps and goes her usual shade of lipstick pink. She crosses one long leg over the other, fiddles with the hem of her cute little mini-dress and shakes her adorable blonde bob in a sort of panicked gesture.

I catch Crow's eye and laugh. She grins.

'Don't worry, I've just guessed,' I say. 'God, I'm stupid.'

'What?' asks Liam, joining the gang and perching me on his lap.

Edie buries her head in her hands. She's muttering something, but I can't hear what it is. Eventually she looks up.

'It may not be me,' she says. 'How can you tell?'

Of course, Edie's been in love with Harry for ages.

Since she was twelve, really, with a brief gap for Hot Phil. I hadn't realised how serious it was, but looking at her now, it's obvious. As for Harry, I'm not sure why I'm suddenly so certain that he's fallen in love with her too. But I think I have a clue.

'He likes kind-hearted, gorgeous women,' I say. 'You're both. Trust me. And don't worry, you have my blessing. Just don't snog him in front of me, OK?' I can handle a lot of weirdness, but even I have my limits.

Ten minutes later, Harry comes over and asks her to dance, while one of his friends minds the decks. Edie ignores our whoops and giggles and soon she has her head buried in his shoulder. I've never seen her look so happy, or him.

'Right,' says Liam, looking at Crow and me hovering on the edge of the dance floor. 'What about the rest of us? What shall we do?'

'Well, where Crow goes, I go,' I say. Maybe it will be to Paris one day, to write for French *Vogue* while she launches her own fashion house, or New York, to be a fashion blogger while she studies art and gets more tips from top designers. But meanwhile, it's back onto the dance floor.

Liam joins us. We throw some crazy moves. We look good.

THE END

What can you do?

Sometimes, it's not about what you can do, but what other people can do for you. If you're living with someone with a mental illness (which a lot of people are), you don't have to cope alone. Charities like SANE (through SANEline and SANEmail) and Childline know what it's like, and they're there to help. Find them on the web. Call them or email them. Find out what they can do.

According to the charity 1GOAL, 72 million children around the world don't have the chance to go to school. That *is* something you can help with. How? Well, charities such as Actionaid and Unicef have some ideas. Check out their websites at actionaid.org.uk and unicef.org.uk. Maybe you can sponsor a child through school. I support SOS Children's Villages. It may not seem like it when exams are looming, but the more children we educate, the better this world will be.

Acknowledgements

Not often, in the course of research, does someone say to you, 'Sorry if I have to answer the phone – I'm expecting a call from Shirley Bassey.' I loved the line so much I borrowed it. I owe a big debt of gratitude to the legendary Don Black, who was charm and courtesy itself, and helped a lot.

Kasia Steyn, Ivan Dubovsky and Alison Clayton-Smith thought they were meeting me for yoga or coffee, but ended up giving me some great insights for the book. That's what happens when your friend turns into a writer. Sorry, and thanks.

Emily and Sophie knew what they were letting themselves in for: a research trip with me to New York. It was a tough job, but somebody had to do it. Ann Ceprynski helped as ever, by suggesting cool places to go. Siobhán McGowan and the team at Scholastic made us feel so welcome when we got there. Felicity Pett didn't come, but told me about the polar bears. Freddie and Tom also didn't come, but wanted to. I owe you. I know.

Jewel Simpfendorfer designed the cover dress and lent us her sample for the shoot. Thanks, Jewel! I still love it as much as I ever did. And thanks to Steve Wells for my lovely cover.

As always, I owe big thanks to Barry, Rachel, Imogen, Nicki and the rest of the Chicken House team. And to Caroline at Christopher Little, who knows the best coffee joints.

Rachel McHale and Jane Ward – thanks for your support. I hope you like the results.

Darling E. Thank you for everything. I couldn't do it without you.

And finally, CJ Skuse, who waited. You know what for. I hope you're happy now.

Two books were very useful and regularly referred to: one new, one old. The new one was 'How to set up & run a fashion label' by Toby Meadows. The old one, which I've had for years, is 'The Queen's Clothes', by Anne Edwards, illustrated by Robb.

About the author

Sophia Bennett would have loved to be an artist, fashion designer, or the lady who does costumes for Jane Austen films. However, not being able to draw or sew very well made those careers unlikely. Luckily, she also loves to write. She is the author of the internationally successful *Threads* series, as well as *The Look*, *You Don't Know Me* and *The Castle*, and has written for *The Times* and *The Guardian*.

She lives in London with her family, and is known for her shoes and her writing shed. You can find out more about her on her website: www.sophiabennett.com

📧 @sophiabennett

📘 SophiaBennettAuthor

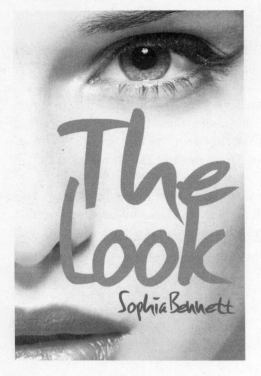

THE LOOK

Ted is tall. Freaky. When she's spotted by a model agency, she can't believe it.

At the same time, her gorgeous sister falls seriously ill.

With her world turned upside down, Ted must choose between fame and family. Can she be a supermodel and a super sister? All in five-inch heels?

'. . . one word, BRILLIANT. A difficult topic, sensitively handled.'
CATHY CASSIDY

Paperback, ISBN 978-1-906427-91-7, £6.99 • ebook, ISBN 978-1-908435-16-3, £6.99

YOU DON'T KNOW ME

Me and Rose. In a band. Singing together, all the way to the live finals of Killer Act.

Only to be told one of us must go.

But no girl would drop her best friend in front of millions . . .

Would she?

If this is fame, it sucks.

Everyone's talking about us, but nobody knows the truth.

'. . . her best yet.'
AMANDA CRAIG, THE TIMES

Paperback, ISBN 978-1-908435-46-0, £6.99 • ebook, ISBN 978-1-908435-80-4, £6.99

THE CASTLE

It's not just the bridesmaid's dress that Peta has a problem with – it's the whole wedding. How can her mum remarry when Peta's army-hero dad isn't dead?

When Peta receives clues that seem to prove he's alive, she sets out on a crazy mission. Somewhere across the sea, her father's being held in a billionaire's castle.

Dad would do anything to save her – and now it's her turn to rescue him.

'. . . a fun, frolicking, and increasingly frightening adventure.'

TERI TERRY

Paperback, ISBN 978-1-909489-78-3, £6.99 • ebook, ISBN 978-1-909489-79-0, £6.99